PLAYING DOCTOR

Running his hands up and down her thighs, he felt her quiver. The air-conditioned room was cool, causing her skin to prickle with goosebumps. She looked up at him, a look of anticipation in her eyes. Watching her lie there, waiting for him to make love to her, made him feel more excited than he could ever remember feeling before. "Libby, you're so beautiful. Everywhere," he added as he scanned her nakedness before him. She shivered again, but smiled sweetly. He wanted to devour her.

Lust's
Betrayal

Debby Conrad

Jocelyn Hollow Romance

Lust's Betrayal by Debby Conrad

© 2006 Debby Conrad
Published by Jocelyn Hollow Romance

For information on Jocelyn Hollow Romances, call 615/514-0173.

ISBN 1-933725-23-0

Design by Armour&Armour
armour-armour.com

First Edition 2006
  2 3 4 5 6 7 8 9 10

Acknowledgments

For my beautiful daughters, Nicole and Ashley: Don't settle for less than your dreams.

To my sister Jacky and my wonderful mother Pat for not telling me to find another dream, and my sister Kitty for the hours of free proofreading.

And for Grandma Helen whose wisdom and encouragement I miss. I wish you could have been here to share this moment.

My first thank you goes to my husband Chuck who does his own laundry so I can spend more time writing. What a guy!

Thanks to my fellow members of the original Lucky 7—Eddie Columbia, Kathy Fuller, Nancy Plisko, Chris Kraft, Jane Sabo, and Peggy Musil—for all your patience and input.

Those late nights finally paid off, as three of us are living proof.

For the rest of the talented group, it will happen to you as well.

Also thanks to June Lund Shiplett for giving so much of her time to help new writers, including me. No one has ever been more generous.

Somehow, you made my writing sound even better than it was.

Thanks to Laura E. Williams who encouraged

me from the beginning even when I had no idea what POV meant or how to insert a page number. You laughed with me rather than at me. Well, sometimes you laughed at me, but I pushed on anyway.

And a special thank you to Mary Campisi for believing in me when I sometimes didn't believe in myself, and for all those kicks in the --- I obviously needed.

PROLOGUE

MEREDITH MCLAUGHLIN WORE her favorite dress on the day she planned to die, figuring, why not look her best? Anyone who knew her would expect nothing less than perfection.

It was a blue floral sundress, and she'd always favored blue. It brought out the blue in her eyes. Her eyes weren't just blue, they were iris blue—at least that's what she'd always been told.

She'd painted her nails this morning with her favorite shade of polish. Hot Cinnamon. And just last week she'd had her blonde hair highlighted for the big event. After all, taking one's own life wasn't exactly an everyday occurrence.

As she tucked her trembling hands into her dress pockets, a warm breeze billowed the skirt softly around her calves, caressing and tickling her skin. Stepping to the edge of the cliff, she peered over and sucked in her breath. Huge jagged rocks lined the way down to a drop of over one hundred feet. The thought of hitting all those rocks made her squeamish. Needing another minute, she quickly stepped back.

Sweat trickled downward between her breasts and along the small of her back. Her palms were clammy, and her mouth was so dry she could barely swallow.

She shouldn't be afraid of dying, because living scared her so much more.

She'd only wanted Ross to love her, and on their wedding day, he'd promised to do just that. But had he even tried? From the first day they were married, Ross had begun to withdraw. Every time she tried to get close, he'd pulled away, until she'd finally accused him of not loving her, and he had admitted the truth. He'd said she was suffocating him.

And then when she'd tried to befriend the rest of the McLaughlin family, they, too, had withdrawn. Couldn't they see she was hurting inside? That all she'd ever really wanted was to be accepted and loved by them?

Swiping at a tear trickling down her cheek, she told herself that the McLaughlins weren't worth her tears. None of them. And they were soon going to be sorry for the way they'd treated her. Her only regret was how Emma would feel. Her two-year-old daughter was too young to understand.

Last week, she'd told Ross they could move away from Falcon Ridge, away from his family and all the gossip, and start over. Just the three of them. But he hadn't wanted to hear about her dreams and plans, or about the new life they could build together.

Listen to yourself, she chided. *You're pregnant*

with another man's child. Do you actually think Ross will forgive you once he finds out?

Sinking helplessly to her knees, Meredith gazed out over the pea-green water, picturing herself floating lifelessly. What if no one cared that she jumped? What if they'd be glad to be rid of her?

Unable to fight back the tears, she stared at the calm lake, hardly a ripple in it. Breathing in the hot, humid, afternoon air, she stayed on her knees for some time, listening to the high-pitched squeals of the sea gulls soaring high above the cliffs. Then, knowing what she had to do, she stood, closed her eyes, and began to inch toward the edge.

She'd been about to take one last step when she heard a noise behind her. A crunching sound—someone's shoe trampling the underbrush. Her eyes popped open as she pivoted around.

"If you're planning to jump, don't let me stop you."

"You'd like that, wouldn't you?" Meredith immediately lost her desire to jump. Suicide was a private thing, and she didn't appreciate having a witness. Squaring her shoulders, she swiped the tears from her cheeks with the backs of her hands and moved away from the edge. "What are you doing here? Did you follow me?"

"Yes, I followed you. I wanted to talk to you alone."

Meredith gazed about. They were high above the sleepy little town of Falcon Ridge, protected by trees and brush. They were definitely alone. "What do you want?" she asked impatiently.

"I want you to leave all of us alone. Ross included." A pause. "You don't belong here. You've tainted everyone you've touched. And now . . . you're pregnant. Does Ross know?"

Meredith wrapped her arms around her middle. "Of course he knows. He's thrilled with the news of being a father again."

"Liar! I know who the father is, Meredith. And it's not Ross. You're not going to destroy us all. I won't let you."

Meredith didn't argue. She just wanted to be left alone.

"Here, this is for you."

Meredith took the envelope, but didn't open it.

"It's a plane ticket to Los Angeles. And I brought money. Lots of money. Because I know it's the only thing you care about."

That wasn't true. She loved Emma, and she loved Ross, in spite of how he felt about her. So what if it had taken her until recently to realize her true feelings for him? Glancing briefly at the black canvas bag on the ground, Meredith quickly turned away and looked out at the water again.

"Aren't you even going to ask how much?"

Meredith didn't care how much money was in the bag. She couldn't stop thinking about Ross and their baby girl. Suddenly, she had second thoughts about killing herself. Right now the only thing she wanted to do was go back in time and start fresh. She could beg Ross to forgive her. Find a way to make him love her this time.

"You only have to promise me one thing, and it's all yours," the voice behind her said. "When you go, you must promise to leave Emma with Ross. I don't want to see him hurt." She heard the rasp of a zipper, the bag being opened. "Turn around, Meredith."

Meredith slowly turned around with renewed impatience. "I'm not going anywhere without my daughter." She held the envelope out, intending to return it. "And I'm not leaving Ross. I love him, and I'm going to make it up to him."

"You little fool. He'll never forgive you." This time money was shoved into her hands. Twenty-dollar bills, stacked in neat little packets. There was so much she couldn't hold it all. Some of the packets fell on the ground near her feet. "Touch it. Smell it."

"No! Leave me alone!" she cried, trying to move away from the edge of the cliff. More money was shoved at her.

While struggling to escape, her heel caught on a tree root, jerking her back. She let out a scream as her arms flailed, trying to catch onto something, but grabbing only air instead.

In the next second, she fell backward and over the edge of the cliff, her cries deafening her own ears.

At the top of the cliff, the person who'd intruded on Meredith's privacy stood in shock for several moments before peering over the edge.

The horrifying sound of Meredith's screams, and then the sight of her lifeless body draped in blue, far below, would never be forgotten.

1

Fourteen years later

HER FATHER WAS a liar! He'd been lying to her for her whole life, and now she had proof. Emma clutched the letter to her chest as she ran through the neighbors' yards, onto the next street, and around a corner. Hot, salty tears streamed down her cheeks, her side aching from running so hard and so fast. But still, she kept going.

She'd repeatedly asked her father over the years about her mother, but he'd always refused to talk about her, other than to say "She was pretty" and "She loved you." But what about the memories? The good times between them? Emma had thought he couldn't talk about the memories because it must hurt too much to remember. She'd tried to understand. But now, after reading the letter, she wondered.

Coming to a halt at the end of the street, she dropped her weary body to the curb, her butt resting on the damp grass. Her pulse thumped rapidly in her chest, and her breathing was strained for a moment. Wanting to calm down and not to cry, she closed her eyes and tried to think. She didn't know what to do next. If she confronted her father, would he continue the charade? Or finally tell her the truth? Travis would be here soon. He'd help her figure it out. He always knew what to do.

Okay, she could understand why her father couldn't talk about her mother, but why wouldn't he want her to know that she had grandparents, aunts, uncles, and cousins, alive and living in Pennsylvania? What other kinds of secrets was he keeping from her?

ROSS MCLAUGHLIN SAT in the dark, his blood pressure rising, and waited for his daughter Emma to crawl back through her bedroom window. How long he'd waited, he wasn't sure. Between finding her missing from her room and discovering several shocking items in her desk drawer, he was still angry and visibly shaken. But right now, he couldn't do anything more than wait for her to return.

He hated being lied to. He'd already had enough lies and secrets to last him a lifetime. And he didn't want, or need, any more.

Max, Emma's shaggy, black and white mutt, sidled over to a corner in the room, his tail swaying slightly. Sniffing out a spot on the rug, he made himself comfortable. He, too, seemed to be waiting for Emma to come home.

A while later, the sound of squealing tires, fading in the distance, had Ross straining to look out the bedroom window. He spotted Emma, her white sneakers highlighted by the moonlight, running across the yard toward the house. He was relieved she'd come home safely, but it was all he could do to keep from going outdoors and dragging her inside.

As the window slowly lifted Max let out a low growl. Ross felt the balmy night air seep in, permeating the cool bedroom. The dog growled a second time, then—as if he suddenly realized who was outside—went to stand beneath the window to wait for his mistress.

One jean-clad leg swung over the window sill, then a second one. "Shush up, Max," Emma whispered, closing the window and locking it.

Seconds later Ross heard a click, and the room filled with the soft glow of lamp light. He raised a hand to shield his eyes, making Emma aware that she and the dog weren't the only ones in the room.

"Dad! You scared me to death! What are you doing?" she asked as Ross got to his feet and held her gaze. A mixture of anger and disappointment clung to his thoughts as he stared at his beautiful young daughter. Her iris-blue eyes were huge with alarm and astonishment, her mouth open wide. Her face was smeared with traces of make-up that she didn't need and was too young to wear. And the remnants of something flowery-smelling lingered on her skin and scented the air around them.

"I was about to ask you the same thing, Emma." Ross tried to appear calm, though he was anything but. God knew he wanted to choke her pretty little neck for worrying him.

She looked just like her mother, he thought. Or at least she had, before she'd whacked off her beautiful, spun-gold hair and added those ugly red streaks to it. It now stood out in two-toned spikes all over her head.

"I couldn't sleep," she began, "so I went out on the patio for a little while . . . for some fresh air."

"Stop it! No more lies! I know you were with that . . . kid." He'd chosen the word *kid* in lieu of *tattoo-covered, long-haired, guitar-picking idiot*, which was how he usually referred to Travis Walker—Emma's so-called boyfriend. "I told you I didn't want you to see him anymore!"

"But—"

"No buts. You're supposed to be grounded, young lady."

"But, Dad," Emma whined again, her bottom lip jutting forward, her eyes darkening as they filled with moisture.

"Emma, you're fifteen years old!"

"I'll be sixteen in less than two months," she argued. "And you still treat me like a baby." Flopping down on her bed, she crossed her arms over the front of her black T-shirt and glared up at him. Max went to her and let out a soft whimper before lying down on the blue plush carpet at her feet. "I *had* to see Travis. It was really important."

"What could have been so important that you'd disobey me and sneak out of the house?"

Emma continued to pout and glare at him. Several seconds later, she blew out an exhausted-sounding sigh, slightly shaking her head. "This," she said, reaching in her jeans pocket. She pulled out a folded sheet of pink stationery and handed it to him.

Ross recognized the letter and didn't bother to unfold it. "Emma . . . I was going to tell you—"

"When?"

Resting a hip against a corner of the dresser, he said, "When you got a little older."

Rolling her eyes, Emma set the letter aside and picked up a stuffed bear from the group of animals on her bed and hugged it to her chest. "Stop treating me like a baby."

He hadn't been prepared for this. "There's a lot of things you don't understand. And it's late. I think it's best if we talk in the morning."

At his reaction, Emma threw her hands up in the air and let them fall noisily to the bed. The bear bounced off Max's head before toppling to the floor, but the dog hardly seemed to notice. "I knew it! I told Travis you'd pull this crap on me."

"Emma, you deliberately disobeyed me tonight, not to mention worrying me half to death."

"Don't try to change the subject, Dad. This is about you lying to me all these years."

"I never meant to lie to you." Ross pushed away from the dresser and stood up straight. "My family and I had a falling out years ago, and I haven't been back home since."

"Did it have anything to do with my mother?"

Yes, everything. "No," he lied. "It's personal, it's between my family and me."

"They're my family, too, and I don't even know them."

"I'm sorry for that, but. . . ."

She snorted. "Yeah, right." After a minute, she added, "According to Grandma's letter, they can't wait to see me. And you, too. It doesn't sound like they're mad at all."

Ross sat down on the blue floral comforter next to her and buried his head in his hands. After a couple of deep breaths, he looked up. "I'm not ready to see them." What he'd actually meant was he wasn't ready to see his brother Barry. And he didn't want Emma learning about the things he'd kept from her for fourteen years.

"What about me? I should be able to decide for myself. Travis said—"

Ross raised a hand. "I don't want to hear what Travis said. You live under my roof, and I make the rules. I don't want you seeing him again. Is that clear?"

"I love Travis, and he loves me. Why do you hate him so much? What has he ever done to you?"

Did she mean besides corrupting his daughter? "Emma," he sighed, "ever since you met this kid, you've been skipping school, coming in past your curfew, smoking and drinking. You're using illegal drugs...."

Emma turned her head away.

"And now you're sneaking out of the house in the middle of the night to meet him and do only God knows what." And Ross didn't *want* to know. "This kid is a loser, Emma. Why can't you see that? He dropped out of high school. He has no future whatsoever."

"Travis doesn't need a high school diploma. He's going to be rich and famous some day. Just wait, you'll see."

"He and his band can't even get a booking in town. Do you actually believe they're going to make it big? C'mon, Emma. You're smarter than that."

"It's just a matter of time before someone notices his talent." Thrusting her chin out, she gave her father a look of defiance and triumph. "Look how long it took you to sell your first novel."

"Emma...." He shook his head, feeling defeated. It was pointless. She'd defend Travis no matter if he told her the kid was an ax murderer. "Okay, fine. Let's say he makes it big soon. Off he'll go to New York, or L.A. Without you. You still have two more years of high school, and then college."

"I'm not sure I want to go to college."

"It's not an option. You're going to college."

"Why? If Travis and I get married right after I graduate, then he can support me."

Ross nearly choked. "You are *not* marrying that kid. Do you hear me? I won't allow it."

"Dad, when I'm eighteen, you can hardly stop me."

"Emma, you're about this far from a spanking." He spread his thumb and forefinger two inches apart for emphasis.

"Get real." Another roll of her eyes as she got to her feet.

His threat *had* sounded pretty weak, since he'd never spanked her in his life. Standing up, he took a deep breath, not that it calmed him in the least. Then he went to her, placed his hands on her upper arms, and looked her in the eyes.

"Listen, no more lies and secrets between us. Promise me. If you want to go out, you come and ask me. You give me the details, and I'll decide whether or not you can go. But you have to promise to respect my decision. Whatever it is."

Her mouth dropped open as she stared up at him. "No way!" she said, jerking away from his grasp. "I'm tired of being treated like a damn baby!"

"Emma! Watch your mouth." Ross's efforts seemed futile, but he somehow got a grip on his temper. "Sit down, please," he said, pointing to the bed. When Emma finally sat, he dropped down beside her, then continued. "Look, I know you and your friends want to experiment with alcohol and drugs and ... *things*." He couldn't bring himself to say *sex*. "And I did the same *things* when I was a kid. But as your father, I expect you to follow certain rules. If you break those rules, you'll be punished. It's that simple."

Emma didn't answer. She looked down at her shoes, rather than look at her father.

"There will come a time when you'll have to choose between making smart choices and your so-called friends, and I suppose I have to trust that when those times come you'll use good judgment. But the lies, Emma. I can't stand the lying."

That brought her head up. "You should talk."

Ross looked at her intently. She was right, of course, but he'd lied only to protect her. Now he wondered if she'd ever forgive him.

"Just forget it." She shook her head violently, making her spiky hair flutter. "I'm tired and I want to go to bed now." At the sound of the word *bed*, Max's ears perked up. Seconds later, he pounced onto the bed and wormed his way under the comforter.

Ross and Emma sat in silence for several minutes. There was so much he wanted to say to her. So much he should have told her. After all, he knew secrets didn't remain secrets forever. But right now, more than anything in the world, he just wanted his little girl back. "You know, I've been thinking. We haven't done anything fun together in a long time."

"That's because you've been doing nothing but writing. You don't even date anymore."

That was mostly true. Ross's first mystery novel hit the *New York Times* best-seller list two years ago. Since then, he'd sold another book and was currently working on the third novel in his mystery series. Had he been paying more attention to his writing career than to his own daughter? he wondered, feeling sick with guilt. Had his neglect somehow driven her to Travis?

"I'm sorry, and you're right. Emma, you're the most important thing in my life. You know that." Ross searched her face, looking for a sign of forgiveness. "Can we make a truce?"

Emma screwed up her face and shrugged one shoulder.

"Why don't we go out for pizza tomorrow night?"

"Can Robin come?"

Robin Schneider and Emma had been best friends since first grade. "Sure, if that's what you want." He felt a little hurt that she wanted to drag Robin along rather than spend time with him alone. Just father and daughter, the way it had been for nearly fourteen years.

"Maybe we could ask Mrs. Schneider to come with us, too?" Emma's face lit up, while Ross grew uneasy. Ellie Schneider had been coming on to him since her divorce two years ago, even though he'd done everything he could think of to discourage the woman. She was a nice person, but there was something missing. Now, lately, Emma had been dropping hints about fixing the two of them up.

"I don't think that's such a good idea, Emma."

"Why not? She thinks you're hot. Robin told me."

Cringing inside, Ross forced himself to remain impassive. "Yes, well. . . ."

"She thinks you've never gotten over Mom, and that's why you've never remarried."

The thought of his love life, or lack of, being discussed with Ellie Schneider didn't set well with him, but he decided to ignore it. "Maybe you're right. That's why it wouldn't be fair to invite Mrs. Schneider tomorrow. I'd feel like I was leading her on or something."

Emma seemed to accept that, and Ross felt instantly relieved. He stood up and was about to say good night when suddenly an idea came to him. "You only have a few more weeks of school before summer break, and I'm almost finished with my manuscript. We should go somewhere this summer. Just you and me. How about a cruise?" he asked hopefully. "You've always wanted to go on a cruise."

"I don't know. Maybe." Her words lacked enthusiasm.

Trying again, he said, "Anywhere you want—you decide. A cruise? Disney World? Hawaii?"

Glancing up, Emma said, "There is one place I'd like to go."

Feeling optimistic, Ross clasped his hands together. "Where? Name it." He and his little girl were going to take a vacation together, he thought, smiling. He could take a break from his writing, and just relax with Emma for the whole summer. With no Travis Walker. He sighed with relief, until he heard her next statement.

"I want to go to Falcon Ridge."

His smile quickly faded at the mention of his hometown. "That's not what I'd meant when—"

"I want to meet my grandparents and my cousins and my aunts and uncles, and I want to—"

Ross shook his head. "Emma, listen to me—"

Ignoring him, she rushed on, "I want to learn about my mother. If you won't tell me about her, then maybe someone else will. Maybe my grandparents—"

"No! Dammit, I said no!" Ross pounded his fist on the dresser top. Several bottles of brightly colored nail polish rattled, and a picture frame toppled over.

"My grandmother is sick!" Emma squealed, ignoring her father's outburst. "How can you just ignore her like that?"

In spite of the mounting guilt, Ross shut off his feelings. Sucking in his breath, he counted to ten before saying what had to be said. "Emma, you don't understand. I love your grandmother, but I can't go back there right now. There were some things that happened years ago, when you were just a baby. Things you're too young to understand." "Well, I'm going. I'm going to see Grandma." Crossing her arms over her chest, she met his eyes, a determined look on her face. "I'm going to write her a letter and ask if I can come, and if she writes back and says I can, then I'm going. And if you don't want to go with me, then Travis said he'd take me."

Ross was sure he was going to have a stroke. He'd kill that punk if he tried to take Emma across the country. Slowly and calmly, he pulled out the desk chair, and dropped into it. "Em—"

"I'm serious, Dad. I'm going to Falcon Ridge this

summer—as soon as school is out—and you can't stop me."

How pathetic he felt over her words, and how true those words were. He couldn't stop her from sneaking out of the house in the middle of the night. How would he stop her from hopping in a car with her hippie boyfriend and heading across the country?

He wished he knew how to make a fifteen-year-old girl understand, but how could he? Emma was determined to meet her long-lost family. She wanted to return to her birth place—Falcon Ridge.

He supposed he should find some comfort in knowing that if he took Emma to meet his family this summer, she'd be away from her wild friends, beer parties, and Travis Walker. But he had a hard time finding comfort in taking her back. Because somewhere in the small town of Falcon Ridge, Pennsylvania, lived a killer. A killer who just might be a member of the family.

2

A S EMMA'S LAST day of school had grown nearer, the more apprehensive Ross had become. He couldn't believe he'd finally agreed to go back home. Emma's constant begging and pleading, and his insurmountable guilt over his mother's illness, had finally won out. Now, here they were. Just father and daughter, on their way back to Falcon Ridge.

As Ross drove through the state of Kansas, he glanced at his sleeping daughter in the passenger seat and shook his head. Maybe Emma had been right about him treating her like a baby. He *had* been overprotective at times, but to think she had been getting into trouble lately just to rebel against his authority . . . well, he wasn't going to dwell on that now.

The sun had started to fade behind them, and the traffic began to thin out. For the past hour, he'd seen nothing but road and vacant land. From the backseat of the Jeep Cherokee, Ross heard Max whimper. Soon after, Ross passed a sign that said a rest stop was coming up. Switching lanes, he watched for it. "Hang on a few more minutes, boy. We're going to stop and let you out." Max's ears perked up with anticipation of a walk.

The good thing about this trip was that it would give Ross a chance to spend some much-needed quality time with his daughter.

The bad thing was that he was not prepared to face the demons of his past, nor did he know how to protect Emma from the things she was about to learn. People gossiped in small towns. Rumors were sure to surface, not only about Meredith, but also about him. How would Emma feel once she found out that fourteen years ago he'd been accused of killing her mother?

"ARE WE ALMOST there?" Emma asked, wiping the sleep from her eyes. She hoped so. She'd had no idea how long, or how boring, this trip would be. Her father had said he was looking forward to driving, rather than flying. He'd said it'd give them a chance to talk about things. Although she had a feeling *things* didn't include her mother.

"Not even close," her father said, making Emma gasp. Surely he was teasing her. Hadn't she seen his mouth curve slightly upward?

Reaching down, she untied her sneakers and slipped them off so she could stretch her toes. She looked across the seat at her father as he drove. She could tell he was tired. There were tiny wrinkles near the corners of his eyes, and he looked like a werewolf with that five o'clock shadow. His dark hair brushed his collar. He was too old, and too conservative, to wear his hair that long. Wasn't *he* the one who'd always said Travis needed a haircut? Oh, well, maybe he'd let her trim it once they got to Falcon Ridge. Surely he wouldn't want Grandma to see him like that.

Emma wondered if her grandmother would even recognize her own son. She'd done some research on Alzheimer's disease, but there were things she still didn't understand. It was scary thinking about it. She couldn't imagine not being able to remember someone close to her. Like her father. Or Travis. Or her best friend Robin.

She remembered the stories Robin had told her about the old man who lived down the street from the Schneiders. He had Alzheimer's disease, and several times a week he'd walk down the sidewalk wearing nothing but his underwear. Emma hoped her grandmother didn't do anything as crazy as that.

"I'm planning on stopping soon. We can grab some dinner and a motel for the night," her father said.

"I thought we'd be there by now," she whined.

"Maybe you should look at the atlas there," he said, "and you'd realize that two thousand miles is a long trip for one driver."

"I said I'd help drive."

He shot her a look, his dark eyes narrowing in on her. "You're fifteen. You don't have a license."

"Sooooo? Travis lets me drive his car sometimes."

It's no big deal." He'd also been teaching her how to operate his motorcycle, but she didn't dare volunteer that information. There was no reason to make her father totally freak out.

"Let's not talk about . . . *Travis Walker.*"

Emma saw a muscle in his jaw twitch and, at the same time, the vein on his forehead seemed to double in size. She hated the way he said her boyfriend's name. Like he was slime. The problem with Ross McLaughlin was that he didn't recognize *cool* when he saw it.

Emma slouched in her seat, but that made her back ache. When she sat up straight, it made everything else on her body ache. She looked out the window but didn't see anything of interest. Just cars and trucks and bare land. "When are we stopping? I'm hungry, and I have to pee."

He sighed. "Emma, this trip was your idea. Remember?"

Yes, she remembered, feeling guilty for complaining. She wanted nothing more than to go to Falcon Ridge, and she certainly didn't regret all the threatening and begging it had taken to make her father give in.

She desperately wanted to learn about her mother. When she was twelve, her father had given her a picture. Meredith McLaughlin had been pregnant with her at the time it had been taken. Her mother had been beautiful. But a picture couldn't satisfy Emma's curiosity. A picture couldn't tell her what she wanted to know. She and her father had moved to Phoenix when she was only two, so she had no memories of her mother, or her grandparents. No warm gushy feelings.

"Emma, what's wrong?"

"Nothing."

"Don't tell me you're having second thoughts about visiting Falcon Ridge. Or that you want to go back to Phoenix so you can see that jerk."

"I thought we weren't talking about Travis. See how you change your mind when it suits you?"

Her father sighed again. "Emma, let's not fight. We have the whole summer to relax, and to sort things out between us. Let's start now. What do you say?"

Feeling childish yet unable to stop herself, she turned her head away and stared out the window. They passed a huge farm where a bunch of black and white cows stood near a fence. Didn't they have anything better to do than just stand there watching the cars go by? Probably not.

Didn't her father understand that Travis was the coolest guy in town? Every girl in her class would die for the chance to go out with him, and he'd chosen her.

"Emma," Ross said quietly. "What do you say?"

Emma turned her head, narrowed her eyes, and glared at him. "I still have to pee."

BEVERLY McLAUGHLIN CLUTCHED the letter from her granddaughter to her breast, careful not to crumple it. She still couldn't believe Emma had written to her, after all these years, asking permission to come for a visit. As if she had to have permission.

Carefully unfolding the letter, Beverly read it again and again. She had to be sure it was for real. Her mind had been playing tricks on her lately, and she wanted to be certain this wasn't a trick. After reading it one last time, she refolded it and placed it neatly under her bed pillow.

Ross and Emma would be here soon. She supposed she should touch up her make-up a bit. Moving to the stool at her dressing table, she toyed with her cosmetics before selecting a pretty mauve shade of lipstick. There was something important she needed to do today, but she couldn't for the life of her remember what it was. Neil would remember if she asked him. Her husband didn't have any problem with his memory, but it irked her to have to rely on him to remember everything for her.

The herbs, vitamins, and minerals he insisted she take daily hadn't been helping at all. Just as Doctor Larson had predicted they wouldn't. Beverly had an incurable ugly disease—Alzheimer's. And no amount of herbs, vitamins, or anything else was going to change that. Not even prayers.

Beverly could accept that. It was Neil who couldn't. She'd caught him crying one day a few months ago, and it had nearly broken her heart. He'd told her he'd do anything if she could just get well, but she couldn't. In fact, she was getting worse.

Looking in the mirror, she saw him standing in

the doorway, watching her. "Neil, you startled me." She picked up her hairbrush from her dressing table and smoothed a few strands of gray into place. The last time she'd seen Ross, there had been very little gray on her head.

"I'm sorry. I came to see if you needed help getting dressed," Neil offered, slowly entering their bedroom. He had aged well. Hardly a gray hair, except at his temples. He was still as lean, muscular, and handsome as the day she'd met him.

"I'm perfectly capable of dressing myself," Beverly insisted as she added a touch of blush to her pale cheekbones. "And, as you can see, I've accomplished the task without your help." She noticed Neil frowning at her in the mirror and spun around to face him.

"What did I do?" she asked in a panic, then looked down at her clothing ensemble. It looked all right to her. Her green chiffon blouse and slacks matched, and there were no buttons missing that she could see. The clothes had even been ironed neatly.

"Nothing, Bev. You look fine."

His patronizing smile told her he was lying. She'd forgotten something again. She was sure of it. "Neil, tell me."

Shrugging, he said. "It's nothing, really. Let's go down to the marina and check on things there. It'll give us something to do while we wait for Ross and Emma to get here."

"Okay," she agreed reluctantly. Maybe she'd been wrong. Neil would have told her if she'd forgotten something important. Remembering Emma's letter, she patted her pockets, but was unable to locate it. She glanced frantically around the room.

A moment later, she sat down on the end of her bed and started to cry. Neil came over and sat beside her. "Bev, what is it? Don't cry. Just tell me."

"I've lost Emma's letter. I can't find it anywhere."

"Shhhh," Neil whispered. "I'll look for it. Why don't you go take your pills? They're lying on the kitchen counter, and I poured you a glass of juice. Go on now."

Once Bev had left the room, Neil buried his head in his hands. This was the fourth time this week Bev had thought she'd misplaced Emma's letter. He didn't have to look under her pillow to know it was there, safe and sound.

Slowly, he rose and picked up the lavender pant-suit lying across the middle of their bed. The pant-suit Beverly had purchased especially for Ross and Emma's homecoming. He took it to the closet, hung it carefully on a hanger, and shut the closet door.

Why did his wife have to be affected by such a horrible disease, and at such a young age? "My poor Bev," he sighed, then went to make sure she took all the pills he'd put out for her. If there were a slight chance that the pills would help, then he'd see to it that she took every last one of them, every day.

But Neil had a feeling Doctor Larson was right, and they wouldn't notice any improvement in Beverly's memory whatsoever. In fact, every day she got progressively worse.

ROSS AND EMMA were coming home for the summer. The McLaughlins had talked about nothing else until April McLaughlin was sick of hearing about it.

To keep from thinking about her brother-in-law and her niece and the past, April busied herself with balancing her checkbook. She'd totaled the outstanding checks twice now, but had come up with two different amounts. "Darn!"

A dull, throbbing headache slowly pushed its way behind her right eye, threatening to explode into a full-blown migraine. Smoothing the loose strands of her nondescript brown hair that had fallen free from her ponytail, she thought about using a rinse to add highlights, knowing she wouldn't bother. What difference could it possibly make? Even if she were to totally change her hair color, Barry wouldn't pay any more attention to her than he would a fly on the wallpaper.

Which reminded her: She'd planned to re-wallpaper the kitchen this summer. She could no longer stand looking at the faded, vine-covered walls.

The muffled whir and vibration from the lawn mower grew stronger and stronger, drawing her attention to the kitchen window. Staring out at the backyard, she picked at a blueberry muffin and focused on her husband as he walked behind the mower.

Barry was on a mission. He'd always been meticulous about the lawn. He made a diagonal pattern with the mower, the way he always did. Each line was sharp and straight and abutted the one before it. It drove April crazy. The few times Barry had relented and allowed her to cut the grass, she'd walked with a crazy non-methodical rhythm that she was sure had made him cringe inside.

Sometimes, April would find herself imagining Barry's teaching their son to mow the grass in an orderly fashion, and scolding him for being careless and missing spots. But that was silly. Because she and Barry didn't have a son, or any children at all. They didn't have much of a marriage anymore, either.

Feeling it might help, she loosened her ponytail, then reached for her empty coffee cup. Caffeine. That might help, too.

After pouring the last of the coffee from the pot, she returned to the kitchen table and flopped down on the chair. As April began to punch numbers into the calculator for the third time, she couldn't help thinking about her niece. Emma would be fifteen now. Almost sixteen. A young woman. Probably beautiful, too, if she looked anything like her mother.

April closed her eyes, trying to ease the pain of her oncoming migraine, but mostly to shut Meredith out of her thoughts. Why did she continually allow a dead woman to intrude in her life? Why couldn't she let go of the past and go forward? Of course, she knew why, although she'd never admit it to herself or anyone else.

She'd never liked Meri. Still, she knew it wasn't

right to hold how she felt about Meri against Emma. Her niece was only a child. Yet April couldn't help but wonder if she'd be able to look at anyone who even slightly resembled Meri without feeling sick inside.

Barry came into the kitchen and set his mug on the counter, snapping April out of her trance. "Coffee's all gone?"

"Sorry," she told her husband, pushing her chair back. "I'll make some more."

"I'll make it," he said, gesturing with his hand for her to stay seated. With his back to April, Barry washed his hands and then fumbled with the coffee making. April breathed in the fresh-mowed grass scent he'd carried with him into the house.

A few moments later, he asked, "I thought you were going to try to cut back on caffeine?"

She knew the reason for her recent migraines, and she doubted caffeine had anything to do with them. In fact, she'd recently read where caffeine supposedly helped. But, a few weeks ago, when Barry had raised the suggestion that she curb her caffeine habit, she'd agreed that perhaps he was right.

"I guess I forgot." April made a pretense of studying the figures in front of her, ignoring the fact that he'd turned around to face her.

"Are you sure you forgot? Or did you just ignore my advice for the sake of ignoring me?"

Glancing up, she saw Barry, dark eyes narrowed, staring at her over his mug. Except for the extra pounds he'd put on over the years, he was still a hunk. And the silver streaks in his hair only made him more distinguished looking.

"You're being ridiculous."

"Am I?" He walked over to the table, snatched up her cup, and dumped the contents into the sink. "I thought you'd be more excited about seeing my brother and his little girl. But if you keep overdosing on caffeine you're probably going to be in bed soon with another migraine."

"I'm sorry. I wasn't thinking."

He let out an exaggerated sigh, shook his head in disgust, then shocked her by filling her cup and setting it in front of her. "Decaf," he said. "I threw the other stuff out." With that, he left the room.

His sacrifice should have made her feel special. Barry was even more addicted to caffeine than she was.

April tried to remember the last time she'd done something nice for him. She didn't mean cooking, or ironing his shirts; something nice, just because. She loved him. Otherwise she wouldn't have stayed with him all these years. Especially knowing that Barry had been in love with another woman. Was *still* in love with another woman. A dead woman.

3

THEY'D BEEN DRIVING for three days. Emma had never realized Pennsylvania was on the other side of the world. Just when she was about to scream that she couldn't take any more, the Jeep veered off the highway and down the exit ramp. A sign told her that Falcon Ridge was seven miles to the south.

"We're almost there, aren't we?" She caught a glimpse of her father as he nodded his head. Straightening her posture, she pressed her nose to the window as she peered out of the air-conditioned vehicle, so afraid she'd miss something of importance.

As they rounded a bend, Emma saw the glistening green water of Lake Falcon. Its edges were dotted with boat slips, while several boats sailed across its middle. "Look, they're water skiing. Cool."

"I can teach you how," her father offered. "It's easy."

Emma jerked her head around. "You know how to water ski?"

"Sure. You don't grow up around a lake and not

learn that." They rounded another bend, and the lake disappeared from view. "We have to cut through town to get to the other side of the lake. That's where we'll be staying."

The town wasn't very big at all. In fact, it was so tiny they drove through it in less than two minutes. She'd noticed a bank, something that looked like a combination drug store and barber shop, a movie theater with only two movie selections—both were films she'd already seen—and a beauty salon. Just outside of town there was a strip plaza with a grocery store, bowling alley, and a few professional offices. Where were all the malls? And she hadn't seen a Pizza Hut. That sucked. Falcon Ridge was sure different from Phoenix.

Emma saw two girls about her own age standing on a sidewalk talking and laughing together. They both had long hair—one had hers braided—and they were wearing girly clothes. Yuk!

Feeling extremely insecure, her hand went to her red and gold spiky hair as she glanced down at her jeans and T-shirt. Emma's friends back in Phoenix thought her hair was the coolest, but here she felt out of place. What if the kids in Falcon Ridge made fun of her?

Oh, what do they know? They probably wouldn't know cool if it jumped up and bit them on the butt.

Still, she was somewhat grateful her father had made her remove the stud from her nose. The kids here would probably think she was some kind of freak, for sure. Besides, the nose piercing had been

Travis's idea. She'd never really felt comfortable with it.

Her father turned down a narrow road, followed it to the end, and stopped in front of a white clapboard house. Emma turned sharply to look at him. "Is this it? Is this Grandma and Grandpa's house?" she asked, unable to hide her anxiety.

He nodded, then stared straight ahead, his body stiff and rigid.

"Dad?" Emma asked softly.

Emma followed her father's gaze. He seemed to be focused on the man standing in the front yard staring back at them. The man raised his hand and waved, but her father did nothing but watch him. He was tall and handsome and looked a lot like her father.

She shoved her feet into her sneakers, tied the laces hastily, then opened her car door. In the back seat, Max pranced back and forth, his tail swishing from side to side. When Emma opened the rear door, the dog dove out of the car and ran toward the man who had waved at them. Emma went around to the driver's side and opened the door. "C'mon, Dad," she said, not understanding why he wasn't hurrying. She waited impatiently until he turned off the ignition and got to his feet. "Let's go say hi to Uncle Barry."

Her father gave her a funny look. "That man isn't your uncle, Emma. He's your grandfather."

"But, I thought he'd be . . . old." Emma raised her hand over her eyes to shield them from the sun as she studied her grandpa. She knew it wasn't polite to stare, especially with her mouth hanging open, but she couldn't help it. That man didn't look old enough to be her grandpa, or anybody's grandpa. Tugging her father's hand, she said, "Well, then, let's go say hi to Grandpa." Feeling a little nervous, she pushed forward, dragging her father along. She'd waited too long for this moment, and nothing was going to stop her now.

ROSS WATCHED AS his father bent over to make friends with Max. Neil McLaughlin had barely aged since the last time Ross had seen him. Maybe a few gray hairs. Hell, *he* probably had more gray than his father, he thought, self-consciously lifting a hand to his head.

Since Neil spent so much time outdoors, his skin had always been a rich, golden brown, his face a little weathered but still handsome enough to turn women's heads. Young and old, the women had always flirted with Neil McLaughlin.

He was sixty-four, yet Ross was the one who felt at least that old instead of his thirty-nine, soon to be forty, years. Ross swore he'd aged considerably the past few months, between worrying about his mother's illness and his daughter's wild behavior.

As his father met them halfway, Ross noticed the slight limp in his walk. He'd almost forgotten about the car accident the summer that Meri had died.

"Hello, Ross," he said casually as he nodded to

his son, his lips parting in a half-smile. He extended his hand, and Ross took it. "It's been a long time." He squeezed Ross's hand rather firmly before dropping it. "I can't tell you how much this means to your mother and me." Taking his eyes from Ross, he looked down at Emma. This time he didn't hold back his smile. "Well, well. Who's this pretty little thing?"

Emma beamed. "Hi, Grandpa," she said shyly, then threw her arms around him, nearly knocking him off balance. He hugged his granddaughter back, rocking with her for a moment. Ross noticed a tear slip from his eye, and he suddenly felt guilty for staying away so long, depriving his parents of their granddaughter.

For several minutes they made idle conversation about his and Emma's trip. Since Ross wasn't quite sure what to say to his father after all this time, especially in front of Emma, he left the two of them alone to get reacquainted and went in search of Max.

The clapboard house seemed smaller to him, but it had a fresh coat of white paint. The shutters were now a dark green instead of the blue he remembered, and there was no longer a basketball hoop mounted above the garage. Naturally, the trees and shrubbery had grown considerably. Creeping myrtle still surrounded the perimeter of the house. The landscaping was dotted with summer annuals— mostly impatiens, his mother's favorite flower.

Looking out toward the lake, he saw the squealing gulls flying overhead, swooping down to splash in the green water and back up again. He took a deep breath. The smell hadn't changed. In all these years, he'd never forgotten the smell. The aroma—a mixture of diesel fuel, damp earth, and sunshine—filled his nostrils, reminding Ross of the first time he'd gone out on one of the fishing boats with his father and older brother Barry. His twelve-year-old sister Meggie had stood on the bank pouting because she hadn't been invited. Fishing was for men, Neil McLaughlin had said. Ross had been a man of seven at the time. That was back when he believed Neil and Barry were the best father and brother in the world—back when he believed they could do no wrong.

Rounding the house, he started for the back door but stopped suddenly, a movement catching his eye. The first thing he remembered when he saw his mother on her hands and knees was the way she used to dig in her garden. She'd spent hours planting, weeding, and fertilizing her seedlings as if they were tiny children in need of her love and affection.

Ross thought she looked smaller than he remembered, more fragile somehow. She was so engrossed in her work, she hadn't realized he'd been watching her.

"Hi, Mom." He waited for his mother to recognize him. But instead, she looked up, a blank expression on her face, and brushed the dirt from her hands and knees. "Let me help you up," he said, offering her a hand.

She ignored Ross's outstretched hand, pushing

off from the ground and straightening slowly. After staring at him for several seconds, she massaged her back and calmly asked, "Do I know you?"

At first, Ross couldn't speak. He'd just assumed she'd recognize him. She'd been writing to him all these years, and although she'd told him about her disease—that she sometimes forgot things, and people, this isn't what he'd expected.

"It's me. Ross." It felt awkward telling her that.

She thrust out her dirty hand. "Nice to meet you, Ross. I'm ... I'm. ..." She took her hand back before he had a chance to do more than brush her fingertips. It was as if she had suddenly realized there was dirt beneath her nails.

She had wrinkles around her mouth and green eyes; her hair was a pretty shade of silver, but she was still a very attractive woman.

"Ross," she said softly. "That's such a nice name. Would you like to come inside for some lemonade? It's fresh. I made it myself."

Swallowing back a lump in his throat, he managed to speak. "Sure, I'd love some," he said, and followed her inside the house through the screen door. The squeaky wooden door slapped shut behind him.

They'd remodeled the kitchen. It used to be yellow with daisy wallpaper. Now, instead of daisies everywhere, Ross saw navy and white checks. He didn't wait for an invitation to sit; he simply pulled out a chair and dropped his weary body into it, making himself at home.

He watched as she squirted Ivory Liquid onto her hands, worked up a lather, then rinsed them under the faucet. Some things hadn't changed. She'd always used Ivory. Reaching for a dish towel, she dried her hands and sat down across the table from him.

He watched her as her eyes darted suspiciously toward the living room and back. "We have to keep our voices down," she whispered, leaning forward.

Ross looked at the doorway, then back at his mother, not quite sure what to expect from this woman who thought he was a stranger. "Okay."

"He's trying to kill me." She wrung her hands together.

"Who?" Ross asked, taking her hands in his, trying to offer comfort.

"Shhh. Keep your voice down."

Ross wasn't sure he wanted to hear this. He didn't know if this was his mother speaking, or the frightened woman without a memory who occupied her body. So he didn't say anything, just listened.

"He gives me pills. Tons of pills, every day. Sometimes I swallow them, because he watches me. But if he's not watching, I feed them to the disposal. They're poison."

"How do you know they're poison?" he asked.

"Do I look stupid?" She jerked her hands away and raised her voice, apparently no longer caring if she were heard. "Who are you? Get out of my house!"

Ross abruptly scraped his chair back and stood,

feeling totally impotent. His heart raced, and beads of sweat formed on his forehead. "Mom, it's me," he said, but his words didn't seem to be registering with her. "Let me get you some of that lemonade."

Reaching for a glass in the cupboard where they'd always been kept, he noticed Emma and her grandfather standing outside the screen door and wondered how much they'd heard. Ross met his father's gaze, then looked away.

His father whispered something to Emma, then opened the screen door. Emma waited outside with Max.

"Bev, it's time for you to lie down," his father said, helping his wife to her feet. His mother didn't argue. After looking at Ross one last time, she simply allowed herself to be led away from the kitchen.

Ross walked to the screen door. It was clear to him that Emma was upset.

Max stood at her side, panting and waiting to be invited inside. "You know, your grandmother is confused."

Emma shrugged. "I know that."

"Maybe she'll feel better after her nap, and then you'll be able to visit with her," Ross said, hoping Emma believed that, wanting to believe it himself. He gestured toward Max. "He looks pretty thirsty. Why don't I bring a dish of water out for him, and a glass of lemonade for us?"

Emma shrugged again. "Okay."

Ross made his way to the refrigerator and pulled the door open, looking for the homemade lemonade his mother had bragged about making, but there was no lemonade in sight. He grabbed two cans of Coke and a plastic bowl from the cupboard, and went outside. After filling the bowl with water from the garden hose, he sat down on the stoop and hugged Emma to his chest.

It was going to be a long summer.

WHILE DINNER COOKED, Meggie hurriedly threw the ingredients together for chocolate chip cookies. Once dinner was over, and the mess cleaned up, she'd bake them. Ross used to love her cookies. Maybe Emma would like them, too. It wasn't much, but it would be something she could take to welcome them home. And after being on the road all those days, surely something homemade would be appreciated.

It had been nine years since Meggie had last seen her brother Ross. Nine years, two months, and twelve days, to be exact. She was sure, because that was the day she'd buried her first husband. Their son TJ had been seven, and Jeremy only a baby, when Tommy had died. They'd been living in Maine at the time. Tommy had accepted a job in Portland as a trial lawyer with a prestigious law firm. A dream he'd always had. A dream that had killed him. His heart just couldn't handle the stress and pressure of his job.

Flipping the switch to On, Meggie stared into the ceramic bowl as the mixer blades churned and whirred, spattering dots of dough here and there. A part of her had died when she lost Tommy. She'd tried to be everything to her boys. Somehow, she thought she could make up for the loss of their father, but she'd been wrong.

She'd been lonely, and she had thought when she met Steve Lattimer, four years ago, that she'd been given another shot at life. Never in a million years had she thought her life would turn into a nightmare.

"Christ, what the hell are you burning now?" Steve shouted accusingly as he stormed into the kitchen, the screen door slamming shut behind him.

Meggie had been so lost in her thoughts, she hadn't smelled the smoke. "Oh, no," she murmured, wiping her hands on the back of her jeans. She slid the skillet off the hot burner. As she lifted the lid, it became obvious that their pork chop dinner was ruined. And so was another night in their *humble* home.

Steve dropped a six-pack of beer on the kitchen table with a loud thud. She wondered why he'd bought only a six-pack tonight, finally deciding he'd probably been short of cash again.

"I'm sorry," she said just as the smoke alarm wailed. Meggie flung a dish towel in the air, using a back-and-forth motion, trying to rid the kitchen of smoke.

"You're sorry?" Steve taunted above the beeping sounds. "Is that all you can say?" Reaching up, he yanked the plastic contraption from the wall and jerked the batteries free, instantly quieting the room.

Meggie knew better than to answer when he was in one of his moods.

Slumping into a kitchen chair, Steve loosened his tie. His nose and cheeks were flushed, his blue eyes dazed. A dark blond strand fell from his neatly combed hair. She'd once thought him so handsome. Even more handsome than Tommy Slade.

"I've been out *all* day looking for a job in this stupid, backward town and you can't even manage to have a simple meal waiting for me at the end of the day."

Steve had slept until way after ten that morning, and he hadn't left the house until noon, according to her sons. From the smell of his breath, she doubted he'd been looking for a job at all. Unless it was taste-testing beer. More than likely, he'd stopped for a drink at Scully's Pub and had perched his butt on a bar stool for the entire afternoon. At least that's where she'd seen his red convertible parked when she was on her way home from work an hour ago.

She'd been up since six, and had cleaned the house, done three loads of laundry, and put in her nine to five at the Marina restaurant. A typical day for her.

"It smells in here," Steve complained. Lately he always had something to complain about. Meggie pulled a pack of matches from the drawer and lit a candle—spiced apple. That should help mask the smoky smell.

Popping the top on a beer can, Steve said, "I saw TJ's bike out on the walk. I thought I told him not to leave it there. Someone's going to steal it. If he thinks I'm going to buy him a car after the way he's treated that bike...." He paused and took a huge swallow from the can.

Meggie knew Steve had no intention of buying her son a car. They couldn't afford it, not with the mounting bills they had. And the lease payments on Steve's car were killing them.

"You can't compare Falcon Ridge with Portland. It's too small a town for someone to get away with stealing a bike."

Slamming his beer can down on the table, Steve glared at her. "Oh, that's right. There aren't any bike thieves in this stupid town. Just a murderer."

She knew he was referring to her sister-in-law Meredith's death. Meggie believed that her death had been a horrible accident, but Steve seemed to enjoy the fact that someone had gotten away with murder. Seeing the look in his eyes, Meggie regretted her words. To keep peace, and to escape her husband's hostility, she went outside to put TJ's mountain bike away in the garage.

When she returned to the kitchen, Steve was on his second beer. "So, what are you making me for dinner?"

Meggie swallowed nervously and opened the refrigerator, praying a home-cooked meal would magically appear. Why she had looked in the refrigerator, knowing it was practically empty, was futile, because Steve now had more than enough ammunition to use against her. She'd let him down again. She should have stopped at the grocery store after work, instead of saving that chore for her day off tomorrow. She knew better. Then why hadn't she stopped?

Because she'd wanted to hurry home and make cookies for her brother's homecoming. That was why. And now, she'd pay the price. Steve would see to it.

4

THE LAKEFRONT COTTAGE was one of the nicer ones. Ross thought his family should have saved it for the summer tourists, instead of giving it to Emma and him. Of course, Ross would insist on paying for it. Although his father and Barry would refuse his offer, and then remind him that he was still a partner at McLaughlin's.

The business had been started by Ross's grandfather and had grown considerably over the years. There was now a good-sized marina, twenty-four furnished cottages around the lake, and a clubhouse with a restaurant and snack bar. There was also a bait shop and several boats for rent: fishing boats and sail boats, as well as a few paddle boats.

Ross had gone to work for the family business when he was ten, but it had never been his life's dream. He'd always known he would be a writer some day.

Their cottage was ideal. Downstairs was a nice-sized kitchen with a breakfast bar, a living room with a fireplace, and a small study for his computer. On the main level were two bedrooms, each with its own bathroom. Outside, a wood deck jutted off the living room and kitchen with sliding glass doors to each room. A footpath led to the stairs and down to the lake, where a twenty-six-foot Sea Ray was tied to the small dock, bobbing with the waves.

Emma slid the glass door open and stepped onto the deck. "I can see the lake from my room." Making her way to the wood railing, she leaned against it and looked out at the water. "It's so pretty here, Dad. How could you have left?"

Emma looked at her father expectantly over her shoulder. A smile spread across her face, lighting her eyes as well. The first real smile he'd seen in months.

Sighing, Ross went to stand beside her. "There were a lot of reasons," he said, but refused to share them with her. She wouldn't understand.

"Where did we used to live?" she asked.

Pointing across the lake and to his left, Ross said, "See that white house over there?"

"The one with all the windows?"

Ross nodded.

"Wow! Who lives there now?"

"I'm not sure." That was the truth.

"Hey, look," Emma said, still staring across the lake. "There's Grandma and Grandpa's house. And the marina."

Down below, Max chased a sea gull off the property, then barked with emphasis to show he meant business. The bird retaliated with a series of screeching sounds. Ross and Emma were so caught up in the scene, neither heard the footsteps behind them.

"Aren't you going to show Emma where her aunt and uncle live?" Barry asked.

Emma spun around. Ross turned around slowly.

Barry had silver-streaked hair, similar to their mother's, and his tanned face had a series of worry lines, mostly around his mouth and eyes. He'd lost his lean athletic build and the hard layer of muscle that used to line his rib cage. In its place was a slight paunch just above his belt buckle. Barry probably didn't play much basketball anymore, now that the hoop was gone from the garage of their family home and his brother was two thousand miles away.

"I knocked, but I guess you didn't hear me. You look good, little brother. Guess you have to keep in shape if your picture's going to be pasted on all those book jackets for millions of people to see." Barry smiled.

Neither brother offered to shake hands. It was just as well. Ross wasn't sure if he would have taken his brother's hand, had it been offered.

Barry turned his attention to Emma. "You sure have grown, little lady. You got a hug and kiss for your old uncle?"

Emma's smile grew wide as she flung herself into Barry's arms. After a long hug, she stood on her toes and placed a kiss on his cheek. "I'll be sixteen in two weeks. I'll be able to drive and everything!" Shifting her gaze toward Ross, she added, "After I get my license, that is."

"Is that right! Maybe I'll take you out for some driving practice," he offered.

"Cool! What kind of car do you have?" Emma asked enthusiastically.

"Well, let's see." Barry rolled his eyes back as if trying to remember. "I've got a Ford Ranger pick-up, but you probably wouldn't be able to reach the pedals on that thing. And I've got a brand new Buick."

Neither of the vehicles seemed to impress Emma, Ross thought knowingly.

"But you'd probably do much better with the 'Vette," Barry offered.

Emma's face lit up. "You have a Corvette? Is it a convertible?"

"Sure is. And it's candy apple red."

"You still have that piece of shit?" Ross remembered when Barry had bought the car. Right before he and April were married. It was a wedding present for April, and it was probably the last nice car they'd be able to afford, he'd said, since April wanted to have at least four kids. So far, after seventeen years of marriage, there were no children.

"Yep. Never found anyone dumb enough to buy it off me, so I guess I'm stuck with it."

"Is it an antique?" Emma asked. "I mean, I don't want to drive it if it's valuable."

Shrugging, Barry answered, "It's just a car, and besides, no one drives it much anymore."

"A 'Vette! That is sooooo cool! I'm going to go call Travis and tell him." She ran inside, then stopped and ran back to the door. "It was nice meeting you, Uncle Barry." She paused, then added, "I mean, I know you probably remember me, but I don't remember you. Well, you know what I mean."

Barry chuckled. "Yeah, I guess I do."

Emma disappeared, leaving the brothers alone.

"Cute kid. Although, she's not going to be a kid much longer."

Ross nodded in agreement.

"You need any help unloading your stuff from the car?"

Ross almost refused Barry's help, then changed his mind. He'd promised himself he was going to make amends with his brother and his father this summer. "Sure, as long as you're offering." They walked back inside the cottage, grabbed the car keys, and went out the front door.

"April asked me to say hello." Barry lifted two boxes from the back of the Jeep Cherokee.

"How's she doing?"

Barry shrugged. "She would have come with me, but she's suffering from a migraine. I told her you'd understand. She said to tell you and Emma she'd come by tomorrow."

"I'll be sure to tell Emma." Ross grabbed his laptop and a few other items from the car and followed Barry inside.

"Dad said Mom wasn't doing very well when you came by earlier."

"No," Ross said bluntly. He didn't consider imagining someone trying to poison you, and forgetting your own son, doing very well, as far as he was concerned.

"She has good days and bad. I guess today was one of her bad ones. When she's feeling better, Dad wants us all to come for dinner."

Ross didn't acknowledge one way or the other. He wasn't ready for family dinners and casual conversation. Although he'd promised himself he was going to try his damnedest to bury the past, some things took time. Sometimes a lifetime. Sometimes more.

Ross and Barry worked in silence as they unloaded the car and distributed the few boxes to the proper rooms. While the brothers worked, Emma continued to talk on the phone, first to Travis, and then to Robin.

Max finally lost interest in the sea gulls when an orange and white tabby wandered into the yard. One look at Max, and the cat scampered up a tree. When Max realized the cat wasn't coming down, he headed up the bank toward the cottage.

When they were through unpacking, Barry asked Ross a few questions about his trip, then said he needed to get back to April and left. Only then did Ross breathe a sigh of relief, massaging the knot in the back of his neck. He tried to tell himself it was from being cooped up in a car for three days, but he knew it had more to do with old fears and uncertainties.

Ross opened a folding chair, eased himself into it, and popped the top off a beer can. Relaxed, he watched the sun set behind a thicket of dense pines. Listening to the waves slap against the boat below, his mind drifted. He thought about another night, the sun setting behind the trees. Although he didn't want to think about Meri, he couldn't seem to stop himself.

It was his first summer out of college. It had been a long day, and Ross was dead tired. After wiping his hands and forehead on a dirty rag, he opened the cooler on the dock and plucked a cold beer from the melting ice. He'd put in a full day at the Falcon Ridge Tribune, *then gone down to the marina to help his father and brother get four boats ready for a group of businessmen who were coming up from Pittsburgh the next morning.*

Neil and Barry had left a while ago, leaving Ross to finish up. That was the deal. Barry stayed late on Friday nights, and Ross got stuck with Saturdays. He was the younger brother, after all. And besides, Ross didn't have a wife to run home to, like Barry. As he drank his beer, he gave serious consideration to diving into the cool lake water to rinse off the grime and sweat that clung to his body.

The sun was about to set, and Ross decided to stay a while longer and watch it. Tossing his empty can into the cooler, he slid off his sneakers, yanked off his sweaty T-shirt, and dove into the lake. The water hadn't warmed up to its potential seventy-six degrees yet. It felt more like fifty-six. When he surfaced he let out a howl that must have echoed across the lake.

He heard a laugh. A giggle, rather. A female giggle. Looking around, he didn't see anyone at first, then he spotted her walking toward the dock. The pretty blonde who seemed to be following him around town. Meredith something or other. Lately, everywhere Ross went, he'd run into her. Of course, he'd never spoken to her—other than a nod or a hello. She wasn't from around here. Visiting relatives for the summer, or something like that, he'd heard.

"Is it cold?" she asked, lifting her long, golden-blonde hair away from her neck. With her arms up in the air that way, her hot pink sundress climbed high up on her thighs. As Ross treaded in the water below, he could see her white panties.

"It's freezing," he said, glancing up at her.

"Mind if I join you?"

Ross shrugged. He watched as she slowly untied the thin straps at her shoulders. She gave him a look of seduction with those big blue eyes of hers before letting go of the ties. Her dress fell below her naked breasts, then skimmed past her hips and thighs, before pooling around her feet. His mouth dropped open in awe.

She stood on the deck, wearing nothing but her bikini panties, as if she didn't have a care in the world. It was Ross who looked around nervously to see if anyone might be lurking nearby. The sun was about to disappear. Part of him was glad, and the other part prayed it would last until this golden goddess removed her panties.

Surely, this was a dream. Beautiful blondes

didn't just appear before your eyes and remove their clothing. He tried to appear casual about the whole thing, but when Meredith tugged her panties over her hips, he nearly swallowed his tongue.

He knew he must look like a real idiot. Would she think he'd never seen a naked girl before? And did he care? Trying to act composed, he let himself sink under the water and swim a few feet away from the dock.

Surfacing, he heard a loud splash and looked over his shoulder. Waves rippled toward him, the last of the sun's glow causing them to shimmer. About two feet away, a head poked out of the water and smiled at him. He could think of only one thing to say. "I'm Ross McLaughlin."

Her smile grew wider. "I know who you are," she said before swimming away. Ross swam after her. He tried to forget she was naked and just focused on swimming, which was extremely difficult, being that he was aroused. The cold water should have felt refreshing, but it was doing nothing to ease his condition.

They didn't talk much, just swam. After nearly half an hour they agreed they were both exhausted and decided to head back. When they reached the dock, she climbed the ladder first. He watched her with interest. What had he done to deserve this? he wondered. Whatever it was, he was going to make sure he did it more often.

"I was disappointed when you didn't strip naked to swim," she said as she wrung out her hair, the lake water bouncing off the dock.

There was no doubt in his mind she was coming on to him, but he decided to play it cool. Let her make the first move, he thought. She'd been doing pretty good so far. He considered himself pretty experienced sexually, but nothing like this had ever happened before. He'd slept with plenty of girls in college, and two during high school. But he'd never had one strip naked in front of him before telling him her name. Not that he was complaining.

He climbed the ladder, and their gazes met. She had beautiful eyes. Even in the moonlight, they sparkled. He was about to tell her so, when he noticed her shivering. "Do you want a towel?" he offered. Ross was cold, too. In fact, he was freezing his ass off.

"Please," she said, her teeth chattering. Ross climbed aboard the Chris-Craft and went into the cabin in search of a towel. He felt the boat rock slightly as she stepped on board. "This is nice."

He spun around. She was practically touching him, she was so close. There were no lights on in the boat, but he knew his way around.

Opening a cabinet, he pulled out two towels, handing one to her and using the other to dry the lake water from his skin. There wasn't much he could do about his dripping wet cut-offs.

She draped her towel around her and tucked it under her arms. "Do you have any beer, or wine?"

Ross stared at her in the dark. "How old are you?"

"Old enough." She sat down on one of the bunk beds. "I know you have beer in the cooler outside. I saw you drinking one before you jumped into the lake."

He figured she was nineteen. Twenty at the most. He supposed that was old enough, as he left her to get two cold ones from the cooler. Why should he care if she drank a beer? He'd only been drinking legally for a year, and here he was acting like a protective big brother. No, big brother wasn't exactly what he felt like at the moment, wanting to kiss her so badly it hurt.

When he returned, he ducked his head and joined her in the cabin, taking a seat on the opposite bunk. He popped the top from a can and passed it to her. There was barely any moonlight coming through the two small windows, but it was enough for him to see the outline of her face and towel-covered body. It was so quiet, he could hear her swallow.

"Aren't you going to tell me your name?" he asked.

"It's Meredith. But you can call me Meri."

Meri, but no last name. Not that it mattered. She was just some girl he'd swum with. No big deal.

Opening his own can, Ross asked, "So, what brings you to Falcon Ridge?"

She didn't answer at first. Then, after another sip from her can, she said, "I'm staying with my grandmother for the summer."

"Who's your grandmother?"

Again, she drank before answering. "Betty Ingall. She lives on Myrtle Street right outside of town. You probably don't know her."

He shook his head. "No." Amazingly, she was right, he didn't know her. That was odd for a small town like Falcon Ridge, where everyone knew everyone else.

"Actually, she just moved here two summers ago."

So that was it. "I was away at school for the last four years," Ross explained.

"I know. Boston College. You studied journalism. Heard you want to be a writer." She leaned back and made herself comfortable on the bed.

How in the hell had she known that? "I am a writer." He was doing his internship at the paper this summer, and they'd promised him a job as a reporter in the fall. It was a start.

"I mean, a real writer. You're going to write a book, right? And become rich and famous. Maybe move to New York City, or San Francisco, or somewhere?"

Of course, he'd dreamed of writing a novel, but he didn't confirm one way or the other. Instead, he asked, "So, how long are you going to be in Falcon Ridge?"

"Who knows? Maybe forever."

"Where's your home?"

"I don't have a home. Anymore," she added quietly. "The reason why I'm staying with my grandmother is because my stepfather threw me out of the house."

She tilted her head and looked at him, then lay flat on her back and opened her towel. He could see the mound of springy hair between her thighs.

His heart rate accelerated. "Why would he do that? What did you do that was so awful?"

"I didn't do anything."

Ross wasn't sure he believed her. "Where's your mother?"

"With my stepfather."

"Can't she do anything?"

"I don't know. I don't care. I don't want to go back."

"Why not?"

She lifted her head. "Trust me, you don't want to know."

"It can't be that bad, can it?"

She rolled her eyes in response.

"Okay, if you don't want to tell me, I understand."

Sighing, she whispered. "I can't go back. My stepfather raped me."

"He raped you?" he asked, stunned. He'd never known anyone who had been raped, and didn't know quite what to say to Meri. "I'm sorry."

She laid her head back on the pillow again.

"Does your mother know? Did you tell her?"

"I don't want to talk about it anymore."

"Okay. Do you . . . do you want me to call anyone? Your grandmother?"

She laughed. "You're joking, right?"

No, he hadn't been joking. He wanted to help her. Just moments ago he'd been thinking about having sex with her, but suddenly the thought of taking advantage of her made him feel like a total jerk. If only she weren't naked, maybe he could put it out of his mind.

"It wouldn't do much good now. Besides, my mother has her convinced that I was the one who seduced Rick."

How could a mother be so unsympathetic toward her own daughter? And how horrible it must have been for Meri, he thought.

"Ross?" she whispered, her voice turning weepy. "Could you hold me for a little while?"

He thought it was a simple request. She was in pain and needed a friend. It wouldn't hurt him to hold her for a minute or two. He stood, hunching over to keep his head from hitting the ceiling, and stared down at her. He tried to forget she was naked, knowing at the same time it was a hopeless cause.

That had been the beginning of their relationship. He'd seen her almost non-stop for several weeks, until she started talking about marriage and babies. That's when he figured it was time to cool it with her.

He wasn't ready for marriage and children. And even if he were, he didn't want to marry Meredith. She was a lot of fun to be around, but he didn't love her. He tried to distance himself from her, but that only made her more clingy. Every time he mentioned that they shouldn't see each other quite so much, she became hysterical, refusing to listen.

She'd accused him of being no better than her stepfather, although Ross had no idea why. He'd never raped her, or used her. They'd had fun together, but it was over. Unfortunately, that wasn't how she saw it.

He didn't learn until much later that Meri was a liar, but by then it was too late. She was already pregnant with his child.

5

AFTER TREATING TWO cases of poison ivy, four allergy patients, one broken wrist, a scraped knee, and a few other miscellaneous complaints, Libby Larson was pooped. That was a lot for a Saturday. She ran her hands through her short dark hair and sighed. She still had at least an hour of paperwork to do, but that would have to wait another day. Right now, all she could think about was a run on the beach, and then a nice cool shower.

Libby couldn't believe how many patients came to see her on a daily basis. She'd been worried that she wouldn't be able to make ends meet if she set up shop in a town this small. But after nearly two years, she had plenty of patients. Of course, that could have something to do with old Doc Sweeney retiring last year.

There was a brand new clinic just over in Newgate, but the people in Falcon Ridge liked dealing with a local doctor. Not that Newgate wasn't local; it was only four miles outside of town. Libby had grown up in Pittsburgh, so anything within four miles was a breeze.

But it was more than not wanting to drive outside of town. Doctor Elizabeth Larson was more than just a doctor to her patients. She was also their friend and confidant.

She was about to lock up and call it a day when Meggie Lattimer limped through the door, her face swollen and bruised, her bottom lip split open.

"My God, Meggie!" Libby cried. "Why do you let him do this to you!" She threw her arm around her friend and led her down the hall to the larger of the two examining rooms. "I'll be right back," she told Meggie as she went back to lock the front door and flip her sign to *Closed*.

Libby shut the door to the small room. Patting her hand on the blue vinyl examining table, she said, "Let me take a look at you."

It was obvious her friend was in pain by the way she moved, slow and controlled.

Meggie didn't look Libby in the eye as she said, "I fell down the basement stairs last night."

Libby knew she was lying. "That's twice this month you've fallen down those stairs." Carefully, she unbuttoned Meggie's blouse and helped her out of it. Seeing what that bastard had done to this beautiful woman made Libby sick.

"I know. I'm so clumsy."

Libby gently pressed the stethoscope to Meggie's chest. Even that slightest pressure caused her to suck in her breath harshly.

"I'm sorry. I didn't mean to hurt you."

Nodding, Meggie smiled slightly, crookedly. Her

mouth was so swollen, it was difficult to smile, had she anything to smile about, Libby thought.

"Why won't you press charges against that bastard? Why won't you throw him out?"

Tears came streaming down Meggie's cheeks, her eyes drifting shut. "I can't. You don't understand."

No, Libby didn't understand. She couldn't understand how Meggie could allow her husband to beat her like this. Or how she could allow him to stay in the same house with her and her two boys. But then, Libby had never understood why her own mother had done exactly the same thing.

Continuing with her examination, she tried her best to comfort Meggie as much as possible. She was so angry with the woman for not standing up for herself.

"Libby?" Meggie whispered.

"Hmmm," she answered, reaching inside a cabinet for a bottle of antiseptic and a handful of cotton balls.

"I think I'm pregnant."

Libby spun around, letting the cotton balls drop to the floor. "Oh, Meggie." She took Meggie's hand and held it in hers while her friend sobbed.

"ARE YOU SURE you're feeling up to this, Bev?" Neil asked.

"I told you. I feel fine." It was the fourth time that night he'd asked her that same question. Bev hated it when Neil treated her like an invalid. She draped her favorite Irish linen tablecloth over the dining room table and straightened the edges.

"We could always go down to the marina to eat. You don't have to go to all this trouble. No one will mind."

"We haven't had the entire family together in fourteen years," she said, sighing. "And I want this night to be special." Brushing past her husband, she headed toward the kitchen to check on the roast. Of course, Neil followed her. Heaven forbid if she were alone in the kitchen. Poor old forgetful Beverly might catch something on fire, or leave the gas on.

She might be forgetful at times, but she'd never do something that crazy, would she? Doubt niggled in the back of her mind, but she refused to give in to it just now. She was having one of her good days, or at least that's what her husband had been saying the past few hours. Nothing was going to spoil it. If that meant putting up with Neil's following her around, then so be it.

"Neil, if you want to help, you can set the table." Grabbing a mitt, she opened the oven door. Carefully, she arranged sliced potatoes and carrots around the meat. Another hour and it should be done.

When Neil opened the kitchen cupboard, she said, "Not the everyday dishes. We're using the good china tonight." She'd told Neil that twice already. Hmmm, she thought. She wasn't the only one losing her mind these days. Smiling to herself, she suddenly felt a little guilty for getting some small satisfaction out of that.

"Don't you want to cut some fresh flowers for a centerpiece?" Neil suggested.

She'd forgotten about a centerpiece. How could she have forgotten that? Her floral arrangements were almost as much fun to make as the dinner itself. It had become her trademark. Even if it were just a family meal, Beverly McLaughlin always had some type of arrangement on her dinner table. Maybe she wasn't having such a good day after all.

Setting the oven mitt aside, Bev grabbed a pair of shears and headed toward the back door.

"Wait, Bev. Let me help you."

Let me help you. She'd heard those words before.

The boys were coming for dinner. It would be just the four of them tonight. Barry spent most of his free time with his new wife and, since Ross had come home from college, he'd been busy working every waking hour. April had been invited, but she had a PTA meeting to attend. Bev was secretly happy—not that she didn't love her daughter-in-law. It's just that it had been a long time since the four of them had shared a quiet meal together.

Bev set the pot of water for rice on the stove to boil, lifted the lid to look at her chicken cacciatore, and took a whiff. Mmmm. Ross's favorite dish. Just as she set the lid down, the doorbell rang.

Hurrying to the front door, she chuckled to herself. It would be just like Barry or Ross to ring the bell. As a joke. The boys both knew this would always be their home even though they each had places of their own now. Barry and April lived in one of the cottages along the lake, and Ross had an apartment in town.

Bev flung the front door open and stared at the pretty blonde girl on her front porch. She didn't recognize her. "Hello," she said, smiling. "Can I help you?"

The girl blinked her big blue eyes and smiled sheepishly. "Hi, I'm Meredith. I was looking for Ross."

Ross? He'd never mentioned knowing anyone by the name of Meredith. "Well, he isn't here, but I expect him any moment. Would you like to come in?"

"Oh, no, I couldn't," the girl said, shaking her head from side to side. "Maybe I could just wait outside for him."

"Well, sure, but you'd be more comfortable inside. We finally sprung and got air conditioning this summer," Bev told the girl. "By the way, I'm Beverly McLaughlin. Ross's mother."

Meredith opened the screen door. "If you're sure you don't mind. It is awfully hot, and I did walk a long way to get here." She stepped inside the house and closed the front door. "Oh, this feels much better," she said.

It was unusually hot for September, with temperatures in the high eighties.

Bev smiled. "Can I get you something cold to drink?"

"No," the girl said, sitting on the edge of the green sofa Bev had just gotten recovered. "I don't want to bother you. I wouldn't have come here at all, except that I have something extremely important to tell Ross, and he's been . . ." She lowered her head slightly, then added, "avoiding me lately."

Bev didn't know what to say. She'd raised her boys right. They weren't rude. And they would never treat a girl with disrespect. The girl glanced at her, then turned away. Bev could have sworn she'd seen tears in her eyes.

"Are you all right, Meredith?" Bev asked, sitting down beside her. "Can I get you something? Are you sick?" The girl shook her head but didn't say anything. "Something's wrong. Please tell me. Maybe I can help."

"I'm so ashamed," the girl wailed, throwing herself at Bev. Bev had no choice but to hold the girl as she cried.

Patting Meredith's back, she said, "There, there. Hush now. Why don't you tell me what it is that has you so upset? I can't help you if I don't know what's wrong."

"I'm pregnant."

It wasn't exactly what Bev had been expecting to hear. Suddenly, she felt numb. "You're preg. . . ." Bev couldn't even say the word. "Is Ross the. . . ?"

The blonde head nodded against Bev's chest. Gently, Bev pushed the girl away and stood up. "What are you going to. . . ? Does Ross know?"

"Nooooo," the girl sobbed. "He hasn't returned any of my phone calls the past two weeks. I don't know what to do. My mother threw me out a few months ago. Since then, I've been living with my grandmother, but now she wants me to leave.

"She said she could barely afford to feed me, let alone my child, too." The girl buried her face in her hands and cried more loudly. Finally, she looked up. "I can't believe it. My grandmother. The only person in the world who I thought loved me. I mean, I can understand her hating me, but not this innocent child. Not Ross's child," she said, placing her hand over her flat stomach.

Bev's insides did a flip-flop.

"The thing that has me so upset is that I thought she was such a good Catholic. But when she mentioned, you know. . . ." Her face went back behind her hands, and Bev heard her mumble, "Killing our baby. Catholics don't believe in abortion, do they?" She became hysterical then, sobbing more and more loudly.

Bev ran off to the kitchen and filled a glass with cold water, then hurried back to the living room and forced it into Meredith's hand. "Drink it, please. You'll feel better."

The girl looked up at her, took the glass, and drank a huge gulp of water.

"Now, please try to calm down," Bev said, her voice a little shaky. "Ross will be here soon, and we'll sit down and decide what to do."

"Oh, God. Do you think he'll hate me? I don't want him to think he has to marry me, or anything like that. I'm sure lots of girls in Falcon Ridge have babies without getting married. Right?"

None that Bev could think of. And certainly none with her grandchild in their belly. It was a small town.

A good town. And the men here faced up to their responsibilities. Especially McLaughlin men. She'd raised her sons to be gentlemen.

Bev could barely think, but managed to come up with a diversion until Ross showed up. "Why don't we take a walk out back. I was going to cut some fresh flowers and make a bouquet."

Meredith rose to her feet, a smile pasted on her face. "I love flowers. Let me help you." The girl swiped at her damp cheeks and beamed, seeming to forget all about her dilemma.

Out back, Bev carefully chose each one of the flowers, clipped the stems, and passed them to Meredith.

The girl sniffed each of the flowers before placing them in a basket to take inside. "When Ross and I are married, I'm going to insist he bring me flowers every week," she said, a dreamy look in her eyes.

Bev swallowed uneasily. Just moments before the girl had said she didn't want to force marriage on Ross, and yet Bev decided that's exactly what she intended to do. She looked up to see Neil at the screen door.

"Something smells good in here," he yelled. Then, noticing the girl, he said, "Hello there."

Meredith's lips turned up into a smile, and she waved at Neil.

Knowing it would be best if she talked to her husband about their guest in private, Bev quickly got to her feet and brushed the dirt off her knees. "Excuse me," she said to Meredith over her shoulder.

Opening the screen door, Bev didn't ask the girl if she wanted to stay for dinner. She went to the kitchen cupboard, pulled down an extra plate, and set it on the table. Something told her Meredith had no intention of leaving.

EMMA HAD NEVER eaten so much in her life, but her grandmother had obviously gone to a lot of trouble to make this dinner, and Emma couldn't hurt her feelings.

Besides, everyone kept saying how skinny she was. She wasn't, of course, but old people always thought you needed to gain weight.

"I wish Meggie and the boys could have come tonight," her grandmother said. Emma noticed there was no mention of her aunt's husband, Steve. She got the impression Steve Lattimer wasn't well-liked by the family, but she wasn't sure why. Something to do with the fact that he couldn't hold a job.

"Emma, more pie?"

"No, Grandma, I can't. Really." Emma pushed her chair back to give herself some breathing space. The snap of her jeans dug into her stomach, and she couldn't wait to take them off as soon as she and her father got back to the cottage.

"Remember that time Ross ate a whole cherry pie?" her grandfather asked, nodding to the group at the table. "He was so sick afterward. He was about ten...."

Emma grinned as she listened to the story about

her father. Everyone in the room laughed, except her grandmother. It was as if she suddenly had no idea what they were talking about. Her father had warned her that her grandma could go from good to bad in a matter of minutes.

Emma watched as the older woman played with her fork, then tore her paper napkin to shreds. Then, right in the middle of another one of her grandpa's stories, her grandmother stood up and asked, "Would anyone like cherry pie and coffee?"

Pie and coffee had been passed around twice already. And she'd made two *apple* pies, not cherry. Emma glanced at her father, but his gaze was trained on his mother. The same as everyone else. Uncle Barry and Aunt April had sympathetic looks on their faces.

"I can't eat two whole cherry pies by myself," her grandmother said. "Someone has to help me eat them."

When no one said a word, Emma couldn't stand it. "I'll have some, Grandma."

Everyone turned her way. Her grandmother stared at her, then sat down, a strange look on her face. "What did you say, dear?"

Emma hoped she hadn't done anything wrong. She was about to repeat her request for pie, when her grandfather intervened.

"Bev, maybe you should lie down for a little while." He stood, pulled out his wife's chair, and helped her to her feet.

"But I made pie. I know I did." Grandma

McLaughlin looked over her shoulder at her family, then sadly turned away. "Neil, will you make sure everyone gets a piece of my cherry pie?"

"Of course, I will."

The room was silent for several moments, and Emma wanted desperately to break that silence. Sliding her chair back, she grabbed her dirty dishes and took them to the sink. She felt so sorry for her grandma, and she hoped she never got that way when she got old.

"Why don't you and I clean up the kitchen?" her aunt suggested, coming up behind her. "It'll give us a chance to get to know each other a little better."

"Okay." Emma hated doing dishes, but it certainly wouldn't kill her. Besides, it was something she could do for her grandmother.

As she and her aunt cleared the rest of the table, she had the strange feeling her father wanted to leave. He kept checking his watch as if he had an important appointment. Emma knew he didn't. She'd noticed how distant he'd acted toward her grandfather and her uncle during dinner, but she wouldn't dare ask him about it. He'd only lie, anyway.

Eventually her father got up from the table and said he was going to take a walk down by the lake. Uncle Barry went to the living room and turned on the television.

Emma and her aunt made idle conversation while they did the dishes. Aunt April washed, and Emma dried. They talked about school, and Emma's favorite subjects, math and English. Her aunt was a school teacher, and she said she missed teaching in the summers. Especially the kids. Emma couldn't help but wonder, if she liked kids so much, why she and Uncle Barry didn't have any. Of course, she knew better than to ask something like that. She had the feeling that even if she'd asked she wouldn't get a straight answer. She was just a kid, after all. And adults just assumed kids wouldn't understand. So, since she couldn't ask her aunt why she'd never had any children, it seemed like the perfect time to ask about her mother instead.

"You knew my mom, right?"

Her aunt stiffened at first, then relaxed and smiled. "Yes. You look a lot like her."

The thought excited Emma. "Do I?"

"Yes." April looked away, and began scrubbing briskly at a pan.

"I have a couple pictures of her. Dad gave them to me." Her aunt didn't say anything. "Were you guys friends?"

Her aunt stood still a few moments, then said, "Not really."

"Oh," Emma said, feeling disappointed. "I just assumed. . . . I mean. . . ."

"Meredith didn't have many friends." April rinsed the pan, set it aside, and drained the water from the sink. "Excuse me, but I didn't realize how late it was. I have to get home. I have a million things to do tomorrow."

Emma stared at the retreating back of her aunt,

watching curiously as she made her way to the living room and whispered something to her husband. She wasn't certain, but it seemed as though April hadn't liked Emma's mother for some reason. And Emma was determined to find out why.

ROSS STOOD ON the dock with his back to his parents' house and stared out into the black lake. The sun had set over an hour ago, and there was only a sliver of moon in the dark sky.

He'd needed to get out of the house to be alone for a few minutes. He was suffocating. If it hadn't been for his mother, he never would have agreed to a family dinner. His father had tried so hard all night to remind them of childhood stories and family events. As if Ross had forgotten them. Oh, he'd tried to forget over the years, but he couldn't.

He supposed that was what made facing his brother and father so difficult for him. A part of him remembered the old days, the fun and love they'd once shared. That's why he could never understand their betrayal.

The rickety old dock squeaked and moaned every time his weight shifted. From the way it looked and sounded, he knew it needed replacing. His father had enough to do with looking after Ross's mother. Ross decided he would come back next week and make the dock sturdier. It was the least he could do while he was home.

He didn't turn around at the sound of footsteps

behind him, figuring it was probably Barry, and he didn't want company at the moment.

"You're not thinking about jumping, are you?" a female voice asked. A voice Ross didn't recognize.

He pivoted around to see a dark-haired woman dressed in shorts and a skin-hugging tank top watching him. Her sneakered feet were jogging in place on the sand, so as not to lose her momentum.

"You see, I've had a long day, and I don't have the strength to save you if you do." She smiled at him.

Ross noticed she still had enough strength to jog on the beach. He stepped off the dock and walked toward her.

She didn't look familiar, but since his return to Falcon Ridge, he'd seen a lot of people he didn't recognize. They all seemed to know who he was, though. He'd seen some of them whispering, gossiping.

The woman thrust her hand out. "I'm Libby Larson."

Ross took her hand. "Ross McLaughlin."

"I know," she said, smiling. "How's your mother? I haven't seen her in a few weeks."

Shrugging his shoulders, Ross said, "She's. . . ." He didn't know how to answer that question.

The woman nodded knowingly. "Tell her to stop by to see me."

"Okay." Wherever that was.

Ross couldn't see the woman's eyes in the darkness, but he could see pretty much everything else. She was tall. At least five nine. And he noticed she wasn't wearing a bra. Her small breasts jiggled slightly as she continued to pedal her feet in the wet sand.

"Well," she said, "nice to have met you, but I have a mission to finish." With that, she jogged past him. Ross watched until she disappeared around a bend.

Libby Larson. The name sounded familiar. Then he remembered Barry mentioning that their mother was seeing a Doctor Larson. A female doctor.

When he was a boy, there'd been only one doctor in town. Old Doc Sweeney. He was so mean, he'd scared most everyone. Young and old.

Apparently, there'd been a few changes in Falcon Ridge, Ross thought, heading back to the house. Finally, a change for the good.

6

BARRY PULLED HIS shirt over his head and tossed it on a nearby chair, then unbuckled his belt. "Did you see how excited Emma got when I offered to take her for a spin in the 'Vette?"

April smiled. "How could I have missed it?" She sat down on the end of the bed, slipped her shoes off, then slowly unbuttoned her blouse. "Did you let her drive?"

"Yeah, but only on the back roads. She made me promise not to tell Ross. He has this *thing* about her waiting until she turns sixteen."

"I seem to remember Ross begging you to let him drive when he was only fourteen. And you let him, as long as he promised not to tell Neil."

"That was a long time ago. I guess he forgot what it's like to be a kid." Barry watched his wife make her way to the closet and hang up her blouse. She re-buttoned each of the tiny white buttons, then unzipped her beige linen shorts and stepped out of them, folding them over a hanger.

In her bra and panties, she walked to the queen-sized bed and folded back the comforter. Pulling open the nightstand drawer, she took out a dog-eared paperback and her reading glasses. Barry realized he was still toying with his belt buckle. Sucking in his breath, he let it out slowly. "I'm going to take a quick shower."

April didn't answer as she retrieved a cotton nightgown from her dresser drawer. At forty-one, she still had a dynamite figure. They'd been lovers since they lost their virginity together their junior year in high school. There was a time when they couldn't keep their hands off each other. They knew each other's bodies well. Although they rarely made love anymore.

Barry stepped under the hot spray of the shower. It wasn't that he didn't want to make love to his wife. He did. In the worst way. But he felt April was simply going through the motions. That she probably preferred he didn't touch her at all.

She'd changed. There was a time when she'd smiled all the time, even while she slept. But that was a long time ago.

Of course, he knew that if, after his shower, he climbed into bed naked and reached for her, she'd come willingly. He just wished she'd reach for him once in a while. That she'd lie naked, waiting for him, wanting him so badly that she'd already be wet between her legs.

Looking down at his semi-hard penis, he wrapped his hand around it and shook his head, feeling disgusted with himself for what he was about to do. Maybe, if he went to her and said something incredibly sexy. . . .

He sighed. There was no sense thinking about making love with April. It was obvious she didn't want him, that she'd rather read her book tonight.

When Barry finally returned to the bedroom, the lights had already been turned off. Since it was only ten-thirty he knew he wouldn't be able to sleep yet. Not wanting to disturb his wife, he fumbled in the dark until he located a clean pair of boxers, then left the room and headed toward the den.

APRIL WATCHED HER husband's back as he left the room. She'd climbed into bed naked, hoping to surprise him. Now she felt like such a fool. Tugging back the covers, she reached for her nightgown and pulled it over her head, brushing a tear from her cheek but refusing to cry. How many nights had she lain in their bed alone, crying helplessly? Wanting Barry? Needing him? They'd been so happy together once, before Meri had wormed her way into their lives and ruined everything.

Meredith—April had never met anyone quite like her, nor did she want to.

"Cool car," Meri squealed as April and Barry pulled into their driveway, their hair windblown from the top's being down. The October day was too cold for convertibles, but they'd dressed warmly in jeans and sweatshirts and defied the weather.

April looked at Barry and rolled her eyes. "Get rid of her," she whispered. "Or you won't get what I promised you." She raised her eyebrows and wiggled them.

Barry grabbed his wife and kissed her full on the mouth. April laughed as she kissed him back. Her husband didn't seem to mind that they had an audience, so why should she?

"Will you take me for a ride?" Meri asked, tightening her sweater around her middle.

Both April and Barry stared at the girl. Meri and Ross had been married for only three weeks, and just last week they'd moved in next door. Since then, Meri had paid them a daily visit. Sometimes twice daily. She was a pest.

April didn't want to be rude to her new sister-in-law, but they had nothing in common. For one thing, April was twenty-four. Meri had just turned eighteen and was extremely immature. And then there were those rumors. The ones she'd heard at Ruby's Comb and Curl. April didn't want to believe them, but Ruby swore that Betty Ingall wouldn't lie about her own granddaughter. Apparently, the little pest had been coming on to her stepfather, and once her mother had found out, they'd sent her away. Though April hadn't repeated the story to anyone except her husband, she found it hard to defend Meri. She was nothing but a flirt with every man—young or old—she came in contact with.

"Not now, Meri," Barry said, hopping out of the car and slamming his door shut. April waited for him to come around and open her door. "My wife and I sort of have plans."

April jabbed her elbow in his side as she got out of the car. He didn't need to broadcast that they were going to have sex in the middle of the afternoon. Ignoring Meri, they headed up the sidewalk toward the house.

"Wait!" Meri shouted to their backs. They stopped walking and turned to look at her. "Barry, please, I need to talk to you about something really important."

Meri looked pleadingly at them both. April was about to invite her in when Meri blurted, "Alone. Please, Barry."

Barry searched April's face, and she smiled reluctantly. Winking, he placed a quick kiss on her cheek. "I'll just be a few minutes. Don't start without me," he teased, and she jabbed him in the side again.

Once April was inside, she went to the den window, the only one that faced the drive. She could watch them from there. She trusted her husband, but she didn't trust Meri, who was nothing but trouble. Peeling back the curtain a fraction, she peeked at the two of them standing on the sidewalk as they talked—and laughed. She counted the number of times Meri touched him. Four. Why couldn't that girl ever keep her hands to herself? she wondered.

When it looked as though Barry was about to come inside, she quickly pulled the curtain shut. Racing to their bedroom, she started ripping off her clothes. Once she was naked, she bounced on the bed, positioned herself in a sexy pose, and waited for him.

She heard the front door open, and she smiled to herself, picturing the excitement she'd soon see on his face when he entered the bedroom.

"April, I'll be back in a few minutes," Barry shouted. The door closed again.

She jumped off the bed, draping her sweatshirt over her. A few minutes? Where the hell was he going? "Barry?" she called out to stop him, but it was too late.

Running to the den, she pulled the curtains wide open just in time to see him driving away with Meri in the car. April's car. Her candy apple red Corvette, a wedding present from Barry.

When her husband finally returned three hours later, April was fuming. He came through the back door, and she heard the keys clatter as they hit the kitchen table. "Honey?" he called out. As if she would forgive him if he called her honey.

"April, honey?" Barry walked into the living room, a guilty look on his face. "What are you doing?"

"What's it look like I'm doing?" she answered in her most irritable tone. "I'm overdosing on chips and dip. If you want supper, you'll have to go get your own bag."

They were supposed to have spent the entire afternoon in bed, and then go out for a movie and dinner. But her husband had rather spend his afternoon with his slutty sister-in-law.

"Honey, don't be mad."

"Don't honey me," she warned, biting into another dip-slathered chip.

Barry hung his head low and turned to walk away. That made April even angrier. Wasn't he even going to try to explain? Not that she'd listen to any of his flimflam excuses. "Aren't you even going to tell me what was so damn important that you would disappear for three hours?"

Turning around, he shrugged. "You know Meri. Everything is a crisis to her."

April glared at her husband. She was on the verge of tears. "What was the crisis this time?"

"She wants to throw a surprise party for Ross next month."

"You talked about a surprise party all this time?"

"Well," he said, pausing a moment. "Not the entire time. We took a drive, too. She wanted to see the top of Falcon Ridge, so we parked the car and hiked up the cliff."

"I see." She and Barry used to go to the top of Falcon Ridge to make out when they were in high school. All high school kids went there to make out. In fact, several of her high school friends had lost their virginity there, April and Barry included.

"Nothing happened, April."

"Why would you say that? What makes you think I suspect something happened between you and that . . . slut?" She crossed her arms over her chest.

"Don't call her that."

"Don't defend her, Barry. Every time I turn around, she's making eyes at you, touching you."

He came closer and took a seat in the recliner. "She doesn't mean anything by it. Meri just wants *people to like her And she's trying really hard to make friends in this town, but with her grandmother spreading all those lies about her...."*

"Please," she said, rolling her eyes.

"She likes you. She told me. She thinks of you as a big sister, and she wants to be friends. In fact, she's going to ask your advice about the party."

April bolted from the couch. She'd heard enough. "If she wanted my advice, she would have asked me to take her up to Falcon Ridge, now wouldn't she?" With that, she turned her back on her husband and headed down the hall toward their bedroom.

"April, wait. We could still go to a movie."

"Go to hell!" April slammed the bedroom door and locked it. Under her breath, she said, "Big sister, my ass! I know exactly what you're up to, little Miss Meredith. And you picked the wrong person to tangle with."

THE NEXT MORNING, Ross drove to his sister's place. She and her husband and the boys were renting a small house just on the outskirts of town. Neil told them Meggie had the flu, which was why she and her family hadn't come for dinner the night before.

But when Ross arrived, he found Meggie outside washing windows. TJ, the oldest boy, was mowing the small front lawn, and Jeremy was sweeping the porch steps with a broom. There was no sign of Steve Lattimer.

Meggie tossed her rag in a green bucket and waved at her brother. She walked, then half ran, to meet him. "Ross."

"Hi, Meggie." Ross picked her up and swung her around. "God, it's good to see you. I missed you last night." She'd always been a small thing. Barely weighed more than a hundred ten pounds except when she was pregnant. As he squeezed her tightly, he heard her quick intake of breath as if he'd hurt her. Carefully, he set her on her feet. That's when he noticed the black and blue marks decorating her face and body. He couldn't see her eyes, hidden behind dark sunglasses.

"My God, what happened to you? Were you in some kind of accident?"

"No. Well, yes. I didn't want to worry Mom and Dad, so I lied about having the flu. Actually, I fell down the basement stairs a few days ago." She quieted when her boys walked up behind her. Ross noticed the older boy roll his eyes when his mother mentioned falling down the stairs.

"Hi, TJ." Ross shook the boy's hand, then pulled him close for a hug. At sixteen, TJ was every bit as tall as Ross. He was a good-looking kid. Lean, dark hair, green eyes, and in need of a haircut. He looked a lot like Meggie. "You playing any basketball these days?" Ross asked, releasing his nephew.

TJ shook his head and sneered. "Nah, basketball's for sissies."

TJ's father, Tommy Slade, had played basketball in high school and college. Ross and Barry had played, too. And no one had better call it a sissy sport in front of Barry, or they'd be sorry.

"Hey, sport," Ross said to Jeremy, rubbing his mop of curly brown hair. Jeremy should be close to ten now. His face was freckled, and he was on the pudgy side, but still a cute kid. He'd taken after his father. "How about you? You think basketball is a sissy sport?"

Jeremy glanced at his brother before saying, "No. I like basketball."

Another sneer from TJ. "You're too fat to even dribble the ball."

"TJ," Meggie said sternly. "That was unnecessary. Apologize to your brother."

TJ did so, reluctantly, and Meggie forced a smile. "Where's Emma?" she asked.

"I dropped her off to visit with Mom, but she's anxious to meet you." Ross turned his attention to TJ. "You know, Emma's only a few months younger than you. I would consider it a favor if you'd introduce her to some of your friends."

TJ shrugged. "I guess I could."

"I'll introduce her to my friends, too," Jeremy chimed in.

"She doesn't want to meet any of your dweeby friends," TJ told his younger brother, thumping him on the top of his head.

Meggie looked helplessly at Ross. It looked to him as if TJ was giving her some problems.

"Why don't we go inside?" she suggested, and Ross agreed. It was a humid eighty-eight degrees in the sun. "Boys, finish your chores." A lot of grumbling followed her comment, mostly from the older boy.

Inside, the house wasn't much cooler. Obviously, there was no air conditioning.

"Sit down," Meggie said, pointing to a kitchen chair. Ross sat. "What can I get you?" He noticed that his sister still hadn't removed her sunglasses.

"Anything cold."

"I have a couple of Cokes in the basement pantry. This house is so small, there's hardly any cupboard space, and there's only this dinky refrigerator."

"Well, then, maybe we should have stayed in Maine," a man's voice said. "We had a nice big house there. But you wanted to move close to your mom and dad."

Ross stared at the man who'd just entered the room carrying a smashed beer can. Steve Lattimer, Meggie's husband. From the looks of him, he'd just woke up. His blond hair stood up on one side, and he obviously hadn't shaved yet. He made a big show of tossing his empty can into the trash.

"Ross, this is my . . . this is Steve," Meggie said, her voice quaking noticeably.

Ross stood up and shook hands with the man. "It's good to meet you, finally."

Steve yawned and pulled out a chair on the opposite side of the kitchen table. "Meg, get us a couple of beers, would you?"

"Sure," she said, hurrying off.

Ross would rather have had the Coke. It was only ten in the morning. A little early for beer, but he didn't want to appear rude, for Meggie's sake. "Thanks, Meggie," he said when she set the cans on the table.

Ross noticed there was practically a whole case of beer taking up space in the small refrigerator, but no room for non-essentials like Coke—Meggie's favorite vice. Or, at least, it had been once.

"I'm going to have that Coke." Meggie opened the basement door and flipped the light switch on the wall.

"Be careful on those stairs, honey," Steve said. "I wouldn't want you to fall again."

Ross noticed Meggie's shoulders tense. Glancing back, she forced a weak smile, and then turned to walk down the stairs.

"I sure love your sister, but she's as clumsy as an ox." Steve took a long pull from his beer, his gaze on Ross the whole while.

Ross tensed with fury. He'd only known this asshole for a total of three minutes, and already he hated his guts. There was something about the man that turned his stomach, and it was all he could do to keep from smashing his fist into his face. Lattimer wasn't a big man—probably five feet ten and a hundred and sixty pounds. It would be simple enough.

He'd never known Meggie to be clumsy. And even if she were, why would her husband taunt her that way? He clenched his beer can as reality struck.

What if she hadn't fallen down the stairs at all? What if Lattimer had caused those bruises?

Ross tried to convince himself that he had a wild imagination. It certainly came in handy when he was working on a book, but he found it intrusive at the moment. Yet the more he tried to ignore his gut reaction, the more it persisted. However, he should give Meggie a little credit. His sister was a bright woman; she'd never stay married to a wife beater. Would she?

When Meggie returned, the three of them sat at the kitchen table and made idle chit-chat, Steve doing most of the talking, mostly about himself. Whenever Meggie tried to change the subject, Steve would interrupt her and bring the conversation back around to him. Several times, while Lattimer had been bragging about one thing or another, Ross had noticed Meggie's forced smiles.

After an hour, Ross had had enough. "I should get going," he said, pretending to study his watch. He looked up at Meggie. "Walk me to my car?"

"Sure." Meggie smiled, but Ross wasn't sure if the smile had reached her eyes. He couldn't see behind her dark glasses.

Outside, Ross slipped his arm through Meggie's and headed toward the car, half pulling her along. "Keep walking. Don't turn around."

"Ross, what are you doing?"

"I want you to get in the car, and lock the doors. I'm going to get TJ and Jeremy."

"What!" Meggie stopped just short of the car.

"You heard me." Ross opened the passenger door. "Get in the car, Meggie. He's not going to hurt you ever again."

"What are you talking about?"

"I'm talking about your husband. I know he did this to you. Now get in the car." Ross gently nudged her toward the open door.

"Meg?" Lattimer called out from the screen door.

Meggie spun around, a horrified look on her face. Her gaze bounced back and forth between her husband and her brother.

"Your mother's on the phone," Lattimer yelled.

"Get in the car, Meggie," Ross ordered. "Now!"

7

SHE'D CALLED HIM crazy. He'd been trying to
help her, trying to save her from that bastard, and
he was crazy? Ross seethed with anger, a huge knot
forming in his chest as he backed out of the drive—
without his sister. She'd refused to get in the car, still
insisting she'd fallen down the stairs.

Had he let his imagination run away with him?
Ross didn't think so. Then, why hadn't he picked her
up and put her in the car? Because he knew Meggie
had a stubborn streak. She would only have climbed
out again.

He sighed, giving up, but only temporarily. On
the way back to the cottage, Ross took a detour and
ended up at Barry's.

"Hey, little brother. What brings you here?"
Barry invited him inside and offered him a cold
beer.

Ross accepted. After his visit with Meggie and
Lattimer, he was ready for one.

He chatted with Barry and April for several
minutes, then April made some excuse to leave,
saying she had some errands to run. Ross was

relieved, since he wanted to talk to Barry in private. After tossing half his beer back, he zoomed in on his brother. "How long has that asshole been beating on Meggie?"

Barry stared at Ross open-mouthed. "What the hell are you talking about?"

"I'm talking about Lattimer. He's been abusing Meggie. You should see her. She's covered with bruises from head to toe." Ross took another pull from his beer and forced it down his throat. He'd been sick to his stomach since seeing his sister.

"How long's it been going on? And why hasn't she ever said anything? Why didn't she come to *me*? Why did she tell you?" Barry fired his questions one after the other.

Ross set his empty can on the coffee table and eased back in the recliner. "She didn't exactly tell me," he admitted.

Staring at Ross, Barry asked, "Well, what *did* she say?"

Ross noticed Barry's fists clenching, his face turning a deep shade of red. Shrugging, he said, "She swore the bastard didn't touch her. But she's lying."

Barry sat forward on the brown leather sofa. "How do you know she's lying? Did you ask her?"

"Yeah, I asked her." Ross looked at his brother as if he were nuts. What did Barry think, that he would just ignore something like that? "She claims she fell down the basement stairs. When I tried to convince her to get in my car and come with me, she told me I was crazy and to mind my own business."

Barry pounded his fist on the table. "Fuck! Meggie *is* our business. She's our sister," he said, as if Ross had forgotten. "I never liked that son of a bitch. He sits up at Scully's most days when he should be out looking for a job. He turned down my offer to have him help out at the marina. Claims he isn't good using his hands, that he's better at using his creative powers. Lazy asshole."

Ross remembered seeing Meggie and the boys doing the household chores, while Lattimer had apparently been lounging in bed, nursing a beer. "Have you ever seen bruises on her before?"

Shaking his head slowly, Barry said, "No." Then, "Wait. A few weeks ago, April mentioned that Meggie was pretty banged up. I was up in Port Clinton. Had to deliver a boat. I was gone about a week, so whatever bruises she had were gone by the time I got back to Falcon Ridge." Ross noticed Barry's mind seemed to be registering something else. "Come to think of it, Meggie told April she'd fallen down the steps then, too. That bastard."

"I think it's time we pay him a visit. Just you and me. We'll have a talk—"

"*Talk*? Are you crazy? You think this guy's gonna leave Meggie alone because we *talked* to him? I say we take him out on the lake, beat the shit out of him, and dump him overboard. He can't swim, you know."

No, Ross didn't know that. But then, he'd only just met the man. What surprised him more than that information was the look on Barry's face as he devised a plan to dispose of their brother-in-law. And Ross was afraid Barry was serious.

"You in? We can do it tonight. After dark."

Ross squirmed in his seat, the heat crawling up the back of his neck. "Barry, what are you saying? That we take him out and . . . kill him?" As much as Ross liked the idea of beating the crap out the guy, he couldn't throw a man overboard and watch him drown. No matter how badly he hated him.

Barry looked away without answering, leaving Ross to feel even sicker inside. Was his brother actually capable of murder?

IT WAS THE third time that week Emma had gone to visit her grandmother. Other than a few brief lapses of memory, she'd seemed perfectly normal. After all, she was in her sixties. Certainly people *that* old forgot things once in a while, didn't they?

Her grandmother smiled. "Hand me the watering can, would you, dear?"

The two of them were tinkering in the flower garden. Although, her grandmother had claimed she'd needed Emma's help, Emma knew better. It was clear to her that her grandmother knew exactly what she was doing when it came to her flowers.

The first two times Emma had visited without her father in tow, her grandfather had stuck to her and her grandmother like glue. Today, however, he'd decided to go down to the marina to see how things were going. Emma suspected her grandfather missed working there. But, she supposed, with his wife so sick, he was unable to leave her most days.

So, in a way, she was helping both her grandmother and her grandfather. Her grandma confessed she liked talking to new people. She had complained several times that her husband hovered. Emma agreed. Her grandpa did hover. But, with all of the things she'd read recently about Alzheimer's patients, she understood his need for concern.

Emma refilled the metal watering can and handed it to her grandmother. "What kind of flowers are these, Grandma? They smell really nice." Actually, they smelled a little bitter, but she wanted to compliment her grandmother's hard work.

"Those are marigolds, dear. And I've started some seedlings in a tray for you to take home. You plant them around the cottage, and be sure to water them daily."

"Thanks, Grandma. I will."

The older woman swiped at her sweaty brow, then plucked several weeds and discarded them. Emma noticed she had tireless energy when it came to her garden.

She looked up. "Are you hungry, dear? Would you like me to make you some lunch?"

Emma smiled affectionately. "No, thanks, Grandma. I'm not very hungry." The truth was, they'd already eaten lunch an hour ago. And this was the third time since lunch that her grandmother had offered to feed her again. "Are *you* hungry? I could make *you* something," Emma offered.

For a moment, her grandma seemed to contemplate. "That's sweet of you, dear. But I think I'll wait and eat with you."

Emma grinned, then crawled in the dirt on her hands and knees. "I love you, Grandma," she said, giving her a hug.

The woman's eyes moistened. "I love you too, Emma. You don't know how many years I hoped that you'd come back to me. When you were just a little thing, you used to love to crawl around out here, just like you're doing now. Once, when I'd turned my back on you for just a minute, you grabbed a fistful of marigolds right out of the ground and started eating them."

"Yuck!" Emma laughed. "Did I like them?"

"No, I don't suppose you did." She sat back on her haunches and removed her garden gloves. "In fact, you burst into tears and wouldn't stop crying until I gave you a cherry Popsicle. You probably wanted to get rid of the bitter taste in your mouth. Though some people actually eat marigolds. You know, on salads and such."

Emma shook her head and scrunched up her face. "Well, you don't have to worry about me doing that again. I think I'm old enough to know better now."

Her grandmother smiled fondly. "You've turned out to be a fine young lady. And I'm proud to have you for my granddaughter." She reached out and touched Emma's cheek. "Your father has done a wonderful job raising you."

Emma thanked her for the nice compliment. "Grandma," she said, pausing a moment, "can I ask you something?"

"Anything, dear."

"What was my mother like?"

She stared at Emma as if she hadn't heard her speak, then picked up her gloves and brushed the dirt from the fingertips.

"Grandma?"

Her grandmother didn't look up. Instead, she grabbed her watering can and re-watered the same flowers she'd drenched only moments ago.

Emma didn't know what to do. Maybe she shouldn't have asked. It was obvious she'd upset her grandmother. Naturally, she'd been distressed by her daughter-in-law's death. Perhaps she still was.

Slowly, the older woman got up from the ground, brushed her knees off, and started to walk in a circle, either totally unaware she was trampling her flowers, or uncaring.

"Grandma, be careful!" Emma shouted. But the woman didn't seem to hear her.

Emma heard her make a gurgling sound in her throat, then watched as she held her ears. It was as if she were blocking out some kind of horribly loud sound. Around and around she went, then she began deliberately stomping her feet, smashing every flower in her path.

"Grandma, what's wrong? Do you want me to call Grandpa?" She watched her grandmother shake her head back and forth violently. "Grandma,

I'm sorry. I shouldn't have asked you about my mom."

Emma was scared and didn't know what to do. She wanted to cry, but that wouldn't solve anything. In the end, she decided to call her grandfather. He'd left the number for the marina on the kitchen table before leaving. "Just in case," he'd said.

Emma ran to the house and made the call, then quickly returned to her grandmother. By this time, she'd begun shouting. Emma didn't understand what she was saying. Most of her words were incoherent.

"Grandma, I called Grandpa. He's on his way." She doubted her grandmother heard her. And she wouldn't look at Emma, either. It was if she had no idea Emma was even there. This time, Emma did cry. "I'm sorry, Grandma. I'm so sorry I upset you."

Several minutes later her grandfather came hurrying through the backyard, dragging his bad leg. "Bev!" he shouted. "Bev, I'm here, sweetheart." Emma was thankful the marina was so close to their house.

Her grandmother continued to ramble, holding her ears, trampling her already ruined flowers.

Seeing the damage made Emma cry harder. "I'm sorry, Grandpa. I didn't mean to—"

"It's okay. It's not your fault. Pull yourself together now, and go inside and call Doctor Larson. Her number's on the wall by the phone."

"Okay, Grandpa," Emma said, wiping her tears and running inside the house again. She made the call and prayed the doctor would be there soon. She watched her grandparents from the screen door, but couldn't make herself go back outside. All of her grandmother's beautiful flowers were destroyed.

A little while later, a woman wearing a long flowing skirt and Birkenstock sandals came through the front door without knocking and made her way to the kitchen. "Hi," she said, a small smile on her lips. "You must be Emma. I'm Doctor Larson. Where's your grandmother?"

Without speaking, Emma pointed to the backyard. She watched as the doctor moved past her and went out the screen door. Doctor Larson talked calmly and soothingly, then opened a small black bag and pulled something from it. Emma suspected it was some kind of needle, and she didn't want to watch. Instead, she called her father at the cottage and told him what was going on, then sighed with relief when he said he'd be right there.

A few minutes later, Emma held the door open for her grandfather, who carried her grandmother into the house. The doctor followed closely behind, and the three of them disappeared, presumably into the bedroom.

Emma pulled out a kitchen chair and dropped into it. She hadn't noticed until then that her hands were shaking uncontrollably.

"Are you all right, Emma?" Doctor Larson asked moments later, pulling a chair up beside her. She set her black leather bag on the table in front of her.

Nodding, Emma forced a half-smile. She wanted to appear brave, grown up. Although, at the moment, she felt more like a frightened child.

"Your grandmother's going to be fine," the woman said reassuringly, reaching for her hand. Smiling, she gave Emma's hand a firm squeeze, then loosened her grip. "Do you want to talk about it?"

Emma jerked her head back and forth. What could she possibly tell the doctor? She didn't really understand what had happened.

The doctor patted her hand. "Okay."

The onslaught of tears surprised Emma. She hadn't meant to cry, but she couldn't help it. The doctor's arms were suddenly around her, comforting her. "It's okay, honey."

"I didn't mean to upset her, Doctor Larson," Emma said between sobs.

"Call me Libby. And I'm sure you didn't mean to upset her," she said between pats on the back. "What happened had nothing to do with you."

The girl looked so pathetic, Libby thought, wanting to comfort her. She gave her time to calm down.

Emma forced her lips into a curl, but the smile didn't reach her face or her eyes. "I wanted to know about my mom. She died when I was little, and I thought...." She shook her head. "My dad never talks about her, and all I know is that she was beautiful, and she died in some kind of accident...."

"Emma!"

Libby and Emma both looked up at the sound of Ross McLaughlin's voice. The man Libby had met on the beach a few nights ago.

"Are you okay?" he asked.

"I'm fine."

"Your grandmother?" Ross looked in the direction of the hall.

Libby stood up, smiled at him. "I gave your mother a mild sedative. Your father's with her now."

Without as much as a word to Libby, he touched his daughter on the shoulder. "I'll be right back," he said, then disappeared around the corner.

Libby didn't know whether the man was rude or simply upset about his mother. Deciding to give him the benefit of the doubt, she concluded it was the latter.

He was much more dangerous-looking in the daylight, she thought, remembering the night she'd seen him standing on the dock, the weight of the world sitting on his shoulders.

Everything about him was dark. Hair, eyes, and complexion. He was tall and lean with broad shoulders. His voice was deep and authoritative, and he was in need of a haircut, Libby mused. Emma didn't look anything like her father. She was fair-haired—except for the red-tipped spikes—blue eyed, and petite. What a contrast father and daughter made.

"I hope my dad isn't mad at me."

Libby stared at her. "How could he possibly be mad at you? What happened was not your fault, Emma. Because you were curious about your mother had nothing to do with what happened. Your grandmother is ill."

"I know, but she was fine until I asked about my mother."

Ross came around the corner, a stern look on his face. "What did you ask her, Emma?"

"Nothing," the girl said, pausing momentarily. "I just asked if she would tell me about my mom. And she got all upset, and—"

Ross came closer and touched his daughter's cheek. "We had this discussion, remember? You promised me you wouldn't mention your mother in front of your grandmother."

Emma looked on the verge of tears again. "I know, but—"

"Emma, promise me."

"Okay," she finally relented.

Ross held out a hand. "C'mon, let's go home."

Emma stood, but didn't take her father's hand. "I think I left the garden hose on." She walked to the screen door. "And I want to clean things up before we go." With that, she flew out the back door.

Probably to hide her tears, Libby thought. The poor little thing. Squaring her shoulders, Libby zoomed in on the girl's father. "Don't you think you were a little hard on her? It wasn't her fault, you know."

Ross looked her in the eye, but didn't answer. He wasn't much of a talker, Libby surmised. Not now, nor the night she'd seen him on the beach.

"The poor thing is just curious about her mother. She feels badly enough already. You shouldn't make her feel worse," she continued to lecture. "What happened to Beverly had nothing to do with Emma. Your mother's had these outbursts before."

Gaping at her with his mouth wide open, he retorted, "Gee, Doc, I didn't know you did family counseling as well as being a general practitioner."

"I'm only trying to help." Libby pretended not to be offended.

"I didn't ask for your help." Ross moved past her and toward the back door. He spotted Emma crawling on the ground. Suddenly, feeling guilty, he wanted nothing more than to go to her. With his hand on the screen door handle, he said, "Thanks for helping my mother, Doctor Larson. But since she's resting now, I doubt there's any reason for you to stick around. Excuse me."

Libby had been dismissed by Ross McLaughlin. She'd thought him arrogant and bossy and rude. And those were just his good points. Realizing she was no longer needed, or wanted, she grabbed her medical bag and left by the front door. As she sped off toward town, her mood darkened even more.

She'd heard the rumors about him. That he may have killed his wife fourteen years ago. Apparently, he'd been arrested for her murder then, after being questioned, was released for lack of evidence. Which was how things worked in small towns. Arrest first, ask questions later.

Some of the townsfolk said that he couldn't have done something so horrible. He came from a good family. The McLaughlins had a fine reputation. Libby knew all about good families and fine reputations. She'd come from one, also. And what went on behind closed doors sometimes never surfaced.

Of course, she'd never paid much attention to the rumors about Ross. And she wasn't the type of person to cast judgment on people she didn't know. Emma said her mother had died in an accident. Maybe it *had* been an accident, after all. Or maybe, Meredith McLaughlin had jumped off that cliff. Then again, no one really knew for sure. No one except for Meredith and God. And the murderer, if there was one.

8

EARLY THE NEXT morning, Ross drove Emma into town to purchase several flats of annuals. Emma insisted she wanted to replant her grandmother's flower garden. While his daughter was busy making her selections, Ross thought of something he wanted to do.

"Emma, I'm going to run a quick errand. I'll be back in ten minutes." He stuffed several bills in her hand and walked out of Sherman's Weed and Feed, headed across the street to the plaza.

He was mildly disappointed to see the *Closed* sign on the door to Doctor Elizabeth Larson's office. According to the hours posted on the door, she didn't open for business for another half-hour. He was about to turn around and leave when he caught sight of her through the door. He tapped twice on the glass.

She spun around, froze in place when she recognized him, then walked slowly to the door and unlocked it. Ross pulled it open and stepped inside. She wore a short khaki skirt today, showing off her long legs, which he tried hard not to look at. Her hair was cropped short, too short for his taste. Her face was plain and free of make-up. And she wore no smile on her unpainted lips.

But those eyes. They were clear and green. The color of the sea.

"Good morning," he said, for lack of anything else. She didn't return his greeting. Folding her arms, she looked into his eyes and stared.

"I. . . ." he started. "How long have you been here? In Falcon Ridge, I meant."

Her mouth opened and shut, then she dropped her arms and relaxed her stiff pose slightly. "Close to two years. Is there something you needed? Is your mother okay? Emma?"

Shrugging, Ross said, "They're both fine." Stalling, he walked around the small reception area, glanced down at a stack of magazines on a coffee table, and looked out the front window at the traffic passing by. "I came to apologize to you." He turned his head to look at her reaction. There was none. "I came on a little strong yesterday. Emma accuses me of being over-protective, controlling. I guess I am. Sometimes."

Libby leaned her hip against the reception desk but didn't say anything.

"And with my mother so sick. . . ." He paused a moment. "I'm afraid I don't understand her illness. I guess I can't believe she can be so . . . normal one minute and out of control the next. I was concerned about Emma, too. I don't want her upsetting my mother, asking her about things she probably doesn't even remember."

"Most Alzheimer's patients remember more about the past than they do the present." Ross nodded in response, watching her fingers toy with a button on her blouse. After a moment, she said, "I have some excellent reading material on Alzheimer's disease."

Without invitation, Ross followed her down a hallway and into her untidy office. Libby rummaged around through some papers and folders until she found what she was looking for. She handed Ross two pamphlets and a soft-covered book. "These may help you and Emma understand some of what your mother's going through."

"Thanks," he told her, taking the items from her. "Well, I should be going. You probably have patients coming in soon."

She walked him to the front door. Neither spoke. For some reason he felt extremely awkward around her. Ross pushed open the door, then turned back to look at her once more. Whatever he'd been about to say, he forgot suddenly. Instead, he thanked her again, and left.

ROSS AND EMMA had stopped to pick up TJ and Jeremy. While Emma planted flowers in his parents' backyard, he and the boys would repair the rickety old dock. Jeremy had been excited and eager to help, but TJ had only grunted and shuffled toward the car.

They'd already replaced several of the boards

when Jeremy shouted, "Ouch! I got another splinter." He held up his finger for emphasis.

"You're such a cry baby," TJ spouted off, not a trace of sympathy for his younger brother.

Ross laid his hammer aside. "Let's take a look." He didn't see any signs of a splinter, nor had he the last time Jeremy cried out. "You know, Emma could probably use some help planting those flowers."

Jeremy's face lit up. "Okay. I'll help her. That is, if you guys can manage without me."

Ross looked at TJ and raised his brow.

With a sneer, TJ said, "Go plant your sissy flowers. You're not any help here, anyway."

Jeremy barely waited for his brother to finish speaking. He was already halfway up the bank.

Ross picked up his hammer and started pounding nails. After a few minutes, he said, "You're pretty hard on your brother most of the time, aren't you?"

"Mom babies him. He'll grow up to be a sissy if I start being nice to him, too."

Thirsty, Ross opened a cooler, snagged two Cokes, and passed one to TJ. "There's a difference between babying your brother and being nice to him."

TJ threw back his head and took a large swallow of his soft drink.

Ross tried again. "I just thought that with all your mom is going through, you could try to be a little nicer to your brother, that's all."

TJ's hand paused in mid-air, then slowly he

pulled the can away from his lips. He didn't meet his uncle's eyes. Setting the can on the dock, he picked up his hammer and started pounding. When the boy went to reach for another nail, Ross interjected. "You get along with your stepfather?"

"Nope."

The pounding began again, and neither of them said anything for a good long time.

A few minutes before noon, TJ announced that he had to go help his Uncle Barry over at the marina. Ross stalled him. "You know, I love your mother. I'd do anything for her. And you and your brother, too." Ross looked him in the eye and was surprised when TJ didn't turn away. "If you ever need me, for any reason, you call. Okay?"

TJ nodded but didn't say anything. Slowly he turned to walk away. But the boy had only taken a few steps when he spun around to face his uncle. "You know, if you were so concerned about my mom, then why didn't you ever come back to visit her before now?"

TJ didn't give Ross a chance to answer. He hurried up the steps and out of sight without a backward glance.

Feeling guilty, Ross sighed, wondering how he could reach his nephew. Wondering if he was too late. Like he wondered if he was too late to help Meggie.

Ross finished repairing the dock alone, but his mind wasn't on what he was doing. He focused on his family instead. There was so much distance between them, and yet there was so much love, too. They'd hurt each other. Betrayed each other. Hadn't he somehow betrayed his sister and his nephews with his neglect? By trying to punish some of his family members, he'd managed to hurt some of the others, as well.

His spirits were lifted a short while later when he hiked up the bank and found Emma and Jeremy engaged in a water fight. Ross's parents watched their grandchildren from the back porch, smiles on their faces. Why couldn't they all be close again? he wondered. But it didn't take long for him to remember why.

HE'D COME HOME for lunch. Not to see Meri, but to see his baby daughter, Emma. Ross parked his car in the drive and opened the door. There was no sign of Meri or the baby, but he heard screams and squeals coming from the backyard. Ross followed the sounds to the back of the house.

The screams stopped when he got there. Meri stood in the middle of the yard wearing a skimpy black bikini. She was drenched, and her hair was sopping wet. His brother Barry, who also was wet, held a garden hose aimed at her.

Ross didn't speak to either of them, just turned on his heel and walked into the house. He went down the hall and quietly opened Emma's door. She was sleeping soundly. Closing the door, he went back to the kitchen and turned on the spigot. Just as he stuck his head under the faucet for a drink of water, Meri walked through the back door, a white towel draped around her shoulders.

"That's disgusting, Ross. Use a glass."

Ross ignored her, filling his mouth with gulps of water and swallowing. Wiping his mouth on a dish towel, he glared at his wife. "Not quite as disgusting as finding my wife and my brother playing water games together."

"Jealous?" she teased, turning her back on him. She wiggled her hips as she walked down the hall to their bedroom. "Maybe if you were home once in a while, I could play with you."

Ross followed her into the bedroom. "Knock it off, Meri. It wouldn't matter if I were with you twenty-four hours a day, seven days a week. You'd still flirt with every man you came in contact with."

"There's nothing wrong with flirting, Ross."

"Barry happens to be happily married. And you know how April feels whenever he's over here with you alone."

Meri unfastened her bikini top and tossed it on the floor. "Well, maybe April should keep a better eye on him before someone takes him away from her."

"Meaning you?" Ross ignored the fact that his wife stood practically naked in front of him.

"I'm not interested in Barry," she said seductively, as she slipped her bikini bottoms over her hips and stepped out of them.

"Aren't you?" Ross asked.

"No. I love you." She moved toward him and smiled, then started unbuttoning his shirt. "Don't be mad at me, sweetheart. This morning, you told me to water the flowers, but I couldn't get the darn hose to work. So I called Barry."

And he ran right over, Ross thought. "What was wrong with the hose? It seemed to be working fine when I got here."

She reached for his belt buckle. "What?"

Ross grabbed her hand to stop her. "What was wrong with the hose?" he asked again, annoyed with Meri and her little games. She always thought she could use sex to get her way.

Taking a step back, Meri laughed. "Nothing. I mean, I guess I had it twisted and the water wasn't coming out. Aren't I silly?"

She reached for him again. Ross nudged her hands away.

Meri pushed her bottom lip out into a pout, then stretched out on the bed in a sexy pose. "I'm innocent, you know. I didn't mean to squirt Barry. The water just came shooting out and the next thing I knew, he had the hose turned on me."

Ross stared at her in disbelief. It seemed that every time he turned around lately, Meri was making eyes at Barry. April had complained to him just last week about the same thing.

"Come over here and let me make it up to you." Meri ran her hands over her breasts and teased her nipples into points. The whole while her gaze was trained on him.

"I have to get back to work." Ross turned around and walked out of the room.

Meri ran after him. "You know, it would serve you right if there were something more going on between Barry and me."

Ross kept walking.

"You know, I could have had any guy in this town I wanted."

Whirling around to face her, Ross asked, "Then why did you have to pick me?"

Meri gaped at him, but didn't answer. Shaking his head, he stormed out of the house, his hunger forgotten.

EMMA AND MAX took a walk around the lake, occasionally stopping to admire the boats dancing across the water while others pulled skiers behind them. It looked like fun. Emma and her father had taken the Sea Ray out a few times, but she hadn't been brave enough to try skiing yet. However, her father had trusted her to drive the boat and pull him along on skis. *That* had been fun.

As Emma followed Max's lead, she wondered if Travis missed her. He hadn't called her in days. He hadn't even responded to any of the recent e-mail messages she'd left him. When she'd first come to Falcon Ridge, they'd talked on the phone every night. Lately, the calls had slowed down. Maybe he was mad at her for leaving him.

When she'd begged her father to take her to Falcon Ridge, she had no idea he'd want to stay for the whole summer. She'd been upset about that piece of news. But now that she was here, she couldn't imagine leaving any time soon. Not with her grandmother so sick. And not before she learned something about her mother.

She'd asked Aunt April and Uncle Barry about her. The first time, her aunt had mentioned that Meredith didn't have any friends, and the second time she'd said it was so long ago, that she barely remembered her. Her uncle had said even less than that, then quickly changed the subject.

She was sixteen, for crying out loud. Or, rather, she would be in a few days. Yet everyone treated her like a baby. Like they couldn't say anything about her mother for fear Emma couldn't deal with it. But they were wrong. Her mother was dead. And she'd dealt with it ever since she could remember.

They were on their way back to the cottage when Max spotted the same orange and white tabby that had been tormenting him since the first day they'd arrived, and took off running.

"Max! Max, get back here." Ignoring her, Max bolted up the bank and into a neighbor's yard in pursuit of the cat. Emma had no idea who owned the property she was trespassing on, and at the moment she didn't care. Because she wasn't leaving without Max.

So she had no choice but to follow. She ran around the side of the house where she'd seen him disappear. "Max," she called, then whistled as loud as she could. "Max, where are you?"

She heard a bark. And as she rounded the corner, she was surprised to see Doctor Libby Larson standing in the front yard, looking up into a huge tree and talking to someone or something. Max stood by her side, barking furiously at whatever was in the tree. Probably the tabby he'd been chasing.

"Max!" Emma scolded. Max quieted and sat down on the grass, looking guilty.

Libby turned her head. "So, Max belongs to you?"

"Yes. Is that your cat he's been chasing?"

"Uh-huh." Libby stuck her head between two branches. "C'mon, baby. He's not going to hurt you."

"What's your cat's name?" Emma asked, moving closer to the tree to get a better look. She spotted the tabby about three feet above her head, his fur standing on end, a vicious look on his face as he clung to a tree branch.

"Smiley."

Emma grinned. Smiley wasn't exactly smiling at the moment.

"He hates heights. Your dog chased him up this same tree last week. I tried to coax him down for nearly an hour before climbing up to get him."

"You climbed up there?"

Libby glanced at Emma and smiled. "Sure I did."

Just when Emma thought Libby was about to climb the tree, she noticed her father's Jeep coming up the dirt road.

"Dad!" Emma shouted, waving her hands.

He stopped the car and stepped out slowly. Removing his sunglasses, he tucked them in his shirt pocket and walked through the front lawn. "What's going on?"

"Max chased Smiley—that's Libby's cat—up in the tree, and he won't come down. He's scared."

Her father looked up at the tree, then down at Max. "Is that true, boy?"

"Dad, you can get Smiley down for Libby, can't you?" Emma beamed at her father and knew he would.

Glancing at Libby first, he said, "Uh, sure."

Libby smiled apologetically and shrugged her shoulders. "Are you sure you don't mind?"

"I think I can handle it without too much trouble," he said, unbuttoning the cuffs of his blue oxford shirt and rolling up his sleeves. He caught a branch and hoisted himself up into the tree with a minimal amount of effort, the muscles in his fore-arms taut.

Emma practically held her breath as she and Libby watched him climb a little higher. Max stood up and watched alongside them, his tail wagging vigorously.

But just as her father came within reach of Smiley, the cat let out a loud hissing sound and struck with his claw. Almost at the same time, her father lost his balance and came tumbling to the ground, landing on his back. Emma heard a loud, "Hmmmph!"

"Dad?" When he didn't answer, she turned help-lessly to Libby.

ROSS GRIMACED PAINFULLY. What the hell had he been trying to prove? All because Emma had looked at him like he was her hero, and he hadn't been able to say no. He tried to move, wondering if his neck or back were broken. Probably both, he thought, picturing himself in a wheelchair for the rest of his life.

However, he quickly abandoned those thoughts when he noticed the claw marks on his hand. *Damn cat probably has rabies*, he thought, glaring up in the tree. Smiley, who Ross thought had no business being called a name he'd never live up to, watched him with interest and licked at a paw while balanced overhead on a branch as if it were the easiest thing in the world to do.

"Dad?" Emma shouted, bending over. "Can you hear me?"

"Yes, Emma," Ross moaned. "I broke my back, not my ear drums."

Emma looked at Libby. "Can you do some-thing?"

Libby stared down at him, calmly. "I'll be right back. I'm going to get some antiseptic and a Band-Aid."

Ross lifted his head and scowled at her. "You're going to fix my broken back with a Band-Aid?"

Shaking her head in dismay, Libby said, "Your

back isn't broken. You just got the wind knocked out of you. The antiseptic and Band-Aid is for your scratch." She pointed to his hand, which was throbbing. Then, turning away from him, she headed for the front door of her cottage.

When Libby returned carrying a pair of dirty, worn-out sneakers and a handful of first aid supplies, Ross reluctantly sat up. His shirt was torn, and his favorite khakis probably had grass stains that would never come out.

Libby knelt beside him. "Give me your hand." Ross complied, and cringed when she dabbed it with a cotton ball that had been doused with something cold, wet, and extremely painful. "Blow."

Raising his brows, he said, "Excuse me?"

"Blow on it." She nodded at his injured hand while she ripped open a Band-Aid. Ross felt stupid, but he blew.

A grinning Emma, who was obviously enjoying the show, dropped to the ground beside him. Ross watched her blue eyes dart back and forth between the unsympathetic doctor and her father.

The doctor was bra-less again. And she smelled delicious. Sweet, like vanilla. She wore a black tank top with a ragged pair of cut-off shorts. Her feet were bare. She wore no polish on her fingernails, yet her toenails were painted a bright red. And a slim silver ring adorned the second toe on her right foot.

"You have a tattoo!" Emma shouted, pointing at Libby's ankle. "That is sooooo cool." She turned her head toward her father. "Dad, I want a tattoo."

"Forget it," Ross said.

Emma rolled her eyes. "But look how cool it looks."

Straining to get a look at Libby's ankle, Ross imagined a huge fire-breathing dragon halfway up her leg and wondered how the hell he had missed it.

Libby sat on the ground and lifted her long, slim leg, showing off her tattoo: a tiny lady bug on the inside of her right ankle.

"A reminder of my college days," she said. "I was pretty rebellious. I guess you could say I still am in some ways."

Ross didn't comment. He didn't care for tattoos. But on the doctor, he supposed it looked okay. Sexy even.

Emma rolled Max onto his back and rubbed his belly. "That's what Dad says about me. That I'm rebellious. You should have seen him when I got my ears pierced. And my nose."

Jerking his head in his daughter's direction, Ross gave her a look. Emma knew perfectly well it wasn't having her ears pierced that he'd objected to. It was the *number of holes* in each ear that had upset him. Four seemed excessive and unnecessary. And he refused to think about her nose.

After slapping a Band-Aid on Ross's hand, Libby shoved her feet in the dirty sneakers, tied them, and stood.

"Next Wednesday's my birthday," Emma said proudly, her fingers playing with Max's fur. "I'll be sixteen."

Libby offered Emma a charming smile. She had a great smile, Ross thought. "Are you going to do something special to celebrate?" she asked.

"We were going to go out for dinner, but I want Mexican, and there aren't any Mexican restaurants in town. So Dad promised to make fajitas."

Libby laughed. "This town does take some getting used to. I love Mexican, too. I'll have to make you some of my queso dip sometime."

Ross felt it coming, and before he could stop her, Emma said, "I know! Why don't you make it Wednesday night and come over to our place for dinner?"

"I'm sure Doctor Larson is a very busy woman," Ross said quickly before Libby could accept.

Closing her mouth, Libby met Ross's gaze, then turned in Emma's direction. Before she could answer, Emma said, "But it's my sixteenth birthday. Surely you could try."

Libby smiled and nodded. "Sure, I'll try." Turning her back on Ross, the pretty doctor threw an arm and a leg over a low-hanging tree branch and pulled herself up, treating him to a nice view of her rounded butt.

"C'mon, Smiley. Come to Mommy." With one hand, she effortlessly reached out and snagged the cat, then jumped to the ground.

Emma seemed impressed.

Ross felt like a moron.

Clutching the cat to her chest, Libby stopped in front of Ross, who was still sitting on the ground nursing his wounds. "Next time you climb a tree, Tarzan, wear sneakers."

As Libby walked to the house, Emma announced, "I like Libby. She is soooo cool."

Ross only grunted in response.

9

AS ROSS DROVE past Scully's Pub on his way into town, he spotted Lattimer's bright red sports car in the parking lot—not that anyone could have missed it. Slamming on his brakes, he made a U-turn. He planned to have a long talk with Meggie's wife-beating husband.

At one o'clock on a Monday afternoon, the place was packed. Most of these people, Ross assumed, were not here for lunch. Unless it was a liquid lunch. Ross opened the door to the smoke-filled bar and glanced around until he recognized the back of Lattimer's head. He was seated at the bar, puffing on a cigarette and flirting with a barmaid.

The faint sound of music echoed from a jukebox in another room, and Ross heard the clanging sound of billiard balls crashing into each other. The place hadn't been updated since he'd left town fourteen years ago. The same scarred wooden booths lined the edges of the room, and the cheap metal tables with the taped red vinyl chairs took up the rest of the space. But the mahogany bar gleamed as if someone had lovingly cared for it all these years.

Ross came up behind his brother-in-law and took a stool. Lattimer barely noticed him as he continued to flirt with the redhead behind the bar.

"C'mon, tell me what time you get off," Lattimer said, stabbing his cigarette into a filled ashtray, and blowing a cloud of smoke into the air.

The woman leaned over the bar, showing off her cleavage. "I told you. I don't date married men. They're bad news."

Lattimer snickered. "Who said anything about dating?"

Ignoring Lattimer and looking at Ross, the barmaid asked, "What can I get you?"

Ross looked at Lattimer's glass, almost asked for a beer, then changed his mind. "I'll have a Chivas and water on the rocks." The woman immediately went to fill his request.

Lattimer looked at him finally. "Well, if it isn't the famous writer. Hey, Ginger. This guy's not married. Rich and famous, too. How about if I fix you two up?"

Ginger looked over her shoulder and smiled sweetly at Ross, showing off a huge gap between her two front teeth. In an attempt to distance himself, Ross leaned back and nearly fell off his chair. She wasn't his type. He didn't go for big-haired, big-breasted women who wore clothes two sizes too small and smelled like dime store perfume.

Then again, tall skinny doctors bearing tattoos on their ankles weren't his type either, and yet he couldn't get Libby Larson out of his head.

Setting his drink in front of him, Ginger licked her lips and gave him her best come-to-me-baby smile. "So, how rich, and how famous, are you?" she purred.

Ross heard Lattimer snicker again. He wanted to knock the guy off his stool. Picking up his drink and tasting it, he smiled over the glass at the barmaid. "Not very rich. And not so famous." He saw Ginger's smile fade. "If I were you, I wouldn't waste your time on me." He winked, laid a few bills on the bar, then turned to face Lattimer. "Why don't you and I find a place to chat?"

"I'm comfortable right where I am."

Ginger interrupted. "You were pulling my leg. Right, Steve?"

"Hey, would I do that?"

"Yes. Last week you told me *you* were rich, and yet your wife had to come down to pay your bar tab. The wife you told me you didn't have."

Lattimer slid off his stool, dug a ten-dollar bill out of his pocket, and threw it across the bar. "Keep the change."

"What change? You mean the quarter? You owe me nine seventy-five."

Ignoring her, Lattimer strolled away from the bar. Ross followed him.

"So, brother-in-law, you want to talk to me? You buying?"

Ross didn't think the jerk needed another beer, but he nodded regardless.

Lattimer slid into an empty booth and yelled

across the room. "Ginger, bring us a couple of drinks. Your best scotch. And make it snappy." He pulled a cigarette from a pack of Camels and lit it with a fancy gold lighter. After a few puffs, he made a face and stabbed it out. "Trying to quit."

Once their drinks had been delivered, Lattimer looked Ross in the eye. "This town stinks. Why in hell would you want to come back here?"

Ross shrugged, took a sip of Chivas. "My daughter was curious about her roots, her family." Squaring his shoulders, he asked, "Why are *you* sticking around?"

Lattimer snorted. "Your sister wanted to come back. Missed her mommy and daddy. I always try to make my Meggie happy."

Yeah, right, Ross thought, remembering the way he'd been hitting on Ginger.

"Besides, TJ was giving her some trouble. Meggie wanted to get him away from the big city and the group of kids he'd been hanging around."

Ross understood completely. He'd done the same with Emma. "How's the job hunting going?"

"Shit, there aren't any jobs here."

None that he'd consider doing, is what Ross figured he probably meant.

"Unless," Lattimer added, "you're counting the new Wal-Mart that just opened." He threw his head back and laughed.

Ross forced himself to chuckle. "Yeah, that wouldn't be a place for a guy like you."

"You're damn right it wouldn't."

Ross saw him make eyes at a blonde across the room. It didn't seem to matter that she was with a man. Nor did it matter to Lattimer that he was married to Meggie. Ross couldn't begin to imagine what his sister had ever seen in this guy.

"Barry seems to have his hands full at the marina now that my father's retired. I'm sure he could use your help."

"I'm sure he could. But I couldn't work for him. If you don't mind my saying so, I wouldn't put a lot of faith in your brother. He doesn't know his ass from a hole in the ground."

Barry's plan to take this guy out and kill him was starting to sound pretty good to Ross. "Really, why's that?" He tossed back the rest of his drink and ordered another round.

"For one thing, I told him he should put up some condos, a hotel, and maybe a four-star restaurant. But he doesn't think it would go over. We could turn this town around. Maybe build a casino on one of those old boats. We'd have tourists coming from all over the country."

"Falcon Ridge is a small town surrounded by small towns. Maybe the people here aren't interested in a bunch of tourists taking up space."

"Look, I know your family has a stockpile of cash. And you must be rolling in some dough—what with two books on the best-seller list? Why don't you spend it? You can't take it with you, you know?" Ginger brought their drinks and set them down. "You know, I could go for a thick juicy steak."

Great. Ross knew he'd be picking up the tab for that, as well. "Order whatever you want."

Once Lattimer had placed his food order, along with another drink order, Ross broached the subject of money. "So, how much start-up capital do you think it would take to get a project like that going?"

Lattimer itched his head, appeared to be thinking about it. "I don't know, a few million."

Ross whistled between his teeth. "That's a lot of money."

"Well, we could start small. How much money they pay you to write one of those books?"

More than he was willing to reveal to this asshole. "Not as much as you think."

"But it's a lot, right? Seven figures? You can tell me. I'm family."

Family, my ass, Ross wanted to say. "How much did you make last year, Lattimer? Oh, that's right. You didn't work last year, did you? How about the year before? Or better yet, how much did you make in your best year?"

Lattimer looked appalled, then slapped his mouth shut. Apparently, Lattimer didn't think it was any of Ross's business how much he'd made. "I'm out of smokes," he said, getting to his feet. "I'll be right back."

By the time Lattimer returned, his meal had been delivered. He jabbed the meat with his fork and cut a piece off, stuffing it into his mouth. "This steak is tough." Dropping his utensils on the table, he pushed his plate aside.

"You know, I bet there are a lot of small towns just waiting to be discovered by a man with your . . . talents." Ross waited for his words to sink in.

Lattimer glared at him, picked up his steak knife and used it as a mirror to check his straight white teeth. "You trying to get rid of me, brother-in-law?"

Ross didn't answer.

"It would take a lot of money to make me skip out on my wife and those kids. Probably more money than you've got. Not that I'd consider doing such a thing." Lattimer looked at Ross with blood-shot eyes. "Meggie needs me. I'm the best thing that ever happened to her."

"Sure you are," Ross answered sarcastically. "And I'd hate to see my sister unhappy. Or my nephews. I think I'd have to kill anyone who tried to hurt them." He couldn't believe he'd added that last part, but he sure as hell wasn't sorry.

"That sounded like a threat."

"Did it?"

Lattimer laid the knife down, slid out of the booth, and said loudly enough for the entire roomful of people to hear, "Speaking of killing, did they ever find the guy that killed your wife? Or, are you still their number one suspect?"

NOTHING HAD CHANGED much at the Falcon Ridge Sheriff's Department in fourteen years. Except that the last time Ross had walked inside the building, he'd had handcuffs attached to his wrists. This time he walked in of his own free will.

Dan Reese sat behind a scarred metal desk, dressed in a gray uniform, a phone receiver balanced between his shoulder and his ear. Ross had been told that Dan, formerly a deputy, had replaced his father as sheriff.

Wearing a matching uniform, a younger man with a receding forehead and a ruddy complexion occupied the second desk. It was this man who greeted Ross. "Can I help you, sir?" His tag read R.H. Maloney, Deputy.

"I'd like to speak to Dan." Ross swallowed. "I mean, the Sheriff." Ross and Dan weren't exactly friends, although they had been at one time. But that was before Dan and his father had accused Ross of killing Meri and arrested him without a single shred of evidence.

"Dan," the deputy shouted, ignoring the fact that his superior was on the telephone, "someone's here to see you."

Dan Reese looked up, met Ross's gaze, and quickly ended his phone conversation. He stood, but didn't move from behind his desk. "Well, I couldn't have been more surprised than if Santa Claus had just walked in. What can I do for you, McLaughlin?"

Dan was a tall man. Nearly six-four, without an ounce of fat. His hair was red, his skin freckled, his eyes a dark shade of olive.

He'd dated Meggie until Tommy Slade had stolen her away from him their senior year in high school. Ahead of Ross by five years, Dan had been one hell of a basketball player, and Ross's mentor.

"I was hoping to ask you for a favor."

Dan couldn't have looked more surprised. "What kind of favor?"

Ross pulled up a chrome and vinyl chair and sat down. Dan followed suit. "What kind of favor?" he repeated.

"I'd like you to keep an eye on Meggie."

Dan narrowed his eyes. "Why?"

Ross blew out a breath. "Because I don't like the guy she's married to."

Dan picked up a pen from his cluttered desk, studied it, then tapped it against his palm a few times. "What does that mean, exactly?"

"It means I don't like the guy. I don't trust him. And—"

"You want me to watch Meggie? Or her husband?"

"Both."

"Give me a reason, Ross. I can't go around bothering innocent people." He resumed the tapping.

Ross gave him a look. *Oh, that's right. Just innocent people like me.* "I think Lattimer is abusing her."

Dan set the pen down. "Did she tell you that?" Splotches of color crept into his face and neck.

"She didn't have to," he said. "I think she's afraid of him. Afraid of what he'll do if she tries to leave him."

Dan took a breath and released it on a sigh, folded his arms across his chest, and leaned casually back in his chair. "You know, Lattimer stopped by here this morning."

Ross sat up straight.

"Said you've been trying to turn Meggie and the boys against him. Said you threatened him."

Ross didn't answer. He'd wasted his time coming here. Dan wasn't about to believe a word he said. He went to stand when Dan uncrossed his arms, held up a hand, and sat forward in his chair.

"I need to hear this from Meggie."

Confused, Ross asked, "What do you want me to do, drag her in here?"

Dan shook his head. "Look, for what it's worth, I believe you. But my hands are tied. And Lattimer strikes me as a complete jerk."

"Meggie doesn't deserve this."

"No, she doesn't," Dan said.

Ross noticed the sadness in Dan's eyes as he stood, and wondered if he still had feelings for Meggie. According to Barry, Dan had lost his wife to cancer a few years ago.

Ross stood too, realizing the meeting was over.

"Ross, I'll talk to Meggie. I usually have lunch at the marina once a week or so. Maybe she'll open up to me."

"Thanks, I'd appreciate that."

"And I'll have a talk with Lattimer, too."

"He spends most of his days at Scully's," Ross told him. "It wouldn't be hard to spot his car when he leaves. It would be too bad if you happened to pick him up on a DUI."

Dan raised his brows as if to say, "You can't be serious," then walked him to the door, a mere twelve feet away. Just as Ross was about to walk out, the door opened and a young man resembling Dan to a tee walked in.

"Hi, Dad."

"Hello, Zack."

The kid stared at Ross as if he were trying to place him. Dan introduced them. "Zack, this is Mr. McLaughlin. Ross McLaughlin. He's staying in one of the lake cottages for the summer. Ross, my son, Zackery."

Ross offered the kid his hand and Zack shook it enthusiastically. "Mr. McLaughlin. Nice to meet you, sir. I met your daughter a few days ago."

"Is that right?"

"Yeah, she stopped by the marina to talk to TJ. I work at the marina on weekends. Or whenever your brother needs an extra hand."

Nodding, Ross glanced at Dan.

"Well, Mr. McLaughlin was just leaving," Dan told his son. To Ross, he said, "I'll be in touch."

EMMA REACHED INTO the kitchen cupboard for a third plate. Maybe her father wasn't expecting Libby to show for dinner tonight, but Emma was. Her plan was foolproof.

Earlier, when Emma had played the message of Libby's voice declining her dinner invitation because of a medical emergency, she'd known it was because her father hadn't gone out of his way to make Libby feel welcome. In fact, he'd done everything he could to talk her out of it, and it had worked.

But Emma wasn't about to take no for an answer. It was her sixteenth birthday, and if she couldn't have Travis or Robin, she could at least have Libby at the dinner table. No matter what her father had to say about it.

Besides, Libby was her only friend in Falcon Ridge so far. She was perfect for her father. And once he got to know her, he'd think so, too.

Emma had made it a point to stop by Libby's house nearly every evening since the cat incident. They'd talked about everything from boys and movies to sex and dating. Even alcohol and drugs. The doctor had even admitted to smoking pot when she was in college. Those were things Emma couldn't talk to her father about. He'd probably have a canary, as Libby would say. Libby was so cool, and so easy to talk to.

"Emma, why are you setting three places?" her father asked, startling her. "You know Doctor Larson can't make it tonight."

"Just in case. You never know. She might show up." She averted her eyes, trying to hide her smile.

"Emma," Ross said impatiently. He'd been secretly happy it would be just the two of them. Father and daughter. They'd been getting along so well since they'd been in Falcon Ridge. It was almost hard to believe. Tomorrow night they were getting together with the rest of the family at the marina restaurant to celebrate Emma's birthday.

Ignoring him, Emma grabbed a bite of tomato from the cutting board and popped it into her mouth. "We should open a bottle of wine."

Ross scowled at his daughter. "*We?*"

"Dad, I'm sixteen. I can have a teeny little sip of wine with my birthday dinner. Just this once."

Ross closed his eyes for a moment and nearly chopped off his thumb. Emma wasn't the type to ask permission. Once her mind was made up, that was that—unless he put his foot down and started a confrontation.

But it was her birthday, and he didn't want to spoil it. Part of it had already been ruined when the florist neglected to deliver the long-stemmed roses that he'd ordered for her. He'd called Rosie's Posies, and the woman he'd talked to had insisted they'd delivered the flowers, but Emma claimed they hadn't arrived while he was out doing the shopping for tonight's dinner and buying a present for her. Tomorrow, he'd go see Rosie in person, and let her know just what he thought of her home-town, friendly attitude.

"Just a sip. That's it."

Flashing a smile, Emma asked, "Red or white?"

"You decide."

"Red. Which one's better?" She held up two bottles. "I don't want any cheap wine for my birthday dinner."

Ross made the selection and shook his head at her in dismay. When he was her age kids drank ripple, Boone's Farm apple wine or whatever stuff they could get their hands on. Obviously kids were more selective today.

He'd just finished sautéing the steak and cutting the vegetables when he heard a tap at the glass door behind him. Before Ross could speak, Emma flew to the door and opened it.

Libby Larson walked into the kitchen, wearing a yellow tank top and matching cardigan, a long floral skirt, and open-toed sandals. Her lips were painted a soft shade of pink, and tiny diamond earrings adorned her ears. She held a small wrapped package in one hand and a covered bowl in the other. "Happy birthday, Emma."

"For me?" Emma asked, snatching the gift from Libby. "Can I open it?"

"Sure."

Max sidled over and received a greeting from Libby and a pat on the head. Libby moved closer to the counter—her vanilla scent permeating the air— and set her dish down. "Hello, Ross."

"Doc," Ross said simply, and quickly returned to his kitchen duties, wondering why she had changed her mind and come.

"Ohhhh!" Emma squealed. "I love it! It's so pretty, Libby. Look, Dad." Ross turned around for a look. Emma held up a sterling silver bracelet. "It's a soft bangle. Help me put it on."

Ross wiped his hands on a dish towel, ready to fasten the bracelet on Emma's wrist, but by the time he'd turned back around Libby had already done it.

"Thanks, Libby," Emma said, placing a kiss on the doctor's cheek.

Libby smiled at Ross over Emma's head. If Ross hadn't known better, he'd think she'd just given him a look. A look that said, "I'm interested in you."

Well, *he* wasn't interested in *her*. There was no point in getting involved with the good doctor, no matter how tempting she looked. He wasn't staying in Falcon Ridge for longer than the summer. And even if he were interested in having a summer romance with the doc, he had no intentions of advertising that affair to the whole damn town. In Falcon Ridge, there were no secrets.

Except for one.

10

AFTER HIS THIRD glass of wine, Ross finally started to relax. Since the cottage had no kitchen table, they'd eaten at the breakfast bar. Emma had strategically placed him next to Libby, while she sat across from them. As he tried to be careful not to touch or bump knees with the doctor, Emma's bright blue eyes darted from her father's face to Libby's throughout the meal. It wasn't hard to see what was going through her head. Emma was playing matchmaker, and she wasn't exactly being subtle about it, either.

Emma picked up the wine bottle. "Have some more wine, Libby."

Libby covered her wineglass with her hand. "No more. I won't be able to walk home."

"No problem. You can stay over," Emma offered. She didn't glance at Ross, or she would have caught his warning look.

Libby looked over at Ross and smiled shyly, her cheeks flushed from the wine and Emma's suggestion.

Ross drained his glass. "Well," he said, getting to

his feet, "we should probably get Libby home before it gets much later. I'm sure she has office hours tomorrow morning."

Emma got out of her chair, threw her arms up in the air, and yawned. "I'm so tired. You don't mind walking Libby home so I can go to bed, do you, Dad?"

Of course he minded. He minded a hell of a lot. He didn't want to walk Libby home alone. He'd assumed he and Emma would do that together. "Emma, you don't want Libby to think you're rude—"

"She wouldn't think that. Would you, Libby?" Emma asked. She quickly kissed her on the cheek, then her father. "Thanks for the bracelet, Libby. And thanks for my pendant, Dad. It's beautiful." She touched the single pearl on the gold chain at her neck and yawned again. "Oh, I'm sorry. I can hardly keep my eyes open. It must be the wine."

She'd only had a sip, so Ross doubted it. If he had his guess, he'd say his daughter was faking the sleepy dramatics so he'd be forced to be alone with Libby Larson.

Emma peered through the glass into the night. "What a beautiful night for a walk on the beach. Well, good night, Libby. Good night, Dad." With that, she was gone, leaving Ross and the doctor alone.

Ross let out the breath he'd been holding. "Well, what do you say we call it a night. I'm kind of beat, too."

Libby smiled. "Sure, but don't feel you have to walk me home. It's only a few doors down—"

"I don't mind, really." He started toward the door when he remembered her bowl. "Do you need this? There's still a little queso dip left."

"Keep it. You and Emma eat it. I can get the bowl next time."

Ross's antennas went up. The doc assumed there'd be a next time. Not if he could help it. Once was enough. He planned to have a long talk with Emma in the morning.

He opened the door, nudged Libby outside into the cool air, and was about to follow when she stopped. "My sweater."

Sweater. Ross turned around, saw her yellow cardigan lying over the chair, and went back for it. She lifted her arms slightly, and Ross had no choice but to help her into it. Her hair brushed the tip of his nose. That vanilla scent he'd noticed all through dinner was in her hair, too, not just on her skin.

"It's chilly," she said with a small shiver.

Ross didn't think so. He welcomed the cool night air after hearing his daughter's blatant invitation for Libby to spend the night. What had she been thinking?

At the top of the steep bank, Libby hesitated until Ross offered his hand. She accepted and held on tightly as he led the way down. At the bottom of the footpath, she didn't let go. They walked hand in hand along the beach, the sound of the waves lapping against the shore. There was a half-moon, just enough to light the path.

"Dinner was great. I love Mexican food."

"Thanks. Your dip was good. Emma liked it."

"I noticed." She moved closer until their shoulders bumped.

"Are you still cold?" he asked.

"Freezing."

Ross dropped her hand and draped an arm around her shoulder, pulling her close as they walked along. Just to warm her up some. She was soft, curvy, feminine, and she reminded him that he hadn't been with a woman in a long time.

"I bought a copy of your book today. *Dangerous Curves*," she said. "I'd like for you to sign it."

"You plan on reading it?"

"One of these days."

They walked in silence the rest of the way. When they reached Libby's house, Ross walked her all the way up the winding wooden staircase to the door, and stopped.

"Do you want to come in for a minute?"

"I should . . . sure," he heard himself say, but he didn't know why. It was a mistake to go inside, yet he didn't want to appear rude. She'd bought his daughter a birthday present. She'd made dip. She'd bought a copy of his first novel. He couldn't be rude.

The back of the cottage showcased a wall of windows, and there was a beautiful, stone, floor-to-ceiling fireplace in the living room. Gleaming hardwood floors set it off. The cottage had the makings of a real showplace, if it weren't for the piles of clutter littering every piece of furniture and corner of the room.

"I could make coffee."

"Don't bother. I can't stay long."

"It's no bother," she said, working her way to the kitchen. Ross followed.

Smiley sauntered into the kitchen and gave Ross a look of annoyance before jumping onto a padded stool and draping his furry body across it.

Libby greeted the vicious-looking animal and scratched him behind the ears. "Don't mind my mess. I mentioned my rebellious streak. This is part of it." She opened a cupboard, took out a can of Maxwell House. There were stacks of junk mail on the counters and table, and dishes piled in the sink.

"My father didn't allow my mother or me to leave anything out of its place. Before I could go to bed at night, he'd inspect my room. If it wasn't in tip-top shape, he'd make me stay up and clean it."

"Your father sounds like he was strict."

"He was a bastard. He still is."

That was putting it bluntly, Ross thought.

"Cream, or sugar?"

"Black is fine."

She made a face. "I have to use extra cream *and* extra sugar to hide the taste."

"If you don't like coffee, you don't have to make it for me."

"The hard part's already done," she said, setting the pot on to brew and flipping the switch. "Besides, I need it to warm me up. Sit down, if you can find a spot." She motioned to the adjoining living room. "The coffee will just be a few minutes."

Libby followed him into the small living room, picked up several magazines and newspapers from the nubby cream sofa, and tossed them to the floor. "Some days, I pick everything up, but thoughts of my father return, and then I toss everything back just the way it was. The dishes in the sink are clean. But I just can't seem to make myself put them away." She pointed to the sofa. "Sit."

On the coffee table, a vase of long-stemmed pink roses stood out. "Nice roses," he said as he sat down. They were identical to the ones he'd ordered for Emma earlier.

Libby sat down beside him and flashed a huge grin his way. "Yes, they are. I was so surprised to see them on my doorstep when I got home from work tonight. It was very sweet of you. Thank you, Ross."

Thank you, Ross. Frowning, Ross looked at the flowers, then back at Libby, who was still grinning, a dreamy look on her face. Her head dipped toward his as her eyes fluttered shut. Her pink lips puckered slightly, as if she expected him to kiss her, but all he could do was stare.

How the hell had she gotten Emma's roses? And why on Earth would she think they were from him? They *were* from him. But they hadn't been meant for *her*.

Her eyes popped open and she stared back at him. "You didn't send them, did you?"

It might have been easier to lie and say yes, but for some reason, he couldn't lie.

"No."

She sucked in a huge gulp of air and moved several inches away from him. Shaking her head back and forth, she forced a smile to her lips. Her green eyes misted over. "I just assumed. . . ." Her voice trailed off for a moment. "I wonder who. . . . Would you like to see the card?"

Ross didn't answer. Libby stood, left the room, and came back a few seconds later. She handed him the card. The one Ross had filled out for Emma. *Looking forward to tonight.*

Emma. This was all her doing.

Ross thought about strangling Emma, and wondered briefly if that would be considered child abuse. At the moment, he wasn't sure he cared.

"I'm sorry, Libby."

She nodded, folded her arms across her chest. "Emma's doing, I presume?"

"These were meant for her. From me," he explained, then told her about his call to the florist when they hadn't arrived.

"I feel like such a fool," she said turning around and walking into the kitchen. Ross trailed behind her. "You must have thought I. . . ."

"What?" he asked, lifting a brow.

"You must have thought I was coming on to you. What am I saying?" She tossed her hands in the air, tugged at her hair, then dropped her hands to her sides. "I *was* coming on to you. All night I kept looking at you, wondering why you weren't looking back at me. I figured you were just nervous with your sixteen-year-old daughter observing us." She tossed her head back and forth again, reached into a cupboard, and pulled down two mugs.

Suddenly, she buried her face in her hands for a moment. "The other day when Emma invited me to dinner ... I thought you didn't want me to come. I made an excuse, left her a message earlier...." She lowered her hands and looked at him. "But when I came home and found the roses...." Her eyes moistened with tears.

"Libby, don't do this." He started toward her, but she stayed him with her hand.

"You didn't want me to come tonight."

He didn't argue with her. There would have been no point.

Blinking back her unshed tears, she braved a smile, wrapped her sweater tightly across her chest. "And since you probably don't want to stay for coffee, I think it would be best if you left now." She lowered her gaze.

Ross wanted nothing more than to hightail it to the door, but his feet remained glued to the kitchen floor. "Look, I enjoyed your company tonight, but I'm not staying."

She glanced up, confusion in her eyes.

"I'm not staying in Falcon Ridge," he explained. "Emma and I are leaving at the end of the summer."

She didn't answer.

"Doc, you don't strike me as the type of woman who would want to have...." He paused, searching for the right word, but couldn't come up with one.

"A fling?" she supplied. "Casual sex? An affair?"

"Yes, those things." What a moron he was.

Libby stared at him, bit at her bottom lip. "Well, now you'll never know. Will you?" Walking to the sliding glass door, she announced, "It's late, Ross. And like you pointed out earlier, I have office hours in the morning."

Ross walked to the door, came up behind her. He touched her shoulder and felt her flinch. He eased back a step and was surprised when she spun around to face him. "The roses," she said. "You should take—"

"Keep 'em," he said. He opened his mouth to say something more—he wasn't sure what—when she pushed him out onto the deck.

"Good-bye, Ross."

The door closed in his face. He'd never felt so much like a jerk in all his life. He also wondered if he'd just made the biggest mistake he could ever make.

MEGGIE WALKED INTO the bank, past the tellers' counter and directly to the manager's desk. She'd known Mr. Thurman all her life. He'd get this mix-up straightened out for her.

"Meggie," Bob Thurman greeted her, showing off his slightly yellowed teeth. He smelled of stale cigar smoke. "How are your boys? Your folks?" He ran a chubby hand over his round bald head.

"Fine, Mr. Thurman. And how is Mrs. Thurman and your family?"

"Couldn't be better," he chuckled. "Fourteen grandchildren now. And Ritchy's wife is expecting next month."

Meggie smiled, pleased with his news. "That's great." She paused, then stated her business. "I came by today because there seems to be some kind of mix-up with my checking account. This morning they refused my check at the supermarket. And they said the one I wrote them last week had bounced. There has to be some kind of mistake."

"Sit down, Meggie," he said, gesturing to a striped velveteen chair in front of his desk, the smile slowly disappearing from his round face. Once she was seated, he went on. "I was going to give you a call later."

"You already know about the mix-up?"

Bob Thurman looked down at his tidy desk, then back at her. "I'm afraid it's not a mix-up. Your account has been overdrawn for quite a few weeks now. I've spoken to your husband about this matter and—"

"You spoke to Steve?" Meggie sat forward, feeling confused.

"Yes. A number of times. And each time he assured me that—"

"Wait a minute. Our checking account is really overdrawn?"

He nodded.

"Then why didn't you just transfer the money from our savings? Do you know how embarrassing this is?" she asked, irritated with him and the bank her family had dealt with ever since she could remember. She got to her feet. "Steve must have written a check out of the account and forgot to record it, that's all. But there's close to twenty thousand dollars in our savings." It was the last of Tommy's insurance money, and she had been saving it for TJ's college fund. She'd made a promise not to touch it no matter how desperate they were, but she could always transfer the money back as soon as the mess was straightened out. "Just transfer whatever money we need."

He refused to meet her eyes. Something was wrong.

Meggie swallowed nervously. "Mr. Thurman, what is it you're not telling me?"

"You no longer have a savings account at the bank, Meggie. Your husband closed it last month."

"There has to be some mistake," she said, slowly taking her seat. "Steve knew that money was for TJ's college. It wasn't his money to take."

"His name was on the account," he said defensively, fumbling with his neck tie. "He told me he was using the money to take you and the boys on a cruise." His mouth opened wide. "Oh, no. Maybe he meant to surprise you, and now I've gone and ruined the surprise."

To save face, Meggie smiled sweetly as she stood. "It's all right. I won't let on that I know. I'll be back tomorrow to settle my account."

Before he had a chance to say anything more, she hurried away from his desk and out of the bank.

Outside, she leaned against the brick building and tried to get her composure back. How could Steve have done something so horrible? she wondered, then laughed as tears ran down her cheeks. The man could beat his wife, yet she was surprised that he'd stoop so low as to clean out their savings account.

Get a grip, Meggie.

The problem now was how to handle the situation. If she confronted Steve, he might lose his temper with her, the way he did so easily these days. When she'd first met him, he'd been easy going and fun to be around. But ever since he'd been fired from his last job, he'd changed. And when they'd moved to Falcon Ridge last year, things had gotten steadily worse.

He'd cried the first time he'd hurt her, and she'd forgiven him. Believed him when he'd said he hadn't meant to hurt her, that he loved her more than anything in the world. That he was so sorry, and so ashamed he didn't want to live anymore.

But after being beaten over and over and over again, she no longer believed his lies. She no longer listened to him when he begged her for forgiveness with tears in his eyes.

He'd said she was heartless. And the night she'd told him she wanted a divorce, he'd threatened to kill her, and himself, if she tried to leave.

Meggie hadn't told him about the baby yet. She was afraid. Another mouth to feed, something else for Steve to be stressed out about. So she'd kept the news to herself, with the exception of Libby Larson. Yet some small part of her had actually imagined Steve would be happy when he learned the news.

Then reality had sunk in.

No, she didn't want to tell Steve about the baby. Not yet. Not until she decided what to do about her marriage. Besides, right now, she had other things to deal with.

ROSS WAS SURPRISED to open his door and find Meggie on the front porch. "Hi! Come in," he invited, kissing her on her cheek. "To what do I owe this honor?"

Meggie stepped inside, smiled at her brother. "I came to ask a favor."

"Sure. Want to stay for lunch? Emma took Max for a walk, but she should be back in a few minutes. We're going to make hamburgers."

Shaking her head, she said, "Thank you, but I can only stay for a minute."

"Okay. At least sit down." He smiled when she gave in and sat on the sofa.

"Ross. . . ." she began. "This is so embarrassing." She folded her hands, then unfolded them.

"Meggie, I'd do anything for you. If you need a favor, all you have to do is ask."

"I need to borrow some money."

Ross looked at her long and hard, hoping she was going to say she was leaving that bastard husband of hers. When she didn't say anything else, he got up, went into his study, and came back with his checkbook. "It's yours. Whatever you want."

Sitting down beside her, he wrote her name on the check, then turned to face her. "How much?"

"Aren't you going to ask me what it's for?" she asked, twisting her fingers together.

"Not if you don't want to tell me."

"It's silly, really." A small smile formed on her lips. "I made a mistake in the checking account, and it seems I bounced a check. I'm too embarrassed to tell Steve. He'll think I'm such an idiot."

"Meggie, let me help you."

A look of surprise came over her. "You *are* helping me. And I'll pay you back. I promise."

"That's not what I meant, and you know it. I'm worried about you. You and the boys." Ross laid a hand over hers. "You don't have to stay with that bastard. I'll take care of you. I talked with Dan Reese and—"

Meggie jerked her hand away. "You did what?" Before he could explain, she tore into him. "Ross, you had no right to do that."

"What am I supposed to do? Sit back and let that sadistic bastard beat on you? Meggie, listen to me. You need to press charges against him. We'll get a restraining order—"

"No!" She stood up abruptly and advanced to the front door. "You don't understand. I shouldn't have come here."

"Meggie, wait. At least take the money."

She turned her back on him, placed her hand on the doorknob.

"Meggie, please," he pleaded.

He watched her shoulders heave, then slowly she turned around. Ross quickly scratched out the check and ripped it from the pad as he went to her. Pressing it into her hand, he said, "I'm here if you need me."

Glancing down at the check in her hand, her eyes became misty. "This is too much. It's way too much. I only needed—"

"Take it," he said, silencing her.

"But I can't pay you back. It's too much."

Ross drew her into his arms, held her tightly while she sobbed. "I don't want the money back. I just want you and the boys to be safe."

"Steve would never hurt the boys. No matter what you think of him. He would never hurt the boys."

Ross pulled away from her, looked her in the eyes. "Are you willing to risk it?"

A look of fright came over her before she turned, yanked the door open, and ran.

"Meggie!"

She ignored him. Sighing, Ross shut the door as she drove away.

11

"FISHING?" EMMA ASKED, her mouth open wide. "You dragged me out of bed to take me *fishing*?"

"Sure, why not?" Ross answered.

"Because it's not exactly on my list of things to do while we're here."

"When my sister Meggie was a kid, she used to cry because she never got invited to go fishing with the men."

Emma rolled her eyes. "Dad, I'm not a kid. And I'm not going to cry."

"You're sure?" Ross asked, smiling to himself as he unsnapped the Sea Ray's canvas tarp.

"Positive. Besides, it will give you a chance to visit with TJ and Jeremy. You guys don't need me hanging around."

Ross climbed aboard the boat and reached for the cooler on the deck. He'd promised to take his nephews fishing, and was beginning to wonder what was keeping them. They should have been here thirty minutes ago. "So, if you don't want to come with us, what are you going to do all day?"

Emma shrugged. "I don't know. Maybe I'll walk

over to Libby's house later. Max and Smiley have finally become friends."

Frowning, Ross kept his thoughts to himself. He didn't like it that Emma spent so much time with the doctor. Lately, every other sentence out of her mouth had Libby's name in it. It wasn't that he thought the doc was a bad influence on Emma, it was that Emma seemed to be so completely drawn to her.

Maybe he was a little jealous. Or maybe it was because Emma still insisted, in spite of his constant denials, that the good doctor was perfect for him.

The last thing Ross wanted Emma thinking was that he was going to take a wife back to Phoenix with him—and a mother for her.

He noticed TJ and Jeremy coming down the bank, their fishing gear in tow, and he watched Emma's face as she recognized the third boy. Zack Reese.

"Dad, why didn't you tell me *he* was coming?"

Ross played dumb. "Who?"

"You know who. *Look at me*," she said, wiping the sleep from her eyes, quickly finger-combing her spiky hair. "I look awful."

She had on the same wrinkled boxers and T-shirt she'd slept in the night before, and no shoes on her feet.

Ross had seen the way she reacted whenever Zack came around. For a girl who hadn't stopped talking since they arrived in Falcon Ridge, she seemed to misplace her tongue whenever Zack got within twenty feet of her.

"Hi, Emma," Jeremy yelled, charging onto the dock. "Hi, Uncle Ross."

Ross and Emma returned Jeremy's greetings. TJ was less demonstrative with his hellos. "Hey," was all he said to his uncle and cousin.

Zack Reese remembered his manners. "Hello, Emma. Hello, Mr. McLaughlin. I hope you don't mind that TJ invited me along."

"Not at all. We have plenty of room," Ross said.

"Emma, are you going too?" Jeremy asked, grinning.

Emma's eyes darted between her cousin and her father, glancing shyly at Zack once, who didn't seem to notice. "I was thinking about it," she said finally.

Ross chuckled to himself knowingly. "Well, why don't you go up to the house and freshen up while the boys and I load the gear."

"Okay." By the time her feet hit the second step, she was racing up the stairs.

Ross smiled. He wasn't exactly thrilled that his daughter had a crush on Zack Reese, but at least he seemed like a decent kid. Totally opposite of Travis.

Jeremy interrupted his thoughts. "We got night crawlers, Uncle Ross."

Staring at his nephew, Ross's thoughts drifted.

ROSS UNSNAPPED THE canvas tarp on the boat and folded it.

"I got the night crawlers," Barry said as he stepped

onto the dock. He set his gear down and yawned loudly. "I'm beat."

Ross seethed inside, staring at his brother. He supposed sleeping with two women could wear a guy out. He told himself he wasn't going to say anything about his suspicions. He didn't love Meredith. He'd told her he wanted a divorce. It shouldn't matter that she'd cheated on him. Yet, it did.

It was Barry's betrayal that bothered him more than anything. Not only had he cheated on April, he'd slept with his brother's wife. What kind of man would do something so low?

And Ross thought he knew his brother so well.

"We need gas," Ross said. "I don't have any cash. What about you?"

Barry touched his back pocket, averted his eyes. "Uh, no. Let me run back to the house and grab my wallet."

"Your house? Or mine?" Ross asked, tossing Barry's wallet at him, hitting him squarely in the chest. The brown leather wallet bounced off his brother's chest and onto the dock. Barry glanced at Ross, then bent over and retrieved it.

"I found it under my bed."

Stuffing the wallet into his pocket, Barry looked him in the eye briefly before lowering his gaze. "Ross, I can explain."

"Can you? What? Meredith had you come over to fix something in the bedroom, and your wallet happened to fall out of your pocket? Save it."

For a few moments Barry said nothing. Then, "I

couldn't help myself. She made a play for me, Ross. And I guess I was too stupid to see that she was just playing games. I swear she wants to break up our family. She's jealous."

Shaking his head in disgust, Ross said, "And that makes what you did okay?"

Barry hung his head low. "No, of course not." He glanced up. "But you don't love her, do you? You told me so the day you married her. If you loved her, I would never have. . . ."

"You son of a bitch." Before he could stop himself, he lunged at Barry, planting his fist in his brother's face.

Barry didn't bother to defend himself, other than ducking before the second blow. Ross hit him several times in the jaw and gut, then managed to knock his brother into the lake.

"What the hell is going on?" Neil McLaughlin yelled, running toward the dock just as Barry surfaced. Ross turned and looked at his father for a moment, then turned away. Breathing hard and fast, he stared down at his brother, who was treading water with one hand and holding his jaw with the other.

"Ross?" his father said, shifting his gaze between his two sons. "What's going on?" he asked again.

"Nothing." Ross ran his hands through his hair, glanced at his throbbing knuckles. "Just a misunderstanding between brothers." He didn't want to involve his father in this. Blowing out a long, harsh breath, he looked down at his brother. After staring at each other for nearly a minute, Ross stomped off without another word.

WHEN ROSS SPOTTED the sheriff's car—with its blue lights flashing on the roof—in front of Libby's office, he slammed on his brakes so quickly, he was nearly rear-ended by the pick-up truck following behind him.

Jamming his vehicle into Park, Ross raced inside. Dan Reese and Deputy Maloney stood in the reception area, both turning their heads in his direction as he came flying through the front door.

"Is everything all right?" Ross asked. "Is Libby all right?"

Both sheriff and deputy exchanged a look, but neither said anything.

"What happened?" Ross asked, annoyed with the two men for not answering his questions.

"There was a break-in sometime during the night," Dan finally said.

"Where's Libby?" He'd no sooner asked the question than Libby came around the corner and into the reception area.

Seeing Ross, she stopped and looked him in the eye, but didn't say anything. She didn't look hurt, he thought. In fact she looked perfectly fine. Damn fine. She was wearing lipstick like the night she'd come to his place for dinner. He'd never seen Libby wear lipstick except for that night, and wondered why she had it on now.

"Nothing else seems to be missing except for the drugs I mentioned," she said to Dan, ignoring Ross completely.

"Well, if you think of anything else, give us a call," Dan told her. "And don't forget to get a better lock on that back door, Doctor Larson."

"I will."

Ross stayed behind while she saw both the sheriff and his deputy to the door. When she turned around, she folded her arms in front of her. "You just here out of curiosity?"

"Yes. No," he corrected. "I was curious, yes. But I was also concerned something had happened . . . to you."

"Well, as I'm sure you can see, I'm fine." She unfolded her arms and spread them wide for emphasis. "Thanks for stopping by."

Her flippant attitude irritated him. And yet he had no idea why. Hadn't he blown her off two weeks ago, and after she'd practically admitted she was interested in him? He supposed that gave her the right to be angry with him.

"Is there something I can do to help?"

"No, nothing."

"I heard you mention that some drugs were missing."

Libby looked at him a long time before answering, as if she were deciding whether or not to bother speaking to him. "Yes. Someone busted the lock on the back door. And it looks like they used a sledge hammer on my storage room."

She led the way to the back entrance, pointing out the damage to the door, then to the storage room. Debris littered the hallway, and the storage room door had been smashed and was lying on its side in the hall.

"Why so many drugs?"

Libby shrugged. "The drug reps offer free samples. Some of my patients can't afford to pay for prescriptions."

Ross bent over, picked up several empty packages, skimmed the labels. "How would anyone know what all this stuff is for? Is any of it dangerous?"

"Most of it's harmless. A lot of antibiotics, allergy medicines, that sort of thing. But some of this stuff can be pretty lethal. There were some heavy-duty pain killers. That's mostly what's missing."

"Why don't I help you clean this mess up?" he suggested.

"That's not necessary, Ross. I'll manage."

Ross shook his head in dismay. "Libby, don't be so stubborn. I'm offering to help you because . . . we're friends."

He wondered what she thought of that idea. After a minute, she thanked him for his offer and handed him a broom. But she still hadn't smiled.

BARRY WALKED THROUGH the back door of his house and into the kitchen. The rich aroma of Italian cooking came tapping at his nose. It was something he hadn't smelled in a long while. He opened the oven door and peeked inside just to make sure he hadn't imagined it. A foil-covered lasagna tray sat inside.

April hadn't made lasagna in years. In fact, she rarely cooked for him anymore. There were four place settings at the dining room table. Reaching across it, Barry snatched a piece of crusty bread from a basket, then went in search of his wife.

He found April in the bedroom, stepping into a pair of black linen shorts, her back to him. "What's going on? Are we getting company for dinner?"

"Just Ross and Emma." She zipped and buttoned the shorts, and stepped into a pair of black flats. "I haven't seen much of either of them since they've been home, and I thought it would be nice to have them over."

He hadn't noticed her hair until she turned around to face him. She'd had it highlighted, or something. There were streaks of gold and strawberry blonde through it, and it was cut in a fuller, bouncier style. She looked ten years younger.

"Look, Barry, I know you and your brother haven't been close all these years, but I thought it was time to bury the past and. . . ." She stopped and touched her hair. "Why are you staring at me like that?"

"Your hair. It looks great. You look great," he said, and meant it.

"Thank you. I needed a change."

Barry smiled and nodded understandingly.

"You're not mad that I invited Ross and Emma for dinner?"

"No, I'm not mad. I think it was nice of you to go to so much trouble."

He thought about what April had said about burying the past, but didn't comment. They stood looking at each other until he finally broke the silence. "If we're having company soon, I'd better get a shower."

The past was all Barry could think of until dinner.

"WHAT ARE YOU doing here?" Barry asked, checking to see if any of his neighbors had seen Meri standing on his front porch dressed in a tank top and some pathetic excuse for shorts.

"You've been ignoring me lately, and I had to see you," Meri said, batting her eyelashes. As if he'd fall for that. Again.

"Look, Meri. I want you to leave."

"If you don't let me in now, maybe I'll just have to come back later when April's home," she said, cocking her hip.

"Don't threaten me, Meredith." Barry caught sight of his neighbor Ben across the street, and quickly changed his mind about sending Meri away. She'd only make a scene. Although it was against his better judgment, it would be easier to invite her in. He swung the door open wide and waited for her to enter, then closed both the screen door and the main door to prevent prying eyes.

"What do you want?"

"I wanted to apologize for upsetting April the other night. I shouldn't have told her what you said about her hair. That was a secret between us."

Barry sighed. "First of all, you should be apologizing to April, not me. And secondly, I never said anything about her hair. You said it would look better if she highlighted it, and for some reason I agreed with you. Jesus, Meri, why would you tell April that I suggested such a thing? Never mind. Don't even bother to answer that. I know exactly why you did it. The same reason you do everything you do. To hurt people."

"Why would I want to hurt her? You're the one who cheated on her."

Barry glared at her, balling his hands into fists. He'd never thought he was capable of hating anyone—until Meri. She'd used him, chewed him up, and spit him out. And now she would never be satisfied until she ruined what was left of him. He had a strong feeling she intended to ruin his marriage, as well. "You're not going to be happy until April finds out about us, are you?"

Tilting her head to the side, she curved her lips upward. "Is it April you're worried about? Or Ross?"

Cringing inside, Barry forced himself to speak. "Ross already knows."

Meredith laughed in his face. "Ross is too stupid to notice what I do. Besides, if he suspected something was going on, he would have said something to me."

"My brother isn't stupid, Meredith. Maybe he just

doesn't give a damn that you're sleeping around." He blew out a long breath. "Look, Meri, what we did was wrong. I was as much to blame as you. But it's over. I love my wife, and I don't want to lose her."

Offering him a sneer, she said, "All of a sudden you're concerned about April. I wonder what she'd do if she knew I was sleeping with you."

"You're not sleeping with me. Do you hear me? It's over. I made a horrible mistake. One I'll live to regret the rest of my life. And no matter how hard you try to seduce me again, it won't work. I'd rather die than sleep with you again."

"Hmmmm. That's funny. That isn't what you told me while you were fucking me." She glared at him, then added, "I wonder what Ross would say if I told him you raped me."

"I think that rape story is getting pretty old, don't you? First your stepfather, and now me?" Barry walked to the door and opened it.

"Wait, Barry. I didn't mean that. I was only joking. You know I'd never do anything like that to hurt you."

He didn't want to hear it. "Get out," he ordered, motioning her toward the door.

"Please, just listen to me." Her voice became child-like, desperate in tone. "I need you. Ross said he's going to file for divorce. Then what will I do? Where will I go?"

She moved toward him, ran her hands up his chest, looked into his eyes. "I thought you cared about me."

"Get out, Meredith. You're not welcome in this house anymore, unless you're with Ross." That was if Ross would ever speak to him again.

IMMEDIATELY FOLLOWING DINNER, Emma begged her uncle for another driving lesson. And it hadn't taken long for Barry to give in.

While they were gone, Ross helped April clean up the kitchen mess. It was the least he could do after the great meal she'd made.

"I put a couple squares of lasagna on a plate for you and Emma to take home," April said, wiping her countertops until they shined.

"Thanks. It was great." He patted his stomach. "I shouldn't have eaten so much. I'll probably pay for it later."

April laughed as she filled two mugs with coffee and carried them to the table.

Ross pulled out a chair for her and then one for himself. Suddenly, her mood sobered. "Barry told me your suspicions about Steve."

Ross took a swig of hot coffee and winced, deciding to let it cool some. "I don't know what to do. Meggie won't talk to me about it. She won't let me help her."

"Maybe she's afraid of what Steve might do to her if she talks." April stared straight ahead as if she were thinking. "Or maybe she's ashamed." She turned and faced him again. "I know you don't want to hear this, but Steve seemed like a decent guy when they first moved here. Then, after a few months, he started changing. Meggie said he was having a hard time dealing with losing his last job." She sipped at her coffee.

"Well, if he is, that's no excuse for how he's treating Meggie. If he's guilty of doing the things I think he's been doing, I don't understand why she stays."

"Maybe she still loves him."

"How could she possibly love a man who hurts her that way? How could she possibly forgive him?"

April shrugged and regarded Ross with misty eyes. "When you love someone, you can forgive almost anything. Forget, never. But you can forgive—if you want to."

Ross looked away. Was she right? Could a person forgive a loved one if they committed a heinous act?

And had April been speaking from experience?

LIBBY HAD BEEN about to go for a run when Emma stormed through her back door without knocking. That wasn't the reason Libby stared at her. She was used to Emma's walking into her house. But this time it was different. Emma had been crying.

"Emma, what's wrong?" Libby asked, going to her and pulling her close for a hug.

Before Emma could answer, she choked back a noisy sob. "Travis doesn't want to go out with me anymore." After she'd let out that devastating news, she wailed for a good ten minutes.

To Libby, who consoled Emma with pats on the back and comforting words, it seemed much longer. But nothing she said, or did, seemed to calm Emma down.

Libby finally had to take control. Grasping the girl's shoulders, she said, "Emma, calm down. I don't know Travis, but I can assure you there isn't a man on this Earth worth that many tears."

She left Emma to get a box of tissues, then quickly returned. Handing Emma one, Libby instructed her to blow.

"Good girl. Now, let's sit down and talk about this calmly." She led the girl to the sofa and cleared a place for them to sit.

"So, he finally returned your calls?" she inquired.

Emma shook her head, dabbed at her wet eyes. "No. I called him. I just happened to catch him at home. I could tell by how quiet he was that something wasn't right. And so, like an idiot, I asked him if he'd found someone else," she sobbed. "And he said yesssss." The last word came out as a whining hiss. "And he wouldn't even tell me her name."

"Men are scum. I know it hurts, honey. But it's better to find out now."

Emma nodded reluctantly. "And to think I almost had sex with him. I even went as far as getting birth control pills prescribed. Thank God I never let him touch me." A look of sheer panic came over her. "Do you think that's why he dumped me? Because I wouldn't have sex with him? He wanted me to, right before Dad and I left for Falcon Ridge, but I chickened out. He was kind of mad about that." Emma sniffed.

"Don't even think something so ridiculous. Any guy who pressures you to have sex isn't worth it. When you decide you're ready to make love with someone, you won't have to ask yourself if you're doing the right thing. You'll know."

"Was it that way for you, Libby? With *your* first?"

Libby thought about lying, and for some reason, couldn't. "No. Not with my first. I was young— seventeen. It was awful, and I'm lucky I didn't end up pregnant or catch some dreadful disease. A few years later, it was better. I met someone who cared more about me than getting laid. Excuse my French."

Emma relaxed her shoulders and giggled. "What happened to...."

"Paul. Paul Denning."

"Why didn't you guys get married? Didn't you love him?"

"Yes, I did. But sometimes things don't work out that way. I went to medical school, and Paul went away to law school. He met someone else."

Emma seemed to be contemplating her words. "He broke your heart."

Smart girl. Libby smiled sadly and nodded. "Yes. But I got over him. Just like you'll get over Travis. The best thing to do is to keep busy. Don't brood. And whatever you do, don't think this happened because of something you did, or didn't do. Promise me."

"I'll try."

"You'll meet someone else, and you'll forget all about what's-his-name."

By the time their talk ended, Libby had gotten Emma to laugh. The girl was going to heal just fine.

12

"C'MON, HAVE SOME lemonade," Bev practically begged her son.

Ross, afraid there wasn't any lemonade in his parents' refrigerator, had already declined twice. This time, however, he accepted. "That sounds great, Mom."

He let out a sigh of relief when he saw a glass pitcher of lemonade appear in his mother's hands. He waited for her to drop several cubes of ice into two glasses and pour.

Barry had asked Neil to come down to the marina and give him a hand with something, so Ross had volunteered to stay with his mother while his father was gone. Today was one of her good days. Her memory, for the most part, was intact, and she was in good spirits.

While Bev had worked in her flower garden, nurturing her babies, Ross had sat on the back porch and watched her. She'd refused his offer to help, and so he hadn't pressed the issue. It made him feel good to see her do something that made her happy.

Now, inside the house, they visited like two

strangers getting to know each other. It saddened Ross to think of all the years that had gone by. He'd never meant to hurt his mother when he decided to leave Falcon Ridge. She didn't deserve to be hurt. She'd done nothing but love her family, and had always been the glue to hold them together. But once Meri had come into their lives, that glue just hadn't been strong enough.

"I'm ashamed to say that I haven't read either of your books yet," she told Ross, setting a glass in front of him and taking a seat across the kitchen table. "I can't seem to remember what I read, so I don't bother anymore."

Ross smiled sympathetically. "That's okay. I could tell you about them, if you'd like."

Beverly looked delighted. "I'd love to hear about them." She listened intently while he gave her the condensed version of each of his published mystery novels and the one he'd just recently finished writing.

Looking at him with tear-glistened eyes, she said, "I'm so proud of you. But it breaks my heart to think that a few hours from now I may not remember what your books are about, or that you'd written a book in the first place."

Ross gave her a long, assessing look. "What kind of things *do* you remember, Mom?"

"Oh, sometimes I remember things from long, long ago, and sometimes I can only remember bits and pieces of things. I mostly forget what I've done yesterday."

She related a few stories she remembered about her childhood in great detail. Ross listened, laughing and nodding at the appropriate moments. They were stories he'd heard before, but not recently. And not with quite as much enthusiasm.

"Then there are the days when I can barely remember my name. And certainly not your father's." She picked up her glass, took a sip, then traced the condensation with her finger. "Some days I wake up wondering why this strange man is sleeping in bed beside me." She blushed. "I don't believe him when he tells me he's married to me. He tries to shove all those herbs and medications at me, and I think maybe he's trying to kill me. There's something about him that I don't trust. But as the day goes on, and Neil is nothing but patient and loving and under-standing, I realize he's been telling me the truth, and that I *can* trust him."

Ross remembered the day he'd come back to Falcon Ridge, when he and his mother had sat at this very table and talked. She'd tried to convince him that someone was giving her poison and trying to kill her. He knew then that she had to have meant his father, but he was confused as to why she would think such a thing. He supposed paranoia could be one of the many symptoms of Alzheimer's, and made a mental note to ask Libby about it the next time he ran into her.

They were interrupted by Meggie, who came to take their mother shopping.

His sister looked better than the last time he'd

seen her. The dark circles under her eyes had disappeared. She didn't look quite as frail, and there were no signs of bruises on her body.

Ross greeted her with a kiss. "You doing okay?"

Meggie glanced quickly at her mother, then nodded at Ross. "I'm fine." Her eyes told him not to mention his suspicions to their mother. As if he would do something so stupid. His mother had enough to deal with; he would never burden her with Meggie's problems. Even though he was worried sick about her.

He'd avoided speaking to Barry about it since the day he'd first mentioned the situation—the reason being that he was afraid his brother could somehow actually convince him to dispose of their brother-in-law.

After the day at Scully's Pub, it wouldn't take much to talk Ross into at least hurting the guy enough that he'd never be able to raise a finger at Meggie again.

"Well, Mom and I are off." Meggie took her mother by the arm and walked her to the front door. "Thanks for keeping an eye on her this morning," she whispered.

"I enjoyed it." His statement had been sincere.

Regret washed over him suddenly as he thought about going back to Phoenix at the end of the summer. He felt badly about leaving his mother's care to the rest of his family and not doing his share. But returning to Phoenix was something he refused to think about at the moment.

"I'M GLAD YOU had such a nice day," Neil said to Bev after she told him about her visit with Ross and talked about the books he'd written. He listened to every word as his wife narrated the stories over and over again. He didn't spoil her mood by mentioning that he'd already read both of Ross's books. Bev had obviously forgotten that a copy of each occupied the book shelf in their living room.

Lately, Ross had been spending a lot of time with his mother, but Neil swore his son tried to avoid him whenever possible. Fourteen years was a long time to pay for his crime. If he could go back and change things, he would. But he couldn't. He'd carry his guilt to his death. It wasn't as if he expected or deserved Ross's forgiveness, but he'd prayed for it. Many times.

NEIL KNOCKED ON Ross and Meredith's front door. When his daughter-in-law didn't answer, he tried the knob and found it unlocked. "Anybody home?" he called out, stepping inside the house and shutting the door behind him.

Bev had insisted he bring them the remaining tomatoes from her garden. She had been canning all morning, and just couldn't do any more. Neil had called Meredith a few moments ago to ask if she could use some. When she said she could use a dozen or so, Neil said he'd be right over. So it seemed odd that she didn't answer the door, he thought.

She was probably out back playing with Emma.

Neil set the basket on the kitchen counter. He'd just say hello to his daughter-in-law and granddaughter, then go back to the house to see if Bev needed a hand.

He stopped at the patio door for a moment. Meredith was lying facedown, sunbathing on the deck while Emma slept in her port-a-crib. A blanket was draped over the top of the crib to protect the baby from the sun.

Neil quietly slid the screen door open so as not to wake Emma. But just as he'd been about to step outside, he noticed Meredith's bare back—she wasn't wearing a top to her bikini. Embarrassed, and not wanting to startle her, he started to close the door and make his escape. But before he could do so, Meredith popped her head up.

"Hi, Neil."

Swallowing before speaking, he finally said, "I left your tomatoes on the counter. I don't want to disturb—"

"You're not disturbing anyone," she said, getting to her feet. Blatantly, she stood on the deck and faced him, a challenging, seductive look in her eyes.

His gaze was drawn to her beautiful, naked breasts. Neil stared for longer than he should have, then turned around. "I'd . . . better be going."

He was angry with his daughter-in-law for not showing the least bit of modesty. She hadn't even covered herself with a towel. It was as if she'd wanted him to look at her breasts. Her next statement let him know that's exactly what she'd wanted.

"It's a shame you have to leave so soon, Neil."

He didn't respond, nor did he turn around to look at her again. Although part of him wanted to. He'd been turned on by her. And he hated himself for feeling that way.

On the drive home, he cursed himself over and over. He couldn't decide whom he was angrier at— himself, or Meredith. He closed his eyes a moment and shook his head. He never saw the traffic light turn red. By the time he opened his eyes, he hit the brakes too late.

THE MARINA RESTAURANT was especially busy for a Saturday afternoon. It was decorated with a nautical flair and offered a view of the lake from three sides. It was open for breakfast, lunch, and dinner and was the most popular restaurant in town.

Ross had stopped by to see Meggie, but other than a few words in between waiting on customers, she wasn't able to visit with him. He supposed the real reason for stopping wasn't to visit, but to make sure she was all right. But seeing her with that haunted look in her eyes hadn't done the least to ease his concerns. It only made him want to seriously hurt the man responsible for putting it there.

Dan Reese had told Ross that he'd paid Steve Lattimer a visit last week, although Ross wasn't sure exactly what had been said. But at least Dan had talked to the asshole, had let him know that they were onto him and that he was being watched.

Lattimer wouldn't like the idea. Ross just prayed he didn't take it out on Meggie.

"Careful, it's hot," Meggie said as she set a large bowl of clam chowder in front of him. "You want another lemonade?"

"Sure."

Just as she hurried off to refill his glass, Ross saw Libby Larson walk in. One of the other waitresses handed her a menu and pointed to the empty booth in front of him. As she worked her way across the room, he noticed the big turquoise dangling earrings swing wildly from her ears. Some kind of tropical birds. He supposed she'd chosen them to match the bright floral dress she wore. It hugged her tiny breasts and small waist, flared out at her hips, and draped her calves. On her feet were black, strappy sandals. And a toe ring, of course.

Libby stopped a few feet away from him, looked over her shoulder as if she were hunting for a quick escape route, then continued to her seat. She gave him the briefest of smiles and a quick nod before sitting down—offering her back to him. For some reason, Ross felt infuriated with her, although he should have felt relief that he didn't have to look at her while he ate his lunch.

So instead, he had to stare at the back of her head and watch those ridiculous birds swinging from her ears. Without thinking, he shoved a spoonful of chowder in his mouth and nearly screamed, it was so hot. The muffled sound he made had Libby glancing over her shoulder at him, then quickly facing the front again. As if she couldn't care less that he'd scalded his tongue and mouth.

Several customers were lined up and waiting patiently at the front door for tables. It seemed silly for them to each take up space in a booth, when they could easily share one. Sighing, Ross slid out of his seat and went to Libby's booth. "If we share a table, someone else could sit down," he offered. "Unless you're waiting for someone."

Libby looked up, blinked twice. She twisted her head, stared at the door, then back up at him. Ross noticed two women across the room whisper to one another as they watched him with interest. Old Doc Sweeney's wife and her sister, Olga Bitmeyer. Ross raised his hand and nodded a greeting at them.

He started to wish he hadn't bothered to ask Libby to share a table when she finally answered.

"Sure, why not?"

Though she'd accepted his offer, she didn't sound very happy about it. Grabbing her purse, she slid out of her seat and into the one across from him.

While his soup cooled, Ross munched on saltine crackers.

Libby buried her face in a menu.

"You and Emma have been spending a lot of time together lately," he said matter-of-factly.

"Yes, we have."

Curt answer, he thought, wondering what to say next. "Have you had any more trouble at your office?"

"No."

Ripping the wrapper from another package of crackers, he stuffed one into his mouth and chewed. "The clam chowder's always good."

"I know."

Leaning forward, he pushed her menu aside and looked into her cool green eyes. "Are you deliberately trying to be rude, Doc?" he asked, annoyance shining through his voice.

Her brows shot up, and she tilted her head to the side. "Not deliberately, no."

Snorting, Ross shook his head. The woman was such an enigma. He couldn't figure her out. He was about to suggest she move back to her own booth when a young couple sat down in it.

Meggie breezed by just then. She seemed surprised to see Libby sitting across from him. "Libby," she said. "I hadn't realized you two were . . . friends." It was almost a question, her dark eyes darting between the two of them.

"Yes, the doc and I are *friends*." Ross punctuated the word *friends*. "Can you bring her something to eat, Meggie?"

"Sure," she said, looking at Libby. "Your usual?"

"That sounds great," Libby said, smiling.

Ross was suddenly annoyed again. "If you knew what you wanted, why were you steaming up the menu for so long?"

"Something to do," she said, shrugging. She nodded at his bowl. "Aren't you going to eat that?"

"It's hot."

She gave him a skeptical look and, without

asking, dragged the bowl across the table and picked up his spoon. Puckering her lips, she blew softly and then brought the spoon to her mouth. Her eyes drifted shut. She was savoring it, Ross thought as he watched her.

"It's not too hot," she informed him. Seconds later, she repeated her moves, licking her lips afterward. He'd be willing to bet she had no idea how damn sexy she looked eating a bowl of clam chowder.

Helping herself to the last package of crackers on the table, she smashed them through the cellophane, tore open the corner, and sprinkled the crumbs into the bowl. She then proceeded to eat his lunch, causing his mouth to water and reminding him he hadn't eaten yet today.

Meggie arrived with another steaming bowl of chowder and a glass of lemonade. She set the glass in front of Libby, but paused before setting the bowl down, not quite sure where to put it, finally setting it in front of her brother.

So, they liked the same food, he thought. Mexican. Clam chowder. Lemonade. Not that that meant anything. It was just a thought.

Libby looked so engrossed as she ate, he didn't want to disturb her. He plopped a few ice cubes into his bowl, stirred, and waited for them to melt. When it looked safe, he dug in. And burned the hell out of his mouth for the second time. He grabbed his lemonade and guzzled it down.

Libby shook her head and smiled. "Too hot?"

She was smart and sassy and sexy. Ross scowled at her as he forced the rest of the hot chowder down. Needless to say, there wasn't much conversation during the rest of their lunch.

As soon as they'd finished, Meggie showed up. "Dessert?"

Libby's face lit up. "Key lime pie."

Meggie looked at Ross. "How about you?"

"I'll have a bite of hers."

"No way!" Libby smiled sweetly, seductively. "Nothing personal, but I don't share my desserts with anyone. Get your own."

Meggie laughed and waited for him to decide. "Never mind. I'll just stare at the doc while she eats hers."

It had been pure torture watching her eat that piece of pie. How anyone could make a dessert last that long was beyond him. Once she was finally finished, she argued with Ross about the check. They finally settled the matter—Ross paid the check, and Libby left the tip. After saying good-bye to his sister, he escorted Libby out the door and into the bright sunshine.

Libby thanked him for lunch and said good-bye. But instead of leaving, Ross tagged along behind her as she made her way to a white Honda Accord.

"Are you following me for a reason?" she asked.

Shrugging, Ross said, "I was just wondering how well you know my sister."

Libby sighed. "As my patient? Or as my friend?"

"Both." He tucked his hands into his pockets and waited for her answer.

She seemed to be thinking. "Sometimes I think I know her pretty well, and other times. . . ."

He narrowed his eyes but didn't ask what he'd originally intended. *Did you ever treat her for injuries sustained from a beating?*

But Libby seemed to know what he'd wanted to ask. Digging a pair of sunglasses from her shoulder bag, she put them on. "Ross, Meggie's my patient."

"I know that, but. . . ."

"The sheriff stopped by last week to see if everything was all right. They have no idea who broke into my office."

Ross didn't say anything.

"Dan also told me your concerns about Meggie." Before Ross could open his mouth, she said, "She's lucky that you care so much about her. And that you want to help her. I just hope she doesn't wait too long before accepting that help."

It was as if she wanted to tell him something more, but couldn't. Ross studied her a little while longer before asking, "Would you promise me something?"

"If I can."

"Would you promise to call me if she ever comes to you . . . hurt?"

Libby's expression turned somber, but she nodded her head.

"Thank you."

She opened her car door but didn't get in. Instead, she turned around, whipped the sunglasses from her face, and looked at him long and hard.

Those green eyes penetrated his, and for some reason he felt like kissing her.

But he didn't. "You know, Doc, I was wondering.... That night I walked you home, if I'd asked you to have a short-term affair, what would you have said?"

Hell, where had that come from? Not that he hadn't been wondering just that for weeks now, but he'd never had any intention of asking her such a thing.

She thought about it for some time, or at least she appeared to. After a few moments, she fixed her eyes on him again. "I'd have said . . . yes." Part of him wanted to jump for joy. Before he had a chance to respond, she added, "Of course, that doesn't matter now. Being that you were never interested." She climbed in her car, plopped her sunglasses back in place, and smiled sweetly at him. "Have a nice day, Ross."

13

"WHAT KIND OF accident did my mother die in?" Emma stared at her father, her bright blue eyes pinning his and waiting. Her spiky hair slapped at her forehead and cheeks as the boat cruised gently through the water. "Was it a car accident?"

The questions had come out of nowhere. But Ross had been expecting them since the first day they'd arrived in Falcon Ridge. He supposed he was lucky that she'd waited this long to start probing.

Today they'd taken the boat out on the lake. Emma had finally consented to learn to water ski. She'd surprised herself when she'd come out of the water for the first time and held the rope for nearly a minute before falling. After that she'd insisted on doing it over and over again until she'd gotten it right.

Ross had enjoyed seeing his daughter laughing. She'd been so sullen and quiet the past two weeks. Since the last time she'd spoken to Travis Walker. When she'd come out of her room that night, tears streaming down her face, he'd asked her what was wrong. Emma had said it was nothing he could help her with, and that she needed to talk to Libby.

Then she'd flown out the door and down the beach. When she'd come back a few hours later, all she'd said was that Libby was right. All men were scum.

Since that night, to his knowledge, she hadn't called Travis again. Although Ross should feel relieved knowing that, it broke his heart to see his little girl so unhappy.

He'd talked to Barry about finding something for Emma to do around the marina to keep her occupied. Barry gave her a job working as a cashier in the bait shop two mornings a week. Emma had been thrilled with the offer. But not as thrilled as the offer that had come from Libby. She'd asked Emma to help her organize her office and do some filing in her free time. Needless to say, Emma had started the same day, and had made herself available to the doctor every afternoon since.

But today was Sunday, and Emma was his for the day.

And she was still waiting for an answer to her question.

As he guided the boat into the slip and cut the engine, he thought about lying. He could so easily answer, "Yes, it was a car accident." But he couldn't do that. He'd avoided her questions all these years. Maybe it was time to be straight with her. At least he could tell her some of what she wanted to know. The rest would have to wait.

"No, Emma. It wasn't a car accident."

She looked at him for some time, digesting the

news. He didn't think she seemed all that surprised by his answer, and he found himself wondering how much she already knew about her mother's death.

She shrugged out of her life vest, tossed it into the storage bin under the seat, and closed the lid. He handed her the rope and watched as she tied the boat to the dock. When she finished, Ross asked her to sit down. For some reason, he had to give it to her straight. As the boat rocked with the waves, he began, "She may have jumped—or fallen—off Falcon Ridge." Before she could say anything, Ross added, "Or she may have been pushed."

Emma's eyes widened with a horrified look, but she didn't say anything.

Tears began to cloud her blue eyes, and Ross reached for her. But she refused to be comforted for more than a few seconds, pushing away from her father and leaning back in her seat.

"What are you saying? That she could have committed suicide, or been . . . murdered?"

Ross swallowed uncomfortably. The hot sun seeped into his skin, beads of sweat forming on his brow. "Yes."

The wind kicked up and blew a chunk of her hair across Emma's eye. She batted it out of the way. Her hair had grown a little, and she'd let the spikes relax some.

"You don't know which?" she finally asked.

Ross didn't answer.

"Why would anyone want to kill her? Or what would have made her want to kill herself? Don't you care? Why haven't you done anything all these years to find out?" Emma stood up, anger and frustration mixed together on her face. Her sudden movements rocked the boat.

"Emma, you don't understand."

Scowling, she said, "You're right. I don't. But, unlike you, I'm going to do something about it. I'm going to find out what happened to my mother." She stepped up onto the dock and glared at him once last time before running away.

"Emma, wait!" It was too late. She'd already disappeared around the bend. Probably heading to Libby's.

Ross swore aloud.

He'd handled things poorly. He deserved Emma's reprimand. She was right. He hadn't done enough to find out how Meri had died. Maybe it was because he didn't want to know the truth.

And then again, maybe it was because he already knew.

ROSS DRAGGED HIS weary body into the house. He hadn't slept well the past few nights. With all that he'd had on his mind lately, it was no wonder.

Meri greeted him with a kiss on the cheek and a bright smile on her face, as if their relationship were perfect. As if he hadn't asked her for a divorce just last week.

"Come see what I made for you," she said, taking his hand and leading him to the kitchen. The smell of

something tempting and edible permeated the room, causing his stomach to rumble loudly. He hadn't eaten a decent meal in days.

"Daddy!" Emma greeted him. She was strapped in her high chair, food smeared across her chubby cheeks.

Ross bent over his daughter and kissed her on the top of her head, the only clean spot on her. "Hi, baby."

"Bite?" she offered, holding her spoon to his lips. Something resembling mashed potatoes and peas was forced into his mouth.

"Mmmmm," he said, swallowing. This time he kissed her on her food-crusted mouth. "Daddy loves you."

"Me, too. Me, too," she squealed.

His heart ached thinking about divorce. How would he ever live without seeing Emma on a daily basis?

"Papa gots a bwoken leg," she announced, as if he had no knowledge of his father's car accident last week. "I writed my name on his. . . ." She seemed to be searching for the right word, then looked up at her mother for help.

"His cast, honey," Meri supplied.

Emma beamed, and nodded her head.

"We stopped to visit Neil again today," Meri announced. "Emma and I baked him cookies this morning. I feel so badly about the accident."

"You keep saying that. But it wasn't your fault."

Or was it? he wondered when she turned away guiltily and opened the oven door.

She peeled back the foil from a corner of a baking dish, then closed the door.

Meri handed him a glass of white wine. "Dinner will be ready in about twenty minutes. Why don't you go take a shower and relax? I'll clean up the monster and get her ready for bed." She grinned at Emma, then shook her head. "I swear she gets more food on her than in her mouth."

By the time he finished showering, Meri had Emma ready for bed. Ross played with her for a few minutes, then hugged and kissed her and tucked her into her crib.

Although he was starving, he had no desire to sit across the dinner table from Meri and pretend every-thing was fine. Everything wasn't fine. And every time he brought up the subject of divorce, Meri would turn into the perfect little wife and pretend nothing was wrong. He wasn't in the mood for it tonight.

"I'm going to go down to the marina and get a sandwich or something," he announced as she was dishing food onto their plates.

"What are you saying? I spent all day cleaning, shopping, and cooking for you, and you can't even sit down and eat the meal I prepared?"

"Meredith, don't start. I didn't ask you to cook for me."

"I'm your wife. Of course I'd cook for you," she said in a hurtful tone, tears quickly flooding her eyes. "I love you, Ross. Why can't you believe that?"

Closing his eyes momentarily, he let his breath out on a whoosh. "Meredith, I told you. It's over. I

don't love you. I don't know if I can say it much more
bluntly than that."

She tossed her hair over her shoulder and glared
at him. "You're being cruel."

"I'm cruel? You showed up in this town, sought
me out for God only knows what reason, and seduced
me. You lied to me about your age—"

"I didn't lie. I just didn't tell you."

"Then you showed up on my mother's doorstep
and announced that you were pregnant. You forced
me to marry you."

"I never forced you."

Ross rolled his eyes. "You haven't given me a
moment's peace since I met you. You're constantly
whining and complaining that I don't spend enough
time with you, that you're lonely, that you're bored,
that you want to move to a big city. It just never ends.
You drove me away. Then to get even with me because
I supposedly neglected you, you slept with my brother.
And I'm cruel?" he asked, closing the distance between
them, the pain still ripping at his heart. He and Barry
had been as close as two brothers could possibly be. It
wasn't Meri cheating on him that hurt so much, but
his brother's betrayal.

Meri forced her bottom lip out. "I said I was
sorry."

Sorry? It was all he could do not to slap her pretty
face. He took a step back, turned away from her, ran
his hands through his hair. Getting violent wouldn't
solve anything. Just as it hadn't made him feel any
better the day he'd beat on Barry, either. That had

been more than a week ago, and they hadn't spoken since.

He felt her hands on his back, and he spun around, forcing her body to stiffen in response.

"Don't touch me," he warned. "I'm telling you for the last time. I want a divorce. And I want custody of Emma." He'd never threatened to take Emma away from her before, but he couldn't stand the thought of his daughter being raised by her. He couldn't stand the thought of not being a part of Emma's life if Meri decided to leave town.

"Well, you're not getting either," Meri declared, folding her arms around her middle. "I'm a good mother."

Ross didn't argue that point. She took good care of their daughter.

"I love Emma, and you can't have her. I'll kill myself first."

Ross stared at her, waiting for a sign to see that she was bluffing. She was unstable. She had to be to say something like that. To be so needy of the kind of attention she craved.

But he couldn't let her threat tie him to a loveless marriage.

So he called her bluff. "Be my guest," he said, without any trace of emotion, and stormed out the door.

ROSS WENT AFTER Emma, knowing she'd be at Libby's. After climbing the stairs to her deck, he knocked on the glass door. Libby opened it and stepped outside. "She's in the living room," she said, obviously knowing why he'd come. "I'll leave you two alone." She slid the door closed, and then disappeared.

Emma was curled in the corner of Libby's sofa, a colorful cotton throw tucked around her. Her hair was still damp, and she was probably chilled from the air conditioning. Her nose and eyes were red and puffy.

"Emma, I'm sorry." Ross sat on the opposite end of the sofa, not wanting to crowd her.

She refused to look at him.

Where should he start? "I couldn't tell you the truth, because I don't know what the truth is. There was an investigation, but the sheriff's office was unable to determine whether...." He noticed her flinch, and didn't bother to put an ending to it.

"But you tried to find out. Didn't you?" she asked in a shaky voice, glancing at him. "You tried to find out what happened to her, didn't you, Dad?"

No, he hadn't tried to find out. He hadn't wanted to know if she'd jumped because of him, because of the things he'd said to her. Because of the threats he'd made.

And he hadn't wanted to know if someone in his family had pushed her to her death. He still didn't want to know.

"Sometimes it's easier not knowing," he said. "Then there's no need to blame yourself, or someone else."

She sat up a little straighter, turned toward him another inch. "Had she been depressed, or something?"

Depressed? Not that he'd ever noticed. Meri had been manipulative, a liar and a cheat. But he'd never known her to be depressed.

"We were young. Immature," he said, as if that might explain everything. Knowing it would never be enough to satisfy Emma's curiosity, he added, "She loved you."

"Then why would she want to leave me?" Emma dragged her fist along her eyes, wiping the moisture away.

"We argued about things. About you. We weren't getting along, but we both wanted you."

Emma stared at him, wide-eyed, but didn't say anything.

"We said some unpleasant things to each other." He let those words hang in the air for a moment. "I don't know. I wish I knew, but I just don't know," he said, shaking his head.

She started to cry again, and Ross leaned forward. "Em, come here." As she lunged forward, she practically knocked him off the sofa. "I'm sorry, baby. I'm so sorry."

Ross held her tightly until she calmed down, smelling the sun and lake water on her hair and skin. Memories of holding her after she'd fallen and skinned her knee came rushing back. He'd always loved her, had wanted to protect her. Even if it had meant lying to her all these years.

A little while later they let themselves out the back door and walked home together—hand in hand.

Libby watched them from her dock, her feet dangling in the cool lake water. Emma had come rushing through her back door, saying her mother may have committed suicide.

Libby thought back to her own youth. Her own mother and father. Bill Larson had abused Libby's mother ever since she could remember. Until her poor mother had finally had enough and decided to get out. Suicide had been her answer.

Her thoughts drifted from her parents to Meggie and her boys. How much more would Meggie be able to take before she decided to do something about her problems? Would she, too, think suicide was an escape? Would she dare leave her boys motherless, the way Libby's mother had left her little girl?

Libby let her eyes drift shut and cried silently.

MEGGIE SQUEEZED HER eyes shut against the blinding light, moaned in protest, and rolled over. Surely it wasn't time to get up yet. She felt as if she'd just fallen asleep.

She was about to drift off again when she heard drawers being opened and closed, then Steve's voice as he swore at her. Her whole body tensed in response.

"Dammit, Meggie. Wake up!" he demanded, his

weight pressing down on the bed beside her. "Where are they?"

"The boys?" she asked, slowly coming to. TJ and Jeremy had each spent the night with a friend. Thank God.

"Not the boys," he said, irritation thick in his slurred speech. "The medicine samples I had in the top drawer of the dresser."

Meggie sat up in bed, looked around the room. Drawers hung open, and clothing had been tossed and scattered around the floor. It looked as if her make-up and toiletries had been swept from the top of the dresser to the floor as well. Maybe they'd been burglarized. "Steve, what happened?"

Steve grabbed her by the shoulders and shook her. "Dammit, where are they? Where the hell's my medicine?"

She blinked, trying to clear her head. *"Medicine?"*

"My drugs! Where the hell are my drugs?"

Meggie jerked her head back. "I . . . I was cleaning the drawers and I threw them out." The slap across her face and mouth had come so suddenly she didn't have time to prepare herself.

"How could you be so stupid? Where did you put them? In the garbage can in the garage?" He started for the door, then turned back to glare at her. "Get out of bed and go find them."

Meggie shook her head as she scrambled to the opposite side of the bed. "They're gone, Steve. I burned them."

"You bitch. Those were mine. You had no right to touch them."

"Like you had no right to touch the savings account," she snapped back. "TJ's college fund." She regretted her words as soon as they'd escaped her lips. But it was too late to take them back. Steve was already lunging across the bed at her.

THE PHONE WOKE Ross at two a.m.

Libby's voice spoke to him. "Ross, I think you'd better come down to my office."

Ross rubbed at his eyes as he yanked the covers back. "What's wrong? Did someone break in again?"

"It's Meggie," Libby said softly. "She had a miscarriage."

ROSS RECOGNIZED LIBBY'S white Honda in the parking lot, parked his Jeep beside it, and raced to the glass door. Tugging on the metal handle, he realized it was locked. He pounded furiously on the glass until Libby appeared and let him in.

"How is she?" he asked, rushing by her in search of his sister.

Libby's hand shot out to catch his arm. "She's asleep. I gave her something for the pain."

He finally slowed down, then stopped, releasing a long breath.

"Thank you. What happened?" he asked, once he'd calmed down some.

"We'll know more once she feels up to talking, but from what I could gather—it was Steve."

"I'll kill that son of a bitch!" Rage tore through him as he marched down the hall to find Meggie. He found her in the room at the end of the hall, sleeping peacefully, an IV attached to her small wrist. Her face and arms were bruised and battered, her lip split and swollen.

"I'll kill him," he repeated.

"Dan's got him behind bars, Ross."

Ross stared at Libby, waiting for her to explain.

"Meggie called Dan to tell him that Steve was the one who'd broken into my office, and that she suspected he was on his way to do it again. Dan got here first, surprised him. His deputy took Steve in. Then Dan went to Meggie's place. He called me and brought her here about an hour ago."

Ross tried to take it all in. Meggie was safe. She was going to get through this, though he didn't know if she'd get over the fact that she'd lost her baby. He knew she'd blame herself for not getting out sooner.

"I didn't even know she was pregnant."

"She was only eight weeks along. She didn't want anyone to know. She was afraid Steve would be upset with her over the news."

Ross swore under his breath. *That no-good bastard.*

"I want to have Meggie transferred to the hospital in Newgate," she suggested.

"Whatever you think is best, Doc." He remembered

TJ and Jeremy suddenly. "Did Meggie mention the boys? Were they awake? Are they okay?"

Libby touched his arm gently and smiled. "Don't worry, they're safe. They're spending the night with friends."

Ross nodded. He'd see to them in the morning. Right now, he intended to pay a visit to the sheriff's office.

"I have something I have to do. I'll call you later to see about Meggie."

"Ross, don't go...." Libby's words trailed off as he disappeared around the corner.

Libby stood there feeling helpless, biting at her bottom lip. She'd never be able to stop him anyway. She just prayed he didn't do something to make matters worse.

HE SAW DAN guarding the front door when he pulled up in front of the sheriff's office. Before Ross had gotten completely out of the car, Dan yelled, "Go home, Ross. We don't need any trouble here."

"I just want to talk to him." *Yeah, right. Like Dan would believe that.*

Dan touched the gun in his holster. "I said, go home. The only way you're going to come inside is if I have to arrest you. Don't make me do that, Ross."

Ross stood his ground for several minutes, sizing Dan up. He was furious with the man, and furious with himself. He swore, pounded his fist on the hood of his car, then got in and sped off.

Dan watched as Ross's taillights disappeared, then went back inside the building and locked the front door. Taking a set of keys from a hook on the wall, he walked through a door and down the hall, then let himself inside Lattimer's cell.

"I just saved your ass from another beating," he announced to Lattimer, who was curled up on the floor, his arms protectively wrapped around his middle, blood still pouring from his nose and mouth.

"I need a doctor," Lattimer rasped.

"Sorry. We're a little short of doctors right now."

"You won't get away with this."

Dan laughed, then spat on the piece of filth lying on the jail cell floor. "I already have."

Turning around, Dan let himself out of the cell and locked it, ignoring Lattimer's pleas. "I didn't mean to hurt Meggie. I'm sorry," he cried out. "Please, I want to see her. I want to tell her how sorry I am."

Dan turned on him. "You so much as even *think* about looking at her again, and I'll kill you." With that said, Dan worked his way to the front of the building.

For the next several nights, he and his deputy would take turns sleeping here. He didn't want any of the McLaughlin men showing up and taking matters into their own hands. Besides, Dan had already done their bidding for them, and was quite proud of himself.

He wasn't a violent man. Truly he wasn't. He'd been a good husband to Nina, and a good father to

Zack. But he'd been in love with Meggie since he was fourteen. And no one hurt his Meggie and got away with it.

No one.

14

MEGGIE STARED UP at the ceiling of her hospital room, feeling empty inside. She had no one to blame but herself for what had happened. If only she'd listened to Ross or Libby, and left Steve.

Closing her eyes, she tried to block everything from her mind. But that was impossible. How could she ever forget that, because of her stupidity and cowardice, she'd lost her baby?

Tears slipped from her eyes and ran down her cheeks and onto her pillow. She didn't bother to wipe them away. It was pointless. Besides, her gown and pillowcase were already soaked from the tears she'd cried through the night.

The knock on the solid oak door startled her, and she looked through tear-clouded eyes to see Ross enter the room. Ashamed, she turned her head away.

"Meggie, don't." Ross moved to the other side of the bed, laid a hand on her cheek. "I'm so sorry. I should never have left you there with—"

"Stop it, Ross. It's not your fault. It's mine," she

sobbed, burying her face in the damp pillow. "If only I'd been honest with you."

Feeling his weight press down on the bed, Meggie half sat and turned into Ross's arms, allowing him to comfort her.

"It's okay, honey," he said. "Go ahead and cry."

And cry, she did. Until she couldn't find the strength to cry any more.

"The boys?" she asked when she could finally find her voice.

Ross smoothed his hand down her back. "TJ wanted to stay with the Reese boy—Zack. And Jeremy's with Barry and April, soaking up all their attention. Barry had him outside working on his dribbling techniques when I stopped by this morning. He and April are planning to bring the boys up later on today to see you."

Shaking her head against his chest, Meggie said, "No. I can't see them yet. I know that sounds horrible, but I. . . ."

"Shhhh. Whatever you say. Whenever you're ready." He held her tighter.

"I know you must think I'm crazy, but I really thought Steve was just having a hard time coming to terms with losing another job. I truly believed that once he found work, that he'd get better. . . ." *And that he'd stop beating me*, she added silently.

She pulled away from Ross, grabbed a tissue from the bedside table, and wiped her eyes. "Now, it all makes sense," she said, her head clearing. "He'd said that his boss had accused him of stealing drugs from the warehouse. Steve had me convinced that the man had used it as an excuse to get rid of him." She paused to blow her nose. "And then Libby's office was broken into. I never made the connection until yesterday when I was cleaning out some drawers and found all those drug packages."

Meggie soaked up Ross's comfort, and he thanked God he was there for her. He stayed with her for the better part of the day, listening to her talk about her shattered dreams, and holding her while she cried.

EMMA STRAIGHTENED THE shelves for the second time that morning. The bait shop had been extremely slow for some reason, and she was bored to tears.

Jeremy was following Uncle Barry around today. She knew the poor kid was lonely, and that he couldn't wait for his mom to come home from the hospital. So she'd given her cousin a few odd jobs to do, which was why everything was already done that needed to be.

Walking over to the picture window, she stared out at the lake and sighed with pleasure at the sailboats cruising along. She'd never sailed before, but she was certain she'd like it. It looked relaxing and fun at the same time. Libby had a sailboat and had promised to take Emma out, but the sails were being replaced. The boat was supposed to be ready some time next week. Emma could hardly wait.

The bell on the door jangled loudly, breaking her concentration. As she spun around to greet her customer, she was surprised to see her cousin TJ and Zack Reese.

"Hi!" she said a little too enthusiastically, excited for the company.

Zack smiled and said hello. TJ gave his usual grumble and avoided looking her in the eye.

"How are you doing, Emma?" Zack asked.

"I'm okay."

Zack nodded, smiled. "That's good. We need a dozen night crawlers."

Reaching into the cooler, Emma asked, "Anything else?"

"That's it. Unless you need something, TJ?"

TJ shook his head, shrugged one shoulder, and walked outside without bothering to say good-bye. Emma didn't concern herself with her cousin's bad manners for very long. She was used to him. And besides, she knew he was upset about Aunt Meggie. Once her aunt was home, and the boys were back with her, maybe TJ would even smile once in a while. At least his horrible stepfather wouldn't be around anymore.

"Looks like you're going fishing," Emma remarked for lack of anything better to say. Zack made her nervous, although she hated to admit it. She'd told herself over and over again there was nothing to be nervous about. He wasn't even her type. But he had this way of looking at her— with that crooked smile—that made her belly do flip-flops and her tongue twist whenever she attempted to speak.

"Yeah. TJ and I are going out early tomorrow morning."

"Oh." *Oh?* Was that all she could think of to say?

"Well," he said. "I'll see you around." He gave her that crooked smile and left.

Emma let her head drop to the counter. *What an idiot I am*, she thought. Moments later, and while she was still admonishing herself for always acting like a fool in front of Zack, Jeremy rushed inside.

"I just saw TJ and Zack," he announced, a neon yellow yo-yo swinging from his middle finger, bobbing against his leg. "They're taking the Patterson twins fishing tomorrow."

The Patterson twins. She'd seen Dena and Darla, although she couldn't tell them apart. Both had long, dark, curly hair, green eyes, and big boobs. Sadly, she glanced down at her own chest. Was that what Zack was interested in? If so, she may as well forget it. Not that she was interested in him in the first place.

He wasn't her type, she reminded herself again.

It's just that he was always so nice to her. Well, at least she used to think so. Any guy who looked at a girl just because of her bra size couldn't be that nice. And it would do her good to remember that. Men were scum, Libby had told her. And she'd never known Libby to be wrong. About anything.

Forget about Zack Reese, she told herself. She didn't need him. Blowing out a long breath, Emma took the yo-yo from Jeremy. "Here, let me show you how to work this thing."

"Okay," he agreed quickly with a smile. "Want a piece of bubble gum?" He reached into his pocket and pulled out a pack of gum.

"Sure, why not?" What did it matter if her teeth rotted and fell out of her mouth? She didn't have to look good. No one was interested in her, anyway. Travis had found someone else. Probably someone prettier. Or more willing. And Zack liked big-boobed girls.

Emma and Jeremy chomped on their gum and blew bubbles while she showed him her yo-yo tricks.

After a long while, the ten-year-old asked, "Why did you do that to your hair?"

"Do what?" she asked, fingering a chunk and lifting her eyes upward.

The boy studied her a moment, and then said, "Make it look all scary like that."

Emma laughed. "You think it looks scary?"

"Nah. But TJ said you looked scary the first day we met you. I told him I thought you were really nice." He slipped his finger through the loop on the yo-yo string and gave it a toss, cheering when he managed to accomplish one of the moves Emma had just taught him.

"Sometimes he says mean things about people," Jeremy said, still referring to his older brother. "He calls me fat all the time. But Mom says he doesn't mean it."

Emma forced a smile. "Of course, he doesn't. And you're not fat. You just haven't talled up yet."

Jeremy seemed to like that explanation. "Yeah, that's what I figured," he said, grinning from ear to ear.

Growing sullen, Emma wondered what Zack thought about her hair. Did he think she looked scary, too?

ON MEGGIE'S THIRD day home from the hospital, Ross brought the boys back to her. She'd spent the first two days at home alone. Although, between Ross, Barry, and April checking on her at regular intervals, they hadn't allowed her much privacy. But she'd insisted she was ready to take care of her kids, and that she was going to be okay.

Ross wanted to believe that. But her emotions still seemed a little too raw, and he was determined to keep a close eye on her, whether she liked it or not.

He walked out of Meggie's, leaving her alone with the boys, and was just about to step into his Jeep and head home when Libby pulled into the drive and got out of her car.

"How's she doing today?" she asked.

Shrugging, he smiled and said, "I wish I knew for sure. Each day, she seems a little stronger, a little more forgiving of herself."

Libby laid a hand on his. "It'll come with time. We can't beat ourselves up forever."

It sounded to Ross as though she were speaking from experience. What guilt trip had Libby been on? he wondered.

"TJ and Jeremy are with her right now. I just dropped them off."

"Oh." She looked at the house, then at her watch. "I don't want to interrupt. Maybe I'll come back in a little while."

"Would you like to grab a cup of coffee, Doc?" The words had jumped out of his mouth with no warning.

She was about to say no, he could tell. But before she had a chance to decline his offer, Ross stopped her. "Just a cup of coffee. Between friends."

"Sure," she said slowly. "I guess I have time."

It was going on five. He assumed Meggie was the last of her patients she would see for the day. Why would she have to hurry home? Unless she missed that beast she called a cat.

"I'll drive," she offered.

They kept their conversation simple during the three-minute ride to the coffee shop. "It's humid today," she said, adjusting the air conditioning controls. "And it's supposed to get even more humid tomorrow."

"I heard that, too," he agreed.

Pointing to the Wal-Mart they passed, she said, "They seem to be pretty busy since they opened last month."

"Uh, huh. Looks that way."

Libby pulled into the parking lot of the coffee

shop, slipped easily into an open space, and turned off the ignition. Reaching behind her seat, she grabbed for her purse. Before she had a chance to step out of the car, Ross met her and caught the door for her.

"Libby, do you think we could talk about something other than the weather and the new Wal-Mart once we go inside?"

She narrowed her eyes at him. "Well, at least I attempted to make conversation. Instead of brooding." She headed for the entrance door and pulled it open.

Ross followed behind her, grabbing at the door when she let it go in his face. "Brooding?" he asked once inside, then lowered his voice. "I wasn't brooding."

"You always brood," she stated emphatically, then told the hostess they wanted a table for two in the non-smoking section.

The place was dated but clean. Ross watched as Libby eyed the glass case filled with pies. She gave each of the desserts a thorough once-over, then hurried to catch up with the hostess.

Once they were seated, a waitress with a blonde, floppy ponytail tied with a bright red ribbon greeted them. She set menus on the table, poured two cups of coffee, and then left them alone.

Ross noticed Libby's cool composure. "I wasn't brooding," he repeated, reopening their conversation.

"You've been brooding ever since I told you I wouldn't sleep with you."

"That's not what you said!" he blurted out.

Assuming he'd embarrassed her, he expected her to glance nervously around the room. He was wrong. Instead, she stared at him, her green eyes wide and focusing on his. She'd worn a pale shade of red on her lips today.

"Well, that's what I meant." She plucked two sugar packs from a basket, ripped them open, and dumped them into her cup. She followed it up with two containers of cream, not stopping until the liquid reached the top, stirred, careful not to spill the hot brew over the sides, and brought the cup to her lips for a huge gulp. Making a bitter face, she set her cup on the saucer. Remnants of her red lipstick clung to the edge of her cup.

"You told me that you would have said yes if I'd asked you to have a short-term affair."

"What does it matter what I said?"

"It matters," he said, meaning it. He nodded at her cup. "And why do you drink that stuff if you have such an aversion to it?"

Shrugging, she said simply, "I need the caffeine."

Ross stared at her in disbelief, and shook his head.

"Don't have a canary," she said.

Ross narrowed his eyes. *A canary*? Emma had been using that same phrase on him lately.

Picking up a menu and eyeing it, she changed the subject, keeping her eyes averted. "They have good pie here."

"If you want pie, get some." He wanted to get

the conversation back on the right footing—their affair—but it was obvious she planned to go in a different direction altogether. Well, she wasn't going to get away with it. "Isn't that what you said?"

She played dumb. "What? That they have good pie?"

Ross sighed out a long breath, then tested his coffee. Still too hot. "We weren't talking about pie, and you know it."

"Oh, Ross, just forget it. I already told you it doesn't matter now. What *does* matter is that we're not going to have an affair, short-term or otherwise. So stop brooding." She signaled for the waitress.

Ross wanted to choke her pretty little neck. Why wouldn't she just admit that she would have said yes? She'd admitted it once. What was so damn hard that she couldn't admit it a second time?

When the young girl arrived at their table, she grinned at both of them. "See anything you'd like?"

"I think I'll have a piece of your Dutch cherry pie topped with French vanilla ice cream, and more coffee, please." Libby looked at Ross, silently asking if he wanted anything.

"Nothing for me, thanks," he said, dismissing the girl.

"You'll be sorry. And don't think you're going to have a bite of mine. Remember, I don't—

"Share your desserts," he finished for her.

She stared at him in amazement, touched a finger to her large, gold, hoop earring, then lowered her gaze. "I'm probably going to ruin my dinner.

Oh, well. I'd only planned to heat up some leftovers anyway."

Ross didn't comment.

"What about you?"

"What about me?" he asked, slowly and distinctly.

"What do *you* have planned for dinner?"

He thought about saying, "You," but knew better. "Nothing."

"Then you should get some pie."

"I don't want any pie. Thank you," he added.

Libby briefly lifted her eyes to the ceiling and drank from her cup.

The smiling waitress returned, set the heaping dessert dish in front of Libby, and refreshed her coffee. Ross had yet to drink more than a sip of his, but the girl topped it off anyway, then roamed about the small room, stopping to chat with two gentlemen at a nearby table.

Carefully lowering his voice, Ross asked, "What if I told you I wanted to have an affair with you? That I find you extremely attractive? That I can't get you out of my mind?"

Libby's head shot up, her eyes giving nothing away. Then, relaxing somewhat, she spread her napkin across her lap. "I'd say, I couldn't possibly make a decision of that magnitude while this piece of pie is staring me in the face."

Ross grabbed her fork and thrust it into her hand. "Start eating."

It was the longest he'd ever seen anyone take to

eat a piece of pie. What was it with her and desserts? The way she savored it had him thinking about other things he hoped she'd savor when and if he ever got her alone. Although she hadn't agreed to sleeping with him, she hadn't exactly said no, either.

The last bite had barely touched her lips when Ross pushed her for an answer. "Well?" He raised his brow for emphasis.

She swallowed, washed it down with a sip of coffee, then tilted her head back and closed her eyes. "It was divine."

Now he really wanted to choke her. She was doing this deliberately. "Stop playing games, Libby," he said impatiently. He'd had an erection for the past five minutes and found it extremely uncomfortable to remain seated across from her, not touching her, not kissing those sweet red lips.

Planting her elbow on the table, Libby rested her cheek in the palm of her hand. A faint smile played at her lips, then disappeared altogether.

"It wouldn't work," she said, finally.

"Why not? And don't tell me it's because of my brooding. If you agree to sleep with me, I'm sure that little problem will correct itself."

Blinking up at him, she toyed with the rim of her cup. "It's because of Emma."

Ross creased his brow and leaned forward. "*Emma*? What does my daughter have to do with us sleeping together?"

Libby shrugged a shoulder and sat upright. "Emma and I have become pretty close."

"So?" He hadn't had time to elaborate on that when their waitress came by to see if they needed anything else. "Just the check," he told her and waited for the girl to make a note on the pad and rip the check free. "Thank you."

He trained his gaze on Libby, and waited for her to explain.

"Your daughter and I talk. A lot. I know *things* about you. And you probably know *things* about me."

Nothing he was willing to admit. Especially not now. He supposed Emma had told him some things about the doctor that she shouldn't have. Like the name of her first real lover. Paul Denning—the man who broke her heart. *The guy must be a stupid bastard.* Suddenly, he wondered what kinds of things Emma'd told Libby about him.

"I'm sure my daughter probably told you that I snore. If you're worried about that, I promise not to fall asleep around you," he joked.

Libby didn't so much as crack a smile.

Ross leaned back in his seat. "What *did* she tell you about me?"

Libby picked up her napkin, dabbed at her lips, then folded it neatly and laid it on the table. "She said you cool your soup in the freezer for several minutes before you eat it."

He didn't argue. That was true.

"And when you get angry, a big blue vein pokes out of your forehead." She pointed to a place above his brows. "In fact, I can see it now."

Ross slid his chair back and reached for his wallet. "I'm not angry."

"You look angry."

"I'm not. You want to leave the tip again?"

She seemed to contemplate the idea. "No. You invited me, remember?"

Yes, and he was starting to regret it. He had a feeling Libby was enjoying seeing him grovel. He threw a five dollar bill down on the table. "Let's go."

Taking her arm, he led her outside.

They didn't speak on the way back to Meggie's place. However, when she pulled into the drive, Ross stopped her from getting out of the car. "Libby, no one has ever made me grovel or beg, but in your case I'm willing to make an exception."

That hadn't seemed to impress her much, so he tried a different approach. "When two people are attracted to each other, it seems only natural that they act on those attractions. Being a doctor, I'm sure you have medical books on animal instincts and behavior."

She grinned and clucked her tongue. "We haven't even kissed yet. I could never have an affair with a man who didn't know how to kiss."

Ross looked at her, a slow smile pulling at his mouth. He'd been dying to kiss those lips for weeks. "Why don't we do a taste test right now?" Pulling her close, he stared into her green eyes, then slowly pressed his lips to hers.

At first, he kept the kiss light, then greed took

over and relieved him of his senses. He refused to settle for a simple kiss, he needed to thoroughly explore her lips, mouth, and tongue. Besides, if he was unable prove to her that he could accomplish at least that much, what chance did he have of taking their relationship any further?

He breathed in her vanilla scent, savoring the delicious smell. Libby ran her hands along his back, neck, through his hair, and let her upper body relax against his, her small breasts pressed against his chest.

Somewhere in the distance, he heard a horn blow, but he ignored the sound. It felt awkward necking in a car in broad daylight, but Ross blocked it out of his mind, as well. At the moment, he couldn't care less who drove by and saw them.

When the kiss finally ended, he sprinkled light kisses on her eyelids, nose, and cheeks while waiting for his breathing to slow down some.

"Well, Doc? Did I pass?"

Libby straightened, pushed herself away from him. She ran a finger across her swollen bottom lip and stared at him. "Tomorrow night," she said breathlessly. "My place. Seven o'clock. You bring the wine."

Ross wanted to scream with joy, but managed to keep his reserve. Before he could say anything, she added, "We'll talk."

Talk?

"And then if we decide...." She reached for the door handle.

What was there to decide? Hadn't that kiss just proved it?

But he'd never pushed a woman in his life. In fact, they were mostly the ones to push him. Determined not to spoil a good thing, he said, "That sounds like a good plan, Doc."

15

ROSS FELT LIKE a teenager going to his first school dance. He'd showered twice and changed his shirt three times before finally settling on a navy blue polo and a pair of khakis. He scratched a note out to Emma, simply telling her he was going out and wouldn't be back until later, then grabbed a bottle of Chardonnay from the refrigerator. He was just about to slip out the back when a knock sounded on the front door.

Glancing at his watch, he noticed the time was two minutes before seven, and wondered who it could be. Before he got to the door, it swung open and Barry stuck his head inside. "Hey, little brother."

"Barry," he said in response. It must have sounded like "Come in," because his brother did just that, closing the door behind him.

"April called and said she and Emma were going to grab a bite to eat when they finished shopping. So, I thought I'd go over to the marina and get something for dinner. I thought maybe you'd like to go along."

"Uh ... I can't tonight." Ross hid the bottle of wine behind his back.

"Oh," Barry said, working his way into the room. "Where are you going?"

Ross looked down at his shoes, trying to think of a response. "What?" he finally came up with.

"I said, *where are you going*?"

"Uh ... I'm going out."

Barry eyed him suspiciously, then raised his hands in surrender. "Hey, if you don't want to tell me...."

"I sorta have a date." There, he'd said it. And by tomorrow, everyone in town would know, too. If not from Barry's big mouth, then surely from Minnie Tottleben who worked as a cashier at the Drug Mart where Ross had picked up a box of condoms earlier today. The old biddy had cast him a censorious look that said he had no business buying such disgusting things.

Resigning himself, Ross walked back to the kitchen and set the wine bottle down on the counter, Barry at his heels. "You want a beer, or something?"

"Nah. Looks like you're ready to leave, so I won't keep you." Barry looked at him, then grinned and punched him in the shoulder. He turned around and headed for the front door. "Say hi to Libby for me," he said before leaving.

Was it that obvious that he had a thing for the doc? Ross wondered. Or had Emma been sharing her wishful thinking with his family?

Ten minutes later, Ross stood on Libby's deck, his face pressed to the glass. He could see her at the kitchen counter, dressed in a red sleeveless top tucked into a flowery skirt that skimmed her calves. Red strappy sandals were on her feet. He tapped lightly on the glass, then slid the door open.

She turned around and smiled at him, her green eyes sparkling, her lips painted a pretty shade of red. "Hi," she said softly.

He returned her greeting, then brushed his lips against hers. "You look pretty. And you smell even better."

Libby blushed. "Thank you. I made some crab dip." She nodded to the tray of crackers artfully arranged around a bowl of dip. Noticing the wine in his hand, she said, "I'll get an opener."

After rooting through a drawer for some time, she smiled satisfactorily as she pulled out a shiny metal corkscrew and handed it to him.

Ross went about opening the bottle, filled the two glasses on the counter, and handed one to Libby. He tapped his glass against hers. "Here's to our . . . affair." He watched her eyes closely as she digested his words and tasted the wine.

After a couple of sips, she set her glass aside. "I thought we were going to discuss this first."

Ross placed his glass beside hers, and closed in on her. "What's to discuss, Doc? I want you. And you want me." He let his breath out slowly when she didn't argue, and pulled her into his arms. "That about covers it, don't you think?"

She tilted her head to the side and looked up at him. "It's been a long time," she whispered.

He pressed his lips to hers and tasted the fruity bouquet of the wine. "For me, too."

He kissed her again, deeper this time, skimming his hands down her bare arms. "We're both a little rusty. We just need some practice," he said kissing her cheeks, her eyelids, nibbling on her ears. "I say we shouldn't waste any more time." He trailed his fingers along the neckline of her silky top.

Laughing, she slapped at his hand. She reached for her wine and, taking a long drink from her glass, smiled at him over the rim. "Don't say I didn't warn you."

She'd always come across as being so sure of herself. He found her insecurities surprising. And sweet. He wondered if she'd noticed his insecurities as well. If not, he wasn't about to volunteer that information. That wasn't exactly the sort of thing a man liked to admit.

They sipped at their wine, staring at each other for a long time, until Ross made the first move. Slowly and appreciatively, he ran his eyes up and down the front of her, causing her cheeks to redden slightly. "Doc, I hate to sound like an overly anxious schoolboy, but if you don't show me the way to the bedroom, I'm going to take you on the kitchen floor." His eyes darted toward the glass doors. "In front of God and everyone."

She leveled her eyes on him. "You sure do know how to sweet-talk a girl."

"If it's talking you want, you've got the wrong guy."

Minutes later they were in Libby's bedroom, their clothing half on, half off. Ross toyed with the straps of Libby's red lace bra before opening the front closure. "Nice touch," he whispered, then lowered his mouth to her breast. Finding her nipple with his teeth, he nipped and teased, enjoying her soft whimpers of pleasure.

The bra tumbled from her shoulders and joined her skirt and top on the floor. She stood in only a pair of red lace bikini panties. She looked vulnerable, trusting, and sexy as hell. Ross knew he'd remember that look in her eyes for the rest of his life.

He pulled her close to him and kissed her as he stepped out of his shoes. She'd already stripped him of his shirt. Her trembling hands reached between them to find his belt buckle, and he allowed her the pleasure of pulling it through the loops and unfastening his trousers. But he stopped her hands from tugging down his zipper.

She looked up at him expectantly, her green eyes glittering in the dimly lit room. He shook his head. "Not yet." Tracing the elastic of her panties with his finger, he said, "First, I want to find out if you taste as good as you smell."

He inched the panties over her hips and down her thighs before lowering her to the bed and kneeling between her legs. She was moist and fragrant with her juices, and Ross nearly lost control tasting her. She squirmed, raising her hips, then pushing him away, only to invite him back again until she finally gave in and tumbled over the edge. Only when she'd stopped shuddering completely did he think about his own pleasure.

He reached inside his pocket, withdrew a handful of foil-wrapped condoms and tossed them on the bed.

Libby's eyes widened. "You were pretty sure of yourself, weren't you?"

"No. I was terrified you'd say no. And even more terrified you'd say yes," he admitted, stepping out of his Jockey's.

She watched him, a cautious look on her face, then she smiled and breathed a sigh of relief. "Thank you for saying that," she told him, reaching for a foil package. Ripping it open, she carefully sheathed him, her fingers brushing playfully along the length of him.

Ross closed his eyes and fought for control until she guided him inside her.

At first, he was very still, enjoying the feel of her, her hands kneading his back and buttocks and thighs. Then, slowly, he started to move with her, their movements quickly escalating to high speed. He heard her labored breathing against his ear, her moans of excitement and pleas to take her higher.

Raising his head, he stared down at her. "Come for me, Libby. One more time." Once again, they picked up the momentum. Her eyes drifted shut, and seconds later she let herself go. Ross immediately joined her, then collapsed atop her body.

It was close to nine o'clock when he opened his eyes and glanced at his watch. He must have fallen asleep. Fragments of a brilliant orange sunset peeked through the mini-blinds with the promise of another beautiful day forthcoming.

Libby's head was cradled between his neck and shoulder. Her soft and steady breath teased his skin. Ross ran his eyes appreciatively over her naked body from her small perky breasts to her ladybug-tattooed ankle.

She stirred slightly and wiggled her toes. A silver toe ring winked at him. He'd never before made love to a woman who had tattoos and rings on her toes. Several delectable fantasies ran through his mind, but before he had a chance to act on any of those thoughts, a familiar voice alerted him.

"Libby?" Emma called out. "Libby, are you home?"

Ross nudged Libby away from him and scrambled to his feet. "Jesus." Raking his hands through his hair, he frantically searched the room for his clothing.

"I'll be out in a minute, Emma," Libby called, cool, calm, and collected, as she slowly sat up in bed and started laughing.

He stared at her as if she'd lost her mind. "That's my daughter on the other side of that door." He shoved his feet through his shorts to find he had both feet in the same leg opening.

"I know that." She got out of bed and strutted across the room stark naked. Ross watched her, an erection instantly forming. Swearing at himself, he yanked his underwear off and tried to get them on right this time.

Libby grabbed a blue terry robe from her closet and thrust her arms inside. Tying the belt at her waist, she smiled at his frustrated attempt to dress himself. "Relax," she said, moving toward him. She kissed his forehead, then disappeared from the room.

"Jesus," he said again. As he hurriedly dressed, he listened to the soft murmur of voices in the hall. Did they have to stand just outside the bedroom door? Couldn't Libby get rid of Emma somehow— before she discovered what they'd been up to? His heart hammered viciously in his chest as all sorts of unpleasantries ran through his mind. What would Emma think of him now?

As the voices grew faint, he tried to relax. Libby would think of something. Ross dropped to his knees to look for one of his shoes, which had mysteriously disappeared. He assumed it was under the bed. He spotted it, and just as he went to reach for it, a dog's bark brought his head up sharp. "Owww!" he yelled, then silently cursed himself. What the hell was Max doing here? he speculated, grabbing his shoe and standing.

As he thrust his feet into his shoes and tied the laces, the sound of Max's whimpers grew stronger, his claws raking on the bedroom door more insistently.

"Max! Stop that!" Emma admonished the dog.

"What's the matter with you?" The door rattled and vibrated until Ross was afraid Max would take it off the hinges. He went to the door and leaned his weight against it, just in case.

"I'm sorry, Libby," Emma apologized. "I don't know what's wrong with him. It's as if. . . ."

Suddenly it got quiet, and Ross pressed his ear against the door to listen.

"You're not alone, are you?" Emma asked.

Ross rolled his eyes and sucked in a breath. Smart girl.

"No, I'm not," Libby answered. Ross seethed at her comment. Did she have to be so damn honest?

"Max!" his daughter hollered when the whimpers and scratching started again. "I'm sorry, Libby. We shouldn't have barged in here."

No, you shouldn't have, Ross agreed silently. But it wasn't Emma's fault. He should have known better and taken Libby to a hotel. Although that would have started some rumors for sure. Maybe he should have just locked the doors to Libby's cottage, instead.

"Don't apologize, honey," Libby said. "It's not your fault."

Max barked again, clawed at the door and rattled it. "C'mon, Max. Let's go. Libby has comp. . . ." Emma's voice trailed off. Then, "Oh, my God. Is it my dad?"

Ross pressed the heel of his hand to his forehead, warding off the sudden shooting pain. He jumped at the sound of someone knocking on the door.

"You may as well come out, Ross," Libby said.

He couldn't come out. What would he say to Emma? Blowing his breath out in a long sigh, he slowly backed away from the door. Why hadn't he listened to Libby when she'd said it wouldn't work between them because of Emma?

Because he'd wanted her too damn much to think logically, that's why. And now he was about to suffer the consequences.

Once he finally had the nerve to open the bedroom door, the only one in the hall to greet him was Max. Ross scowled down at the mutt. "Traitor," he whispered.

Following the sound of voices, he ended up in the kitchen. Emma was perched on the countertop, her sneakered feet dangling. She was busy munching on crab dip and crackers. "Mmmm, this is so good."

"Thanks. Have some more," Libby said with pride, pulling out a kitchen chair. "Ross, how about you? Hungry?"

He was starved. "No. Thank you." He couldn't look either of them in the eye. Then suddenly an idea came to him. Turning toward Libby, he winked and said, "I think I got your toilet working again."

Libby stared at him, her brow creasing. "My toilet?"

He winked again. Was she dense? "Yes. Remember you asked me to look at your toilet? *That's* why I was in your room." He flashed his gaze toward Emma, trying to tell Libby to play along.

"Oh!" Her eyes lit up. "My toilet! What was wrong with it?" she asked, grabbing the lapel to her robe and stuffing a cracker into her mouth.

Shaking his head, he said, "It was the . . . you know . . . that *thing*." He scowled at her. What the hell did he know about toilets? The one and only time he'd ever had a problem with one, he'd called a plumber.

"Oh, that thing again," she said, fighting off a grin.

Emma followed the conversation, her gaze shifting between the two of them. She jumped off the counter, helped herself to another cracker and dip. "So, are you two . . . doing it?"

"No!" Ross insisted.

Libby only laughed.

Ross had never been so embarrassed in his life. "What are you doing here, Emma?" he asked rather impatiently, rubbing his sweaty palms against his pant legs.

Emma rolled her eyes. "I came to see if Libby would help me color my hair." She grabbed a small brown sack from the counter and opened it, pulling out a box of Clairol something-or-other.

"What color?" he asked warily, staring at her red spikes, remembering the first time he'd seen them and how he'd reacted.

"My natural color. Blonde. I'm kind of tired of the red in it. And I thought," she said, turning toward Libby, "that I could use a new hairstyle, too."

"Of course I'll help you," Libby said, smiling warmly. "Excuse me while I get dressed."

Ross finished off the glass of wine he'd poured earlier, and stuffed a few crackers in his mouth. He refused to look at his daughter, for fear his face would show that he'd been lying. He wondered if she'd bought his toilet story. Obviously not.

It was Emma who finally spoke. "I told you Libby was perfect for you."

Ross glanced at his grinning daughter, and shook his head in defeat.

Libby returned a moment later wearing frayed jeans and a white T-shirt. She had a towel, a comb, and a pair of scissors. "When I finish with her, I'm going to trim your hair," she said to Ross, snapping the scissors and winking.

Ross watched as Libby draped a towel over Emma's shoulders and opened the box of hair color. The two women chatted incessantly as if he weren't even there. Noticing Smiley sneering at him from a stool in the corner of the kitchen, Ross pulled up a chair, sat beside the cat, and brooded along with him.

Watching as the doc fussed over his daughter, he tried to keep his lusty thoughts at bay. It was hard to forget the look on Libby's face when she'd come. Or the tiny little sounds that had echoed from her lips while he'd been inside her. He wanted nothing more than to drag her back to bed and make love to her until morning.

Fat chance. At least not tonight.

So, instead, he satisfied himself with watching Libby transform his daughter into a beautiful young woman. And waited for his turn in the chair, the feel of Libby's hands and fingers in his hair.

"SO, WHAT DID you buy?" Barry asked as April tossed her shopping bags on the bed.

"I got a new blouse and a pair of sandals." She took the shoebox from the bag and placed it on her closet shelf.

"Let's see the blouse," he suggested.

April dug a yellow blouse from the bag, and pulled the tissue paper away from it. Holding it up, she shrugged. "It was on sale. You know what a sucker I am for a bargain."

"It matches your eyes," he said, lowering himself to the bed. April stared at him awkwardly. "The tiny gold flecks...."

She forced a smile, turned, and took her new purchase to the closet and placed it on a hanger.

"What did you do while I was gone? Did you eat anything for dinner?"

"Nah, I wasn't hungry."

"I could make you something," she offered.

Barry patted his stomach. "Thanks, but skipping one meal won't hurt me." He lay back on the bed, folded his arms behind his head. "Actually, I *was* hungry earlier. I stopped by Ross's place to see if he wanted to go over to the marina and grab a bite."

April studied him. "Didn't he want to go?"

Barry released a small chuckle. "He said he would have, but he'd already made other plans. He had a date."

April's gold-flecked eyes lit up. "With Libby Larson," she said knowingly.

"Yeah. You were right."

The night they'd had the family dinner at his parents' to welcome home Ross and Emma, April had seen Ross talking to Libby down on the beach. She'd made her prediction then about his brother and the doctor getting together, although he hadn't put much stock in her words at the time.

"I didn't think he'd bother to get involved with anyone," he said, "since he's not planning on sticking around."

"Love can get in the way of carefully thought out plans."

"*Love*? Ross barely knows her. He's probably only talked to her a half dozen times."

"For some people, that's all it takes." Barry let his wife's words sink in. She was right. That's all it had taken for them to first fall in love. Now it seemed like such a lifetime ago.

"I missed you tonight," he admitted and waited for her reaction.

"Did you?"

He swore he saw a tiny shudder escape her lips.

"Yes." He slowly got to his feet and made a move toward her. She backed up a step and glanced nervously around the room as if she were looking for an escape route. "April," he whispered, reaching for her hand. "I want to make love with you."

He thought for a moment she was about to run. But then he saw the tears form in her eyes. "Don't cry, baby." Pulling her close, he picked her up and cradled her in his arms. He dropped to the bed and held her while she trembled. Once she'd calmed down, he placed his hand under her chin, lifted her face up to his, and kissed her. "God, how I've missed you."

"I don't go shopping that often."

Barry laughed and kissed her again. "I didn't mean just tonight."

"Oh," she said, looking surprised by his confession. Then *she* kissed *him*, causing his hopes to soar. Hopes of having his marriage back. Was there a chance they could put all of the pain and distrust behind them and go forward after all these years? He'd give anything to have April back. And her forgiveness.

After all, he'd forgiven *her* . . . a long time ago.

16

"ARE YOU IN love with her?" April asked, biting at her bottom lip, searching his face, his eyes.

Barry shook his head, sadly. He figured he would have felt less shame if he had been in love with Meri. At least he would have felt as if he had a good reason for what he'd done.

"Then why?" she asked in a shaky breath, folding her arms protectively around her.

He lowered himself into the recliner, and hung his head. "I don't know."

She covered her eyes with her hands and started to cry. When he went to get up, she dropped her hands from her eyes, and said, "Don't. Stay right there. Don't touch me. Right now, I couldn't stand for you to touch me. Not after you've been with her."

Barry closed his eyes. He'd finally confessed his affair with Meri. Although, April had been hinting for weeks that she suspected he and Meri had been up to no good. He'd never meant to hurt April. Looking at her pain-filled face, how could he not have intended to hurt her? Didn't he realize how she'd feel if she knew he'd betrayed her? He supposed he hadn't cared much at the time. All he'd thought about was his own selfish pleasure.

"April, listen to me. It's over. I don't love her. I love you."

"You couldn't possibly love me and do what you did. And what about Ross? Whatever you felt for Meredith must have been pretty strong to risk your marriage and your relationship with your brother. You must have thought you were in love with her."

Barry shook his head. "No. I thought I could love her, once. But it was different from what you and I have." He paused. "I can't explain it. What I felt for her was more like . . . lust. I couldn't stay away from her. And I hated myself for what I was doing. But I never stopped loving you."

"Please," she tossed at him. "I don't want to hear any more. I hate you for what you've done to me, to us. And I hate her even more. I wish she were dead."

Barry shuddered at her words. Would she ever forgive him? he wondered. He'd do anything to make it up to her. Anything. She only had to say the word.

"WHY DO I have to go with you?" TJ asked, looking more annoyed than anything. "I don't even remember your mom."

Emma stared at her cousin, hurt by his words. "If you don't want to go with me, then fine. I'll go by myself. I just thought since you know Sheriff Reese that maybe he'd tell me what he knows about my mom if you were with me." She paused for a moment before adding, "And I thought since we're cousins that you'd want to help me. I guess I was wrong. You only care about yourself and your own problems."

"I don't have any problems." TJ picked up a rock and tossed it into the lake, watching the waves as they undulated in an expanding circle.

"Yeah, right. What about your stepfather?" She regretted her words, but before she could apologize, TJ cut in.

"All right. I'll go with you, but you ask the questions. Okay?"

Emma beamed at him. "Okay! Thank you." She reached up, planted a kiss on his cheek.

TJ scowled at her, his face turning red. After a few moments, he said, "I like your hair better this way than before."

Touching her blonde curls, Emma smiled gratefully. "Thanks, TJ."

TJ HAD BORROWED his mother's car. The Reeses lived in a small brick ranch just on the fringe of town. Since TJ and Zack were friends, the sheriff naturally invited them in. Once inside, Emma immediately noticed the pictures of Zack's mother adorning the living room walls. TJ said Mrs. Reese had died a few years ago.

The only photos Emma had of her own mother were kept in her bedroom. Her father had never framed or hung them on the walls of their Phoenix home. He obviously didn't want any reminders of the woman he'd married. That saddened Emma. She'd always thought it was because her father thought it was too painful to look at his wife's pictures hanging on the walls, but now she wondered if there was another reason. Maybe he wasn't sorry that she'd died.

Sheriff Reese led them to the kitchen. "Have a seat. Can I get you two something to drink? Coke? Iced tea?"

Emma declined the offer. TJ said, "I'll have a Coke. I'll get it." She knew TJ had stayed with the Reeses when his mom was in the hospital. He obviously felt comfortable here.

"So, what's this all about?" the sheriff asked, once they were all seated.

Glancing at TJ for support, Emma opened her mouth to speak. But it was TJ who started the conversation. "She wants to know about her mom. About how she died."

Emma swallowed nervously. She watched the sheriff's face for some clue as to what he was thinking. There was none. After a long, uncomfortable silence, he leaned back in his chair and studied her, gnawing on his bottom lip. "What has your father told you?"

"Not much," she said. "I just want to know what the big secret is. Why no one is willing to talk about her. You have to remember something."

He blinked a few times, then sighed. "After a long investigation, your mother's death was ruled an accident," he finally said. "I'm afraid I can't tell you much more than that."

"So, she fell off Falcon Ridge?"

"Yes, it seems she did. I'm sorry."

A part of her felt relieved. She'd waited so long to hear what had happened fourteen years ago. Now she knew. But for some reason, knowing how she had died didn't seem like enough. She wanted to know more about her mother. About the kind of person she was. "Did you know her?"

"Sure. Although I didn't know her very well. She was very pretty. You look just like her, you know?"

Emma smiled. "Thank you."

The sheriff explained how Meredith's mother and stepfather had moved away before Meredith died. No one had been able to find them fourteen years ago. And then Meredith's grandmother had died shortly thereafter.

Sheriff Reese wasn't as helpful as Emma had hoped. She was disappointed, but at least he'd told her more about her mother during the past ten minutes than her father had in fourteen years.

They hung around for a few minutes more. TJ finished his Coke, and then they got up to leave. "Thanks, Sheriff Reese," she said.

"Sure."

Emma was halfway to the car when she noticed TJ wasn't behind her. He stood on the front porch, saying something to the sheriff. Probably thanking him. Opening the passenger door of the car, Emma got inside and waited for her cousin.

"You didn't tell her Uncle Ross was arrested for her mother's murder and then let go," TJ said to Dan.

Dan had had a feeling that's what TJ was going to say. "I thought it would be best if it came from her father. If she needs to know at all."

Tilting his head to the side, TJ glanced at his cousin in the car, then back at Dan. "Yeah, you're probably right."

"How'd you know about that, anyway?"

He shrugged. "People talk. I hear things."

Dan thought about that, and nodded his head. "You watch out for her. She seems like a nice girl."

"She's okay, I guess," TJ admitted.

Dan breathed a sigh of relief as the boy drove off. It wouldn't have been right to tell a sixteen-year-old girl about his suspicions surrounding her mother's death. And besides, he—and his father, who had been sheriff at the time of Meredith McLaughlin's death—still didn't know for sure what happened all those years ago. Oh, they thought they knew. But proving it would be another story. So, Dan and his father had decided maybe it was best to just leave it alone.

"I DIDN'T KILL her, Dan." Ross's gaze shifted between Dan and his father.

"Just tell us where you were Saturday between noon and three," Sheriff Reese demanded between puffs on his cigar.

Walter Reese was a big man, six feet, four inches and two hundred forty pounds of solid muscle. Dan had a slighter build, taking more after his mother than his father.

"I already told you."

"What? That cock and bull story about your boat running out of gas on the lake?"

"It's the truth," Ross said defiantly.

"Who towed you into the marina?"

The sheriff blew a puff of smoke directly at Ross. Dan noticed Ross's eyes water.

"I've already told you all of this."

"Tell us again." The sheriff dragged a chair noisily across the tile floor and dropped his weight into it. He sat directly across the table from Ross. Dan remained standing near a corner of the small room they used for booking criminals.

Shaking his head, Ross said, "I don't know their names. Two guys, around forty to forty-five years old. They were up here from Pittsburgh. That's all I know."

"And they're not staying in one of your family's lake cottages?"

"I don't know," he answered impatiently. "I don't think so. I didn't recognize them."

"What was the name of their boat?"

"I told you. I don't remember."

Sheriff Reese kicked the chrome leg of the chair beside him, toppling the chair over and sending it flying across the room. "You grew up on that lake. You've been around boats all your life. You really expect us to believe that?"

Ross didn't answer. Dan set the chair on its legs and received a scowl from his father for his efforts. He was sweating, and so were his father and Ross. The room had no ventilation, and the oxygen seemed to be spent.

Sheriff Reese stubbed his cigar out on top of an empty pop can, wiped his brow with a dirty paper napkin, and resumed his questioning. "So, if you didn't kill your wife, who do you think did?"

Dan looked at Ross, studying him, anxiously awaiting his answer.

Ross looked away as he spoke. "I have no idea."

"Was she playing around? Seeing someone else?"

Ross jerked his head up, looked over at Dan. "No, not that I know of."

Dan knew he was lying. He'd heard the rumors. Meredith hadn't been faithful since the day she'd married Ross, nor had she been discreet.

"Ross," Dan interjected. "We're talking about a possible murder here. By lying, you could be protecting your wife's killer."

"I thought I was supposed to be the killer. Isn't that why you arrested me?"

Dan took the chair next to his father. "We found several packets of twenty-dollar bills on top of the cliff. All together, there was several thousand dollars. And a plane ticket to LA. One way."

Ross didn't so much as flinch.

"You have a total of three hundred dollars in your savings account. Where did she get the money?"

Ross still didn't answer.

"Had you two been getting along lately?"

Blinking, Ross hesitated, then answered, "Yes. Why?"

Dan and his father exchanged a look. Then Sheriff Reese took over. "Look, here's how we see it. Your wife was playing around behind your back. Probably with someone you know. She was planning to run off and leave you. Maybe take your baby daughter with her. You couldn't stand the thought of losing your wife, or your child. You couldn't stand the thought of another man having her. You were angry. You argued and fought. You lost your temper and pushed her off that cliff."

"It wasn't me," Ross stated in a huff.

"No? Who was it, then?"

Ross closed his eyes, slowly opened them. He said nothing.

"Who are you trying to protect, Ross?" Dan asked.

They sat quietly for a few minutes—not a sound except their breathing—until Sheriff Reese broke the silence.

"Did you know she was pregnant?"

Ross didn't move for a minute, then he sat up straight, a look of sheer misery on his face. "I'm not answering any more questions," he announced slowly, distinctly, "until I have a lawyer present."

The sheriff rotated his eyes toward his son, then back at Ross. "Suit yourself."

"WHERE ARE YOU taking me?" Libby asked as Ross

careened his Jeep through winding back roads, managing to hit nearly every pothole in their path.

"Somewhere we won't be interrupted." Ross kept his gaze straight ahead, focusing on the dark road.

He hit another pothole, causing Libby to bounce off her seat. "Owwww," she moaned, shooting him a nasty look. "You made me bite my tongue."

"Sorry," he said, easing up on the accelerator. "But I was only going to bite it later anyway."

Libby tried not to laugh at his lame joke. She felt like a teenager sneaking into the woods with Ross. He'd waited until Emma was asleep before slipping out of the house and showing up on her doorstep.

He'd brought a cooler along, packed with a bottle of Chianti, cheese, and crackers. Her first picnic in the dead of night.

After a few more bumps and turns, he finally pulled off to the side of the road and eased onto a path. Fifty yards or so farther, he stopped, opened the sun roof, and turned off the ignition.

Checking out their surroundings, Libby reached into the cooler at her feet and grabbed a piece of ice. "This looks like a cornfield." She popped the ice into her mouth. It felt good against her sore tongue.

"That's because it *is* a cornfield, Doc." He released his seatbelt, pressed the automatic locks into place, and slid closer to her. Reaching across the console, he nibbled on her ear, breathed in deeply, and toyed with the button on her blouse. "You always smell so good."

Ross smelled good, too. Like soap. His hair was

damp against her cheek from a recent shower. And his face was smooth. Freshly shaved.

There was a starlit sky and a full moon, adding just enough illumination for what they were about to do.

"What if somebody sees us?"

"Trust me, no one's going to see us out here." He unfastened her seatbelt, then slid his seat back. "If you hand me the wine and the corkscrew, I'll do the honors."

After the wine was opened, Libby held plastic cups while Ross filled them. She sniffed, then tasted, the liquid. "Mmmmm," she whispered. "Heaven."

"I brought you a dessert, too. But I haven't decided if I want you to eat it before we make love, or after."

"What kind of dessert?" Libby rooted through the cooler. Her hand came in contact with a cellophane package and she picked it up. "A Twinkie?"

Ross grinned at her and shrugged. "I know how much you like sweets."

"And so you went all out." She tossed the snack cake, hitting him squarely in the chest.

"It's all I could find on such short notice. I risked my life as it was sneaking it from the kitchen. It was the last one. Wait until Emma discovers it's missing." He set the Twinkie on the dashboard. "There's going to be hell to pay."

"I can't believe I'm about to have sex in a corn-field with a guy who's trying to woo me with a Twinkie. Not to mention all the bruises I'll probably have tomorrow." The cramped quarters didn't offer much in the way of leg room.

"Pretty romantic, huh?"

Libby laughed, choked on her wine. Ross patted her on the back. "You okay, Doc? You're not going to have a *canary* or anything, are you?" he teased, tossing her favorite phrase in her face.

They sipped on their wine, nibbled on cheese and crackers, and giggled like two teenagers about to make love for the first time. When they'd finished the bottle, Ross looked into her eyes. With his index finger, he flicked the bright orange earring dangling from her ear.

"Why don't you get rid of those ... whatever they are?"

Libby tried to look offended. "They're fish. I'm a Pisces. Get it?"

Ross scowled. "Got it. Get rid of them. And anything else you'd like to take off is fine with me." His look was dark and sexy. Libby felt a little chill run up her spine. She'd had enough wine to make her feel daring. With Ross watching, she carefully unfastened the earrings and laid them on the dashboard. Next she shed her tangerine cardigan and matching tank top. She hadn't bothered with a bra this evening, knowing it would be just the two of them, and knowing she wouldn't be wearing it for very long, anyway.

She tossed the garments over the seat. Before she could straighten, Ross's hands and mouth were all over her, touching her breasts, neck, and face.

"Do you know how sexy you are when you don't wear a bra? Do you have any idea what knowing that does to me?"

Libby ran her hand between his thighs, boldly touching his zipper. "I have an idea." Quickly, she withdrew her hand.

"Tease," he said, snatching her hand and placing it where he wanted it. "Touch me."

Libby obeyed his order, gladly. She enjoyed touching him, feeling him, exploring him. As they kissed, she helped rid him of his pants and briefs, pulling them down around his ankles when he lifted his hips. "Did you come prepared?" she whispered against his lips.

"Pocket," Ross moaned, trying to reach his pants.

"I'll get it," she offered, maneuvering herself to reach the condom in his pants pocket. She pulled her hand out, sat up, counted. "Four?"

Ross shrugged, kissed her again. "I'm optimistic."

"Or you're praying for an early death."

"Have some faith in me, Doc." He pinched her nipples lightly. "Why don't you take off your panties and sit on my lap?"

Slipping out of her panties and skirt, she crawled over to Ross's seat, fitting him inside her perfectly. Together they rocked, slowly, then quickening their pace. Slowing again, until bringing themselves to completion.

Feeling cramped, they later moved to the backseat

and cuddled together spoon-fashion. He'd removed all of his clothing, and she could feel his chest hairs against her back, his muscular legs entangled with hers. He ran his tongue on the back of her neck, causing her to shiver slightly.

The sounds of chirping crickets and the occasional bull frog grunts reminded her they were in the middle of nowhere. Alone. "It's so quiet. Peaceful."

"I like the quiet. That way I can hear those little sounds you make when you come," he said.

Libby giggled. "What little sounds?" She was thankful for the darkness and the fact that Ross was behind her and couldn't see her blush.

"You know. . . . Oooh, oooh, uhhhh," he moaned, exaggerating the sounds. At least she hoped he was exaggerating. She didn't remember sounding quite like that.

"Your mouth opens," he continued, "and you make little panting sounds." Knowing he was teasing her to some degree, she elbowed him in the ribs.

Ross buried his face in her hair, nuzzled her neck, his hot breath on her skin. "What made you decide to settle in Falcon Ridge?" he asked, surprising her that he wanted to talk. He rarely asked questions about her personal life or her past.

And he never shared anything personal about himself. The few times she'd asked him questions, he'd answered evasively and then changed the subject.

"My grandparents used to vacation here when I was a little girl. I loved it. The quiet, the peacefulness. I used to pretend I lived here and that nothing bad could ever happen to me as long as I stayed here."

Wrapping his arm tightly around her middle and pulling her close, he asked, "What kind of bad things were you afraid would happen if you left here?"

She contemplated whether or not to share her deep, dark, family secrets and for some reason decided to tell him. "My father abused my mother. Similar to Meggie's situation."

She heard Ross suck in his breath, grow still. "Did he ever hurt *you*?"

Libby shook her head. "No, not in the way you mean. Not physically."

"Your mother. . . . Is she. . . ?"

"She committed suicide when I was seventeen."

He didn't say anything for a long time. She assumed he was thinking about Meggie, comparing the two abused women. "I'm sorry, Libby." He didn't use her name very often. When he did, he was always so serious-sounding.

Libby flipped over on her back, bent her knees, got comfortable. Looking into Ross's face, she smiled. He seemed to be studying her, memorizing every detail of her face—her mouth, eyes, nose, and cheeks.

The windows had steamed up in spite of the sun roof's being open. Her skin felt damp from the humidity and their love-making.

"Why are you looking at me like that?" she asked

when it looked as if Ross would never stop staring at her.

"No reason. I was just wondering if you were ready for your Twinkie."

Libby slapped him on the shoulder, closed her eyes, and laughed. He kissed her, long and thoroughly, running his hands along the length of her. When she opened her eyes, there was a spotlight shining through the Jeep's window, illuminating their naked bodies.

Before she had a chance to react, a man's voice shouted. "Please step out of the car. Sir, ma'am."

"Shit!" Ross swore as he tried to shield her nakedness from the intruding light.

17

ROSS LIFTED HIS head, tried to see out of the Jeep's windows. But he couldn't see anything except for the light shining on them.

He had no idea who was out there. But from the way the man had asked them to step out of the car, he assumed it was a voice of authority. Not Dan Reese. He would have recognized Dan's voice. Probably his deputy.

"Do you think you could shine that light somewhere else?" he shouted toward the open sun roof.

"No, sir. Please step out of the car," the man repeated.

"You mind telling me who you are?" Ross fired back.

Libby lifted her eyes. "Just listen to him," she whispered, trying to scoot out from underneath him. Ross stilled her with his hands and his weight.

"I'm Deputy Maloney with the Falcon Ridge Sheriff's Department. Now step out of the car. Please."

"Well look, Deputy Maloney, my name is Ross McLaughlin, and I'd appreciate it if you would shine that light somewhere other than on my bare ass."

"I know who you are, sir. You're the only one in town with Arizona plates on his vehicle."

Libby rolled her eyes, tossed her head back and forth on the seat. A small smirk appeared on her lips. He wondered how funny she would think the situation was once he stepped out of the car and the light was on *her* naked body. Not that he had any intention of letting Deputy Maloney get a look at her without her clothing.

"Look, Maloney. Why don't you go back to your patrol car and let the lady and me get dressed?"

The light moved around the vehicle slowly. "Are you all right, Doctor Larson?"

Ross swore aloud. How the hell had he known it was Libby beneath him? Was there no such thing as privacy in this town?

Libby broke into a fit of giggles, but managed to say, "I'm fine, Deputy. But you're making Mr. McLaughlin a little uncomfortable."

Ross shot her a look.

"Oh," then, "Oh, sure, I understand."

The light went out.

Through the steamed-up windows, Ross could make out Maloney's figure. He was alone, apparently.

"Since you seem to be the only one who can talk to this idiot," Ross whispered to Libby, "why don't you see if you can get rid of him?"

"I'll do my best," she said, smiling sweetly.

Raising her voice, she said, "Deputy, if you could move away from the car, we'll get dressed and come out. Okay?"

Maloney hesitated for a moment, then said, "I guess that would be all right. Sure. I'll wait in the patrol car, Doctor Larson."

"Thank you," Libby shouted, trying not to laugh.

Ross immediately got to his knees, began digging for his clothing. "This isn't funny, Doc." He tossed her tank top at her, managed to find his slacks and one sock, but not his underwear. Fumbling in the dark, he complained, "How the hell am I supposed to get dressed in here?"

"The same way you got undressed."

"I seem to remember I had a little help. Do you think you could sit up and give me some room? I can hardly move."

Libby sat up, calmly pulled her top over her head, found her skirt, wriggled into it. She opened the car door, bathing the vehicle in light.

"Where are you going?" he snapped.

"To tell Deputy Maloney that we're sorry, and to go home. I'll tell him that you didn't drag me out here to rape me. I came willingly."

Ross looked at her, the ceiling light shining on her flushed face. "Very funny."

A few moments later, Libby came back to the car, got into the passenger seat in front. Ross heard a car pull away. He opened the door, stepped out of the car. Gravel and dry, brittle grass stabbed at his bare feet. With the light, he managed to find the rest of his clothes. He dressed quickly and got in behind the wheel.

They drove in silence for the first few minutes, then Libby's soft voice broke the spell. "Tomorrow, you'll be laughing about this."

"I doubt it. But everyone *else* in town will be laughing when they hear about it."

Libby shook her head. "Don't start brooding, Ross."

Why did she always accuse him of brooding? Did he?

"You know, you're a lot like your character in your book. Roman Vazquez," she said as if simply saying the name made her ill. "Very cynical. But at least *he* has a sense of humor."

Ross eyed her occasionally as he drove. He wasn't anything like Roman. True, he and Roman were a *little* cynical, but what did that have to do with anything? Roman was still a great guy.

As far as his own personality, he supposed Libby was right—he didn't have much of a sense of humor. He'd been so absorbed in his past all these years, he'd forgotten how to live. How to have fun. Although, he had no intention of admitting those faults to her.

When he pulled up in front of Libby's house, she grabbed her big, orange, fish earrings from the dash and leaned over and kissed him on the cheek. "Thanks for one of the most *interesting* nights of my life."

She started to open the car door, but his hand snaked out, grabbed her arm, stopping her.

"Libby," he said, simply, pulling her close. He ran a finger across her bottom lip. Her eyes widened as she stared at him, a questioning look on her face.

Instead of saying anything or apologizing, the way he'd intended, he kissed her.

A kiss that went on forever.

A kiss that spoke of promises, and tomorrows. Although they both knew their relationship was only temporary.

"WHAT WOULD YOU like to do to celebrate your birthday, Grandma?" Emma asked as she opened a bottle of nail polish.

Bev not only couldn't remember that she had a birthday coming up, but how old she'd be as well. She hid her embarrassment by avoiding looking her granddaughter in the eye as she tried to figure out which birthday she'd be celebrating. Sixty-something, but she'd be darned if she could remember. At her age, most women wouldn't want to remember their age, but Bev desperately wanted to.

"I haven't really thought much about it," she finally said.

"We could have a party," Emma enthusiastically suggested.

Bev hesitated. "I don't know. . . . I don't really feel comfortable around large groups of people."

"We could have a small party, you know, just family."

"That sounds nice, dear."

"And Libby, of course."

Bev jerked her head up. "Libby Larson?"

Emma grinned. "Yeah. My dad and her are sort of seeing each other."

"I didn't know." No one had told her. Of course, no one told her much these days. Too afraid she'd forget, or get upset. Bev felt hurt, and wondered if Neil knew about Ross and Libby.

Then again, maybe Neil had already told her about their son and the doctor, and she'd forgotten. Was that possible?

While she finished folding a basket of clean towels, Emma applied another coat of ice-blue, glittery polish to her nails. Bev didn't care for the color, or the sparkles, but kept her opinions to herself. What did she know about teenagers these days?

Just like the hat Emma wore. It was khaki-colored twill, frayed around the edges, and reminded her of one of Neil's old fishing hats. Not very becoming for a young woman. But Emma seemed to like it.

"There," Emma said, replacing the cap on the polish, staring at her outstretched hands. "As soon as my nails dry, I'll make us some sandwiches."

Smiling, Bev nodded, then returned to her folding. She wasn't helpless. She knew how to make sandwiches. She even knew there was sliced turkey breast in the refrigerator.

Or was it ham?

It didn't matter, she told herself. Anyone could

forget small details like that. At least, lately, she remembered the important things.

Except for her birthday.

But she remembered she had two sons and a daughter. Three grandchildren. That's all that mattered. And Neil. They were her family, her loved ones. All of them pampered and coddled her, wanting to protect her, keep her safe. She understood. She didn't like it at times—felt claustrophobic—but she understood.

Just like she'd done for them most of her life. Until she'd been stricken with Alzheimer's. But she wasn't going to think about that now. No sense feeling sorry for herself.

Lifting her chin, Bev smiled at her granddaughter. Such a sweet little thing. Nothing like her mother, who'd been selfish and conniving. Meredith had nearly ruined their family, had come between them. Ross, Barry, and even Neil had been fooled by her. They'd all thought once that she was just young, immature, and starved for affection. They'd had no idea how vindictive she could be until it was nearly too late.

Because of Meredith, Ross had moved away. But he was back in Falcon Ridge now, where he belonged. And slowly, the McLaughlins were healing. All of them were now willing to put the painful past behind them.

"Grandma, do you want to eat now?"

"Sure. I'm going to put these towels away while you make lunch. How's that?" Bev lifted the laundry basket from the table.

"Okay," Emma said, reaching for her hat and pulling it from her head. Blonde curls popped out, framing her heart-shaped face and transforming her into another woman. A woman Bev despised.

Staring at her, Bev almost dropped the laundry basket. Quickly, she sat down. "Meredith," she whispered, unable to take her eyes off the young woman in front of her.

"WHY DO YOU think men cheat?" April asked.

The question came out of nowhere. Bev gaped at her daughter-in-law, not quite sure what to say, when April asked, "Do you think Neil would ever cheat on you?"

Bev looked at April, shocked that she'd asked such a question. "Heavens, no!"

April stared at her for a moment before pivoting in the other direction. She turned on the kitchen faucet, washed the greasy cookie dough from her hands, and dried them on a dish towel. When she turned back around, a shameful look came over her face. "I'm sorry. That was so careless of me to ask something like that."

Noticing April's eyes as they filled with moisture, Bev set her rolling pin on the table. They were baking sugar cookies for St. Carmichael's bake sale on Saturday. "Honey, what is it? What's wrong?"

"It's nothing," April said, shaking her head. "Forget I said anything." She carried a tray of unbaked cookies to the oven and placed them on the middle rack, closing the door.

"Does this have something to do with you and Barry? Meredith said you two haven't been getting along lately."

At the mention of Meredith's name, her daughter-in-law spun around. "That little bitch!"

Bev tried not to look upset. She bit her bottom lip, wanting to give April time to calm down and tell her what this was all about. But April didn't say anything. She lifted several dough shapes from the flour-covered table and arranged them on another baking sheet. Bev noticed a tear slip from her eye, just as April brought her shoulder up to catch it on the fabric of her T-shirt.

'Sit down, honey. Let's talk," she finally said. "You haven't been yourself lately."

"I'm fine. Or rather, I would be fine if little Miss Meredith would stay away from us. If I were you, Bev, I'd never leave that little slut alone with Neil."

She digested April's words. What had she meant by that statement? Meri and Emma were at the house visiting Neil at this very moment. Ever since his car accident, Meredith had been giving him special attention.

Neil seemed to look forward to her visits. She was always baking him something, or stopping to pick up something special for him. Once it was a pound of his favorite cheese, another time his favorite brand of cigars—although Bev had refused to let him smoke them in the house. Broken leg, or no broken leg. He could wait until he was getting around better, and then enjoy them somewhere where she wouldn't have to smell that awful scent—out in the middle of the lake, she hoped, where he usually smoked.

"All men will cheat if they think they can get away with it," April stated bitterly.

It took a while before Bev finally gathered the courage to ask, "Do you think Barry has been unfaithful to you? Is that what this is all about?"

April threw her head back and laughed. At the same time, she dropped into a kitchen chair and lowered her head to the table. Her brown ringlets dusted the floury table as her shoulders heaved.

"Honey, don't cry. I know Barry. He would never—"

April's head popped up, the ends of her hair tipped with white, her face wet with tears. "No, Bev. You don't know him. I thought I knew him, too."

Bev didn't know what to say. Barry was her son. He was a good man. He loved April. How could he possibly have done something so cruel? She tried to keep an open mind, at the same time telling herself April had made a terrible mistake. "Do you know ... who the woman is?" she asked, dreading the answer and feeling sick inside.

Suddenly April became hysterical and flew out of her chair. "My, God, Bev. Don't be so naive! Your son ... my husband ... has been sleeping with ... Meredith!"

Bev closed her eyes, feeling shame for her son. She prayed it wasn't true. But somehow she knew in her heart it was.

* * * * *

"ARE YOU DONE with my laptop?" Ross asked his daughter.

She had her legs curled beneath her on the kitchen chair, the computer on the table in front of her.

"I have to work on a few revisions for my editor."

"I just want to check my e-mail real quick." While Emma waited for the connection, she poured Frosted Flakes into a bowl and doused them with milk. "You've got mail," she mimicked the male voice that came from her computer. She jabbed a spoon into the bowl, then into her mouth as she scrolled through the list of messages.

Ross poured a cup of coffee and took it to the table, sitting down across from her. He watched her eyes and face as she read something of particular interest, giggled, then typed a few words in reply. She fed her mouth another spoonful of cereal, then became absolutely still. She glanced up at him.

"This one's from Travis." Emma seemed to hesitate, then clicked the button on the mouse, presumably opening the letter.

Great, he thought. Just what they needed. That slime bucket. Why couldn't he just leave her alone? The jerk had already broken her heart, why did he have to write to her after all these weeks? "Don't even bother to read it," he suggested.

She rolled her eyes at him. Then hissed a "Shhhh" at him and grew still, her blue eyes scanning back and forth. Suddenly her eyes stopped moving. Whatever she'd just read caused her face to go pale. Several seconds later, he heard the familiar voice tell her good-bye. She pushed her chair back and carried her uneaten bowl of cereal to the sink.

"Em, what's wrong?"

"Nothing."

Ross sighed.

"Nothing that you can help with, anyway. If you were a woman. . . ."

"Why do you always do that?"

She turned around and looked at him as if she had no clue what he meant.

"Why do you shut me out? I'm not such a bad guy. You can talk to me."

Folding her arms across her chest, she snapped, "Why? So you can lecture me?"

He looked at her, feeling hurt. "Is that how you see it?"

"It's exactly how I see it."

"I'm sorry if I lecture. I don't mean to. I care about you so much, and I worry about you. I don't want anyone to hurt you. So, maybe I overcompensate by lecturing, or questioning you." He slid his chair back, but didn't stand up. He had a feeling if he tried to get close, to touch her, she'd bolt from the room.

Instead, he tried a different approach. "We lost your mother when you were only two. She used to do everything for you. She was a good mother. Knew exactly what you were going to do and say before you made a move."

The scowl on Emma's face softened at the mention of her mother.

"I, on the other hand, was scared to death of you. You were so fragile and tiny. And then, there we were. Alone. Just the two of us.

"I had no clue what to do with you. I went to the bookstore one day and armed myself with at least two dozen books on raising children. I was so confused when I finished reading them all, I almost cried. So, I decided to wing it. My biggest fear was that you'd grow up hating me some day for all the wrongs I did."

She stared at him, wide-eyed and innocent. "You didn't do so bad."

He smiled.

And after a minute, she did, too. "I'm sorry, Dad. I don't mean to shut you out. It's just that sometimes I need to talk to a woman. Libby's been great to talk to."

Nodding his head in agreement, he said, "I'm sure she has been. But when we leave here...." He didn't finish that sentence.

Emma walked back to the table, slid into her chair. "No lectures?"

"Scout's honor," he said, raising his two fingers and holding them in the air.

"Travis wants me back."

Ross cringed, but managed to hold back his tongue.

"I don't think I want to go out with him again, though."

Yes! He hid his reaction, bringing the mug of coffee to his face and taking a drink. Damn, it was still scalding hot. He slammed the cup onto the table but didn't say anything.

Apparently, he didn't have to. Emma stood, yanked open the freezer, and grabbed an ice cube. She tossed it into his cup and took her seat.

"Travis told me he'd been seeing Robin, that she'd started flirting with him as soon as I left town. But she broke up with him yesterday." She shook her head in disgust. "We're supposed to be best friends. I can't believe she betrayed me like that."

Welcome to the real world. He reached across the table and squeezed her hand, then let go.

"Travis wants to know if I can come back to Phoenix at the end of the month instead of the end of summer," she said, as if she couldn't get over his nerve. "He said he missed me, and that's why he started seeing Robin." She looked up at him. "That jerk."

"What are you going to do?"

"I'm going to tell Travis where to go." She looked at him sheepishly. "Well, you know what I mean."

He sure did, he thought, nodding. "And you have my permission to use the word. Just this once."

She grinned. "Don't be mad, but I have to go tell Libby. She was right. Men are scum." Her eyes grew large, her mouth fell open. "I'm sure she didn't mean you, Dad."

He laughed. "What are you going to do about your friendship with Robin?"

Standing, she thought for a moment. "I guess I'll ask her for her side of the story." When he raised his brows at her, she shrugged. "We've been friends a lot longer than I've known Travis. I'd at least like to hear what she has to say."

Pushing her chair beneath the table, she said, "And then I'll probably forgive her. I won't want to at first, and I'll probably still be mad at her, but. . . ." She eyed him closely. "Does that sound stupid? That I want to keep her as my friend?"

"Not at all." Ross stood up, not giving a damn if his daughter wanted a hug or not. She was going to get one anyway. He pulled her close and held her tightly. "I'm proud of you."

He just wished he could forgive as easily as Emma.

18

MEGGIE'S EYES FLEW open at the sound of shattering glass. Immediately, she threw back the covers and got to her feet. She didn't need to turn on the light. It was already on. Since returning home from the hospital, she'd become accustomed to sleeping with the light on.

She'd told herself it was because she'd recently developed a phobia for darkness. But that wasn't exactly true. It was Steve she was afraid of. Even though she knew he was locked up behind bars. But he'd be free some day. That was, if he ever got anyone to post his bail. Then he'd probably come after her. Which was why she'd bought a gun.

Quietly sliding open the nightstand drawer, hands trembling, Meggie picked up the small silver pistol and took a deep breath. She hadn't told anyone she'd bought the gun, not even her boys.

Tip-toeing down the hall, she stopped just outside the kitchen before peeking around the corner. She didn't see anyone, but she heard someone. Noises. A scraping sound, glass tinkling.

Then she saw him, just a figure in the shadows,

wearing jeans and sneakers. He was bent over with his head hidden in the broom closet. Raising the gun, her heart pounding viciously in her chest, she took aim and charged into the kitchen.

"Don't move or I'll shoot!" she hollered.

He moved.

But she couldn't pull the trigger.

"Mom?" TJ whirled around to stare at her, his mouth gaping wide open. "What are you doing?"

Meggie tossed the gun to the floor and screamed, "Oh, my God! TJ, I could have shot you." She hurled herself at her son and wrapped him in her arms. "I'm so sorry. Oh, dear God, I am so sorry."

Now she understood when they said most shooting accidents happened in the home. What had she been thinking when she'd bought that thing? She could have killed her own son.

"Mom, you're suffocating me." TJ extricated himself from her. "Where did you get that gun?" He bent over and reached for it.

"No!" Meggie shouted. "Don't touch it. I shouldn't have done something so stupid. So dangerous." She cast a look at the gun and made a disgusted face. As she averted her eyes, she saw the shards of broken glass on the floor.

"I was going to have some orange juice."

That was typical for TJ. Still growing. Always hungry and thirsty. Every hour of every day. Even after midnight.

"I'll clean it up," she offered.

Before she'd taken more than a step, TJ glanced

at her bare feet and said, "You'd better be careful." He went to the broom closet and came back with a dustpan and broom. "I'll clean it up. Go back to bed."

Meggie smiled. "You're sure?"

TJ just shrugged.

"I love you." Meggie didn't wait for her son to respond. He wasn't good at showing affection or even saying something that simple. Jeremy, on the other hand, told her he loved her at least ten times each day. She turned, lifted the hem of her nightgown a few inches, and carefully inched toward the hall.

"Mom?"

Meggie turned around.

"Aren't you going to take your gun?"

"Oh, yes. I guess I'd better put it away." She bent down, picked up the cold piece of steel, and held it away from her.

"Maybe *I* should keep it," he suggested as he swept pieces of glass onto the dustpan. Meggie started to argue, but he cut her off. "Well, we don't want Jeremy to get ahold of it and shoot himself in the foot or something."

Meggie almost laughed. Poor little Jeremy was as clumsy as he was inquisitive. TJ was the opposite. He'd always been so sure and confident. Glancing at the gun in her outstretched hand, she tucked it behind her back and out of sight.

"I think I'll take the bullets out and hide it in a safe place. It's not as though we'll ever need it. I don't even know why I bought it in the first place," she lied, trying not to alarm TJ with her fears.

"I do. And I'm glad you did. Because if that jerk ever comes back here, I'll kill him myself."

Meggie shut her eyes and hung her head. "TJ—"

"Go to bed, Mom."

She opened her eyes and stared at her son. He looked bitter, angry, and full of hate. And it was all her fault. She'd married Steve so the boys would have a father. Some father he'd turned out to be.

It was the middle of the night. This wasn't the time to be having a discussion, especially one of this magnitude. Maybe tomorrow, when her nerves were calmer. "Good night, TJ."

Meggie had already started down the hall when she heard him whisper, "I love you, too, Mom."

ROSS BANGED HARD on the glass door. He knew Libby was still inside because her car was in the parking lot. It was shortly after five. Office hours were over, and the door was locked for the night. He assumed she must be inside doing paperwork of some kind.

Peering through the glass and feeling impatient, he banged on the glass again. Finally, Libby came to the door, keys in hand.

"What are you doing here?" she asked, after opening the door and locking it again. "I thought you and Emma were picking me up at my place at seven."

He and Emma were taking Libby to dinner at a new Japanese restaurant in Newgate. "We are," he told her, folding his arms around her waist and pulling her close for a kiss. "But I wanted to see you first."

She kissed him back, wrapping her arms around his neck and toying with the hair at his nape. He liked it when she did that.

"Mmmmm," she said, pulling away slightly. "What was so urgent that it couldn't wait until later?"

"Emma will be with us later." Ross kissed her again, this time letting her know fully his intentions. "I want you, Libby," he breathed against her ear. "And both times we've been together, we've had interruptions."

Libby laughed softly and tried to wriggle away, but Ross wouldn't let her. "If you're thinking what I think you're thinking. . . ."

"I am," he admitted. A mischievous look appeared in her eyes, then disappeared suddenly.

"You can't be serious." She managed to break free this time.

He'd never been more serious, he thought as he continued to look at her. Slowly, he ran his gaze down the front of her, then back up to meet her eyes.

Shaking her head vigorously, she grabbed the edges of her white lab coat and pulled them closed. "We can't do it here."

Ross glanced behind him. "I didn't mean right here in front of the door." He took a step toward her, took her hands in his.

"But there's nowhere—"

"We'll find a place." He moved closer. With each step he took, she took a step backward until they'd moved into the hall. Libby's eyes shifted nervously around the hall walls. "We're alone, aren't we, Doc?"

"Yes, but—"

Ross grinned wickedly. "Where's your sense of adventure?" He steered her down the hall and into an examining room.

"I think you used that same line on me the night you took me parking in the cornfield. Did you bring another Twinkie with you?"

He held out his hands. "Sorry, I was all out of Twinkies. But I promise to buy you a gooey, fattening dessert after dinner tonight."

She looked at him skeptically, but her green eyes twinkled with amusement.

"Scout's honor," he said, although he'd never been a Boy Scout.

Libby reached around him, flicked off the light switch on the wall. "Well, I've never known a Boy Scout to lie."

Turning off the lights hadn't done much to dim the room. The sun continued to soak through the tiny cracks in the mini-blinds.

"Did you want to play doctor?" Libby asked teasingly, her eyes appraising their surroundings.

"Now that sounds like a plan."

She was in his arms instantly. They kissed and touched one another, taking their time. He breathed in her scent while he ran his hands over her hips.

Pulling her close, he smiled satisfactorily, knowing she could feel his erection and how badly he wanted her. All day he'd thought of nothing else.

He heard her little moans and gasps of pleasure. He knew she was ready, even without testing her wetness. But she'd have to wait just a little longer, he thought. Guiding her toward the examination table, he said, "Why don't you hop up there and let me look at you?"

She hesitated for a moment, then did as he suggested. The sanitary paper crinkled as her weight pressed down on the vinyl-covered table. Her legs and feet dangled over the end, and he edged his way between them. As he kissed her, he slowly worked her skirt up over her hips, then—with her help—slid her pantyhose and panties down and off.

"Lie back," he whispered.

The paper crinkled again. Running his hands up and down her thighs, he felt her quiver. The air-conditioned room was cool, causing her skin to prickle with goosebumps. He nudged her legs apart and placed her feet into the cold metal stirrups. She looked up at him, a look of anticipation in her eyes.

Sliding a stool to the end of the table, he eased himself onto it and gazed at her. Watching her lie there, waiting for him to make love to her, made him feel more excited than he could ever remember feeling before. "Libby, you're so beautiful. Everywhere," he added as he scanned her nakedness before him.

She shivered again, but smiled sweetly. He wanted

to devour her, then thrust himself inside her again and again. And that's just what he intended to do.

"You'd better hold on. After I finish examining you, it could get a little rough."

"LIBBY SAID WE could bring Max with us," Emma informed her father. Max barked at the sound of his name and went to stand at the door.

"Well, if Max isn't afraid of speedboats, he certainly shouldn't be afraid of sailing," Ross answered as he tied his sneakers.

Emma couldn't wait to go sailing with Libby. Just the three of them and Max. Like a real family. Just like last night's dinner. Only Max hadn't been invited to the restaurant, of course. But they'd brought him a steak bone, and all was forgiven.

Her dad liked Libby. A lot. And Libby liked him, too. She'd known all along they were meant for each other. Hadn't she told him so?

"Put your cereal bowl in the sink, Em."

Emma picked up the dish and carried it to the sink. While her father wiped off the kitchen table, she rinsed the last soggy Frosted Flake down the drain. "Last night was fun, wasn't it, Dad?"

"Yep."

"Libby's so interesting to talk to, don't you think?"

"Yep." Ross rinsed the dishrag, wrung it out, then yanked a paper towel from the roll and dried his hands.

"Did you know that Libby wants to buy the house she's renting? It's pretty big. There's two more bedrooms upstairs and another full bath. Of course, she doesn't use the second floor. But if she were to get married or something. . . ." She chanced a look at her father, then went on. "Her house has a great view, too. Better than ours."

She knew he was staring at her, but she pretended not to notice. "Look, Max is waiting to go."

"Emma—"

"You know, I think Grandma really enjoys my visits, don't you?" She pushed her feet into her sneakers, but didn't bother to tie them. "And Uncle Barry and Aunt April like it that we're back in Falcon Ridge. And even TJ has been acting civil toward me lately—"

"Emma," he said sternly.

Emma pulled out a kitchen chair and dropped into it. "What?" She felt a lecture coming on.

"Don't do this. Libby and I are just friends."

She rolled her eyes. Yeah, right. She knew they were doing it. She wasn't an idiot.

"Quit fantasizing about weddings and—"

"But, Dad, don't you love her?"

"I . . . I care about her. Very much. But that doesn't mean—"

"How does she feel about you? I think she loves you."

"Emma, stop it."

The vein on his forehead had surfaced, which

meant he was mad. But she didn't care. Maybe he just hadn't realized yet that he was in love with Libby. Sometimes men could be really stupid about those things. She'd read a couple of romance novels and, honestly, some of those heroes had to be practically hit on the head before they realized what had happened to them.

"Libby no more wants to get married than I do," he said, shocking her to her senses.

"How do you know? Did she tell you that?"

"Not in so many words. But we have an understanding between us. She knows I'm—we're," he corrected, "leaving in a few more weeks."

"But—"

He shook his head. "Trust me. She's not in love with me. Do you actually think she'd want to marry an old guy like me with a teenaged daughter to care for?"

He wasn't exactly old, she thought, even though he'd be forty soon. And he was only seven years older than Libby. It wasn't like that was a big deal or anything.

"She'll naturally want to get married *some* day," he went on. "And then she'll want babies of her own. In the meantime, she's busy building her practice and doesn't have time for marriage and kids."

His words left Emma feeling crushed. She'd thought that Libby liked her, even loved her, maybe. She'd assumed Libby would want to marry her dad, become a family with them. Now she felt stupid.

But if Libby didn't like her, why did she spend

so much time with her? Emma wondered now if she'd pushed herself on the doctor, and Libby had just been too polite to tell her she didn't want to be friends, let alone be her stepmother.

"Em, are you okay?" He reached out to touch her.

She leaned back and out of his reach, forced a smile to her lips. "Of course. I wasn't serious about all that love and marriage stuff." He looked as though he didn't believe her. "I wasn't!" She rolled her eyes for emphasis. "Get real."

He sighed, a painful expression on his face. "Okay. You ready to go? Libby's probably wondering what happened to us."

She stood up. "Not yet. I don't think I like this shirt. I'm going to go change." With that, she ran to her room and shut the door. Only then did she let her tears fall.

"LET'S SEE," LIBBY said, digging into the cooler. "You can have your choice of turkey or tuna salad sandwiches."

"Tuna? Ugh." Emma wrinkled her nose. "I don't want either. I'm not hungry."

Libby saw Ross scowl at his daughter, apparently making her reconsider. "Fine," Emma snapped. "I'll take turkey."

Libby handed her a Saran-wrapped sandwich. "How about you, Ross? Turkey or tuna?"

"I'll try the tuna." He worked the cork free from

a bottle of Chardonnay and poured a small amount into two plastic cups.

"I made potato salad, too," Libby said proudly. It was her mother's recipe. "I brought some grapes and brownies for dessert. Oh, and Max, this is for you." She tossed a dog biscuit onto the grass and watched the dog lunge for it. Several crunches later it was gone.

"Sit down and eat," Ross said. "You don't have to wait on us."

Libby sat down on the rickety old picnic table, causing it to wobble. The three of them—and Max— had sailed her catamaran across the lake to a public beach area.

Ross slid one of the glasses of wine toward her and set the bottle down. When Emma reached for the wine bottle, both Libby and Ross yelled, "No wine!"

"Jeez. Chill out." Emma made a face and shifted her eyes between Libby and her father before reaching into the cooler and grabbing a Coke. She sat down with a thunk, and the table wobbled again.

Libby glanced at Ross, who was seated on the bench next to her. He only raised an eyebrow. She'd noticed Emma's foul mood earlier. It was as if she were being forced to be here, although it had been her suggestion to go sailing and have a picnic.

"I'll take some potato salad," Emma said, holding her plate out to Libby.

"Oh, sure. Let me get it." Libby had already half-stood when Ross's arm snaked out and stopped her.

"Emma can get it. We're used to waiting on ourselves."

Emma shot her father another look before sliding to the end of the bench and lifting the cooler lid. As Emma dished potato salad onto her plate, Libby tasted her wine and watched the boats cruise by.

The putt-putt of the engines and the chop-chop of boats jumping waves made her smile. The smell of gasoline and lake water permeated the air around her. To Libby, nothing smelled better. It smelled peaceful. If there was such a smell.

When Emma finished dishing potato salad, she dragged the bowl across the table, placing it in the middle. Libby took Ross's plate. "Would you like some?"

Ross took the plate from her. "I'm not helpless."

He'd been acting strangely today, too. If they got a moment alone, Libby planned to ask him about it. In the meantime, she just wanted to relax, watch the boats, and enjoy their picnic lunch.

There was a family picnicking close by. Libby watched as the father tossed a Frisbee in the air and his children ran to grab for it. There were two boys around the ages of five and seven and a little girl with blonde ringlets who looked barely old enough to walk. But that didn't stop the girl from trying to keep up with her older brothers. Occasionally the boys would let the Frisbee drop to the ground, and she'd pick it up and squeal with delight.

Libby smiled at the child. She wondered if

Emma had looked like that when she was a baby. Certainly the child's hair resembled hers.

Max barked at the kids, wanting to join in their game. Soon, they invited him to play along.

"Do you like kids, Libby?" Emma asked, bringing Libby's attention back to their table.

"Of course I do." Her gaze shifted toward Ross, who didn't look back. He took another bite of his sandwich and chewed.

Emma went on. "Do you like babies?"

Ross stopped chewing and stared at his daughter.

"Naturally." Libby took a sip of wine.

"But babies take a lot of time. I mean, if you had a baby, how would you work every day?"

Libby's gaze wavered between father and daughter. The look they exchanged told her that something was going on. But she had no clue. "Well . . . I'm not sure."

"Older kids would be easier, don't you think?"

"Well—"

"Emma, why don't you go get Max? It looks like those people are ready to sit down and eat, and I don't want him begging for food."

Emma ignored her father. "Do you like being a doctor?" she asked. "I mean, on a scale of one to ten, how important is it to you?"

Libby looked at Emma's liquid blue eyes before answering. "Ten," she said honestly. Emma stared at her as if she'd said something unforgivable, then bolted from the table and ran to get Max.

"What was all that about?" she asked Ross.

He shook his head and shrugged, took another bite of his sandwich. But Libby didn't believe him. "Ross?"

"It was nothing. You know how teenagers are. They're always asking a lot of questions."

"But it sounded as if Emma was asking me those things because she thought I was going to have a baby . . . or something."

His gaze darted to her stomach, then to her face. "You're not, are you?"

She paused before answering. "No, we've been careful." It annoyed her that he looked so relieved. "So, why would she be asking me questions like that?"

He scratched his cheek, but didn't answer.

"Maybe I should go talk to her—"

His arm shot out and touched her forearm. "She'll be all right. She just had this crazy idea that we were in love and should get married."

Libby's eyes widened, and she swallowed hard. "What did you tell her?"

"I told her . . . the truth."

She wondered briefly what the *truth* was. It was obvious that he'd been appalled by Emma's idea. She hadn't expected his answer to hurt so much. But it had. Suddenly she had this empty feeling inside, and she couldn't swallow. She'd lost her appetite. Trying to smile as though what he'd said had no effect on her whatsoever was difficult, but she managed before looking away.

She busied herself with cleaning up the dirty dishes and loading the picnic basket, mostly so she wouldn't have to face him.

"Libby?"

She forced the cork into the wine bottle with the heel of her hand. "Hmmm?"

"Is something wrong?"

"No. Nothing."

She watched as Emma walked to the shore and sat down in the sand, Max at her side, looking as if she'd lost her last friend in the world.

"Kids come up with the most outrageous things, don't they?" he asked, jokingly.

Libby's lips thinned into a smile, but she couldn't find her voice. Instead, she nodded her head and turned away from him. She wouldn't let herself cry. After all, she was a big girl and had entered into this relationship knowing full well Ross didn't want to form any attachments.

And his recent words couldn't make it any plainer.

19

STEVE PACED THE floor of his eight-by-eight-foot cell. Where the hell was Meggie? He'd told that damn deputy that he needed to talk to her. And he was supposed to call her and ask her to come down here. That was yesterday. And she still hadn't shown up.

This morning, when he'd accused Maloney of not placing the call, he'd sworn up and down that he had. And then he'd told Steve not to count on his wife coming.

The stupid fuck. What the hell did he know about Meggie? She *had* to come. She couldn't leave him sitting in this piss hole forever. He'd learned his lesson already.

He was sure that was what this was all about. He was sorry for hitting her. But it wasn't his fault. If she'd just left the drugs alone, he would have been fine. He'd gone a little crazy, that was all.

But it wouldn't happen again. He should have told her he was taking them for medicinal purposes—maybe that he had some rare disease—and that sometimes the drugs made him act a little weird.

If he could get her to drop the assault charges against him, he'd be out of here. They'd questioned him about the break-in at that bitch Doctor Larson's office, but there was no way they were going to add robbery to his crimes. They had nothing. Because he'd been careful not to leave any prints behind.

He'd talked to some stupid lawyer, but the jerk had told him no one was willing to post his bail. When Steve had asked the lawyer if *he'd* post it, the man laughed in his face and said the McLaughlins were family friends. What the hell did that have to do with anything?

When he got out, he planned to sue the idiot. But right now he just wanted to go home. Not that the shack he and Meggie were renting was really their home. It was just temporary until they could buy something more suitable. Besides, interest rates were sky-high right now. They really should wait a while longer before they started looking.

Steve yanked at his hair, then smoothed it into place. Who the hell was he kidding? He didn't have a job. No bank would lend him money to buy a house when he didn't have a job.

And then there was the matter of a down payment. He didn't have one of those either. He'd told Meggie he'd invested the profit from the sale of their home in Maine to use on their next home, but he'd lied.

Unknown to his wife, there'd been a second mortgage on the house, and he'd spent the small bit of equity left after the sale on drugs and alcohol.

Okay, so maybe he had a drug problem. But he could control it. And if he had a job as a drug rep again he could get any drugs he wanted. Nothing dangerous, just a few things to help take the edge off.

It was hard being responsible for a wife and two kids. Especially two kids who weren't yours. First it was a big house, and then the new cars. And the boys wanted everything under the sun. Expensive sneakers, designer label clothes, video games, mountain bikes, soccer camp, not to mention the orthodontist bills. At first, he'd said yes to everything they'd asked for, not wanting to disappoint Meggie. She'd rather her sons have nice things than herself. It was a good thing she never asked for much. Hell, there'd barely been any money left over between paychecks to spend on himself.

Blowing out an exhausted breath, he dropped onto the roll-a-way bed. *Some bed.* The first night here he'd almost fallen out when he tried to roll over. The night the sheriff had beat him up.

Where the hell was Meggie? he wondered, slamming his fist into the flimsy mattress. He had to talk to her. They had a lawsuit to file against the sheriff and the county. People couldn't go around pounding on citizens just because they felt like it. With the money he'd get they could get out of this one-horse town and maybe go to San Francisco or Sacramento. He'd always wanted to live in California. Meggie would love it there, too. Away from her nosy family. Especially her famous author brother.

He didn't know what was so damn special about Ross McLaughlin. He'd read one of his books once after Meggie had said how wonderful it was. Christ, he could write a better book than that. As far as he was concerned, the guy was just an overpaid, talent-lacking nobody.

Steve stood up, went to the metal bars, and peered down the hall toward the closed door. It was quiet. Not even a phone ringing in this place. Not much crime going on in Falcon Ridge—not these days, anyway.

"Deputy!" he shouted. "Maloney, dammit, I want to talk to my wife!"

No one answered him. Not even when he threatened to sue them.

"WHAT'S ALL THIS?" Barry asked as he walked into the kitchen. April was cooking scrambled eggs. Bacon sizzled in the pan next to the eggs, and a muffin tin full of blueberry muffins sat on the countertop cooling.

She smiled shyly. "Nothing much. I just thought you'd be hungry this morning."

He was starving. Making love to her the night before, and this morning, had exhausted him.

Barry opened a cupboard and reached for a mug. Before he lifted the coffee pot, April said, "That's decaf. I made you regular. It's in the thermos." She nodded her head toward the island counter behind her.

"Thanks." He poured himself a cup and sat down at the kitchen table. The newspaper lay off to the side. He chanced a look at his wife. He wasn't used to being waited on. At least not in the past fourteen years of their marriage. But he had to admit that he liked it. A lot.

They'd been making love nightly for weeks now. But there had been no mention of any of the things that had soured their marriage in the first place—the most significant one being his affair with Meredith.

He'd been feeling insecure at the time. The only woman he'd ever had sex with had been April. He supposed that was the reason he'd cheated on her. Just to see what it would be like with someone new. That and the fact that Meredith wouldn't take no for an answer. She'd done everything in her power to seduce him, including stripping naked right before his eyes one afternoon.

He'd known it was wrong, and he'd hated himself for doing it. He still hated himself, in fact. If there was anything he could change in his life, it would be that. It had changed everything between him and April, him and Ross. For years, he'd been suffering the consequences. He'd lost his brother's trust and respect, and a piece of April, as well.

Meredith had paid with her life.

April dished a heap of eggs onto his plate. "Do you want more coffee?"

"I can get it."

"Let me. I'm already up. Read your paper."

By the time April sat down, he'd already eaten half his breakfast.

She didn't look at him for any length of time. Instead her gaze wavered between his face and the food on her plate as they ate in crystalline silence. It was as if they were two strangers sitting in a restaurant. Funny how you could sleep beside someone for seventeen years and still be strangers.

"April," he started.

"Do you want more bacon?" she said, scooting her chair back.

Barry lifted a hand to stay her. "No."

"Oh, did you want some juice? I have orange and grapefruit."

He shook his head. "We need to talk," he said softly.

She looked at him then, long and hard, before her gaze drifted from his face.

"Look at me."

Slowly, she lifted her head. "Just leave it alone, Barry. Things have been ... nice the past few weeks. Let's not spoil it. Why can't we just forget about everything else?"

"Because we can't. And you know it."

She stood up, whisked her plate off the table. "I don't know any such thing." She turned her back on him and went to stand at the sink.

He hung his head and sighed loudly enough to be heard across the room, and noticed her shoulders tense. "April, it's been fourteen years and not a word about—"

"Don't!" She spun around to face him, her eyes glistening with unshed tears. "Don't say her name in this house. I don't want to talk about her. Not now, not ever."

Running a hand through his hair, he said, "But *I* need to talk about her. I need to get rid of this guilt I've been carrying around all these years. She's dead . . . because of me."

"And I'm glad she's dead. She deserved to die." The tears spilled onto her cheeks as she ran by him and out of the room.

"Oh, God, April," he whispered, his worst fears nearly confirmed. All these years he'd tried to convince himself his wife could never have murdered someone. But now, he didn't know what to think.

"HI, EMMA. HOW'S it going?"

Zack's voice startled her. Emma dropped one of the tackle boxes from the stack in her arms. At least she hadn't fallen off the stepstool. From the back room, she hadn't heard the bell ring when he entered the bait shop.

"You need some help?" he asked.

Looking over her shoulder, she smiled awkwardly at Zack, who stood in the doorway. "No, thanks. Go ahead and look around, and I'll be with you in just a minute."

"Sure. Okay."

What a clumsy idiot she was. Before returning

to the front of the shop, Emma peeped her head in the restroom to take a quick glance in the mirror. She was appalled to find dirt across her cheek, but thankful she'd had enough sense to check her appearance before Zack got a better look at her. She grabbed a paper towel from the dispenser, dampened it, and swiped at her face. It would have to do.

Then she made her way out front. "Finding everything okay?"

Zack looked up from a display of bobbers. "Yeah." He moved in front of the counter and shoved his hands into his jeans pockets. "What are the fish eating today?"

"Minnows, mostly."

He nodded.

"Do you want some minnows?"

"No, thanks. Not today. I was just curious." He rocked back on his heels. "So, you like working here?"

"It's okay," she said. "I get to meet a lot of people."

Nodding again, he said, "That's cool." He fiddled with a bucket of fishing lures, as if he were trying to find something special.

"Do you need some help?"

"What? No, I just . . . I like your hair that . . . color."

Emma's hand slowly lifted to her blonde curls, twisting one between her fingers. "Thanks."

"Is that your natural color?"

"Yes, why?"

He shrugged and went back to the bobber display. "Just wondered. Would you like to go to a movie tonight?" he mumbled, only half looking at her.

"You mean with you and TJ?" She and Zack and TJ had gone to the movies together the week before.

Looking at her head on, he said quietly, "I didn't ask TJ to go."

"Oh," then, "Oh!" Was this his way of asking her out on a date, and if so, why now? As her father had so bluntly pointed out, they'd be leaving Falcon Ridge in a few weeks. What was the point of getting to know Zack better when she'd only have to end their friendship soon?

She didn't want any more heartaches. She didn't know how she was going to go back to Phoenix when her grandmother needed her here. And then there was Libby. Except their friendship was already over. Maybe by the time summer came to an end, she'd forget all about Libby. Then she wouldn't have to miss her, too.

Zack stood staring at her, rocking back and forth on his heels, fumbling with his Pirates ball cap, eyebrows raised in question. "Are you still thinking about it?"

Forcing a smile, she came up with a lie. "I'm sorry. I can't tonight. I already have other plans."

"Oh, okay." He looked surprised at first, then a little disappointed, but Emma was sure he'd get over it. And probably sooner than she'd like. "What about tomorrow night?"

Her mouth dropped open. "I . . . I can't go tomorrow either."

"I see." His gaze wandered around the shop. "Well, I'd better let you get back to work." He smiled his crooked smile. "I'll see you around."

Emma couldn't say anything. Her lips thinned, trying to form a smile, but they couldn't. When the door closed behind him, she swallowed back the lump in her throat and kicked the cooler with her sneakered foot.

She knew she'd done the right thing. She didn't need another person to leave behind. But why did doing the right thing have to make her feel worse?

ROSS DIDN'T BOTHER knocking. From the deck, he saw Libby in the kitchen. She was hunched over Smiley, who was perched on a stool. Her lips were moving as if she were engaged in a deep conversation with the cat. She wore her blue terrycloth robe, and her feet were bare. Apparently, she hadn't gone to her meeting tonight, and he was curious why she hadn't. Sliding the glass door open, he stepped inside.

"Hi."

She straightened. "Ross, what are you doing here?"

"I wanted to see if everything was all right."

"Of course it is." She looked away.

"Libby—"

"Look, Ross," she started, her voice louder than

normal. "We don't have to spend every evening together. I have a life of my own, you know." She folded her arms in front of her. "And I need some space."

He narrowed his gaze, studying her. Again, she looked away. Shrugging, he said, "If you needed space, all you had to do was say so. You didn't need to lie to me."

She lifted her eyes toward his. "I'm sorry. There wasn't any meeting tonight. I shouldn't have lied, but that still doesn't give you the right to spy on me."

He started to move toward her, but stopped when she backed away. He held up his hands, a signal that he wouldn't come any closer. "I wasn't spying. I was taking a walk, and I noticed your lights were on. You didn't sound like yourself on the phone earlier, so I thought maybe you weren't feeling well and had decided not to go tonight."

She had the decency to look guilty. "I said I was sorry. I don't know what else I can do."

"You could tell me the truth. Apparently, I've been crowding you. You should have said something sooner."

This time she looked at him, long and hard. "This isn't working. I can't do this anymore."

"Do what?"

"This. *Us*," she stressed. "It's over. I mean, we both got what we wanted, didn't we?"

"Did we?" he asked, not quite sure of his feelings, though he knew he wanted much more than sex from her.

She closed her eyes and tilted her head back, showing off her slender neck. It was all he could do to keep his hands off her. She breathed in deeply, then let it out slowly before opening her green eyes and focusing them on him. "You wanted no strings attached, remember? Just a casual summer romance. Some frills, some thrills." She licked at her lips. "Let's end it before it gets boring."

Ross didn't say anything. Hell, he didn't know what to say. She was right; that's exactly what he'd wanted. In the beginning, that is. Before he'd gotten to know her better, before he'd made love to her. But now, what was it that he wanted?

She moved to the door, slid it open. His invitation to leave. He took it.

But at the door he turned around, ran his gaze over her face. "Libby, you mean more to me than a casual summer romance, and certainly more than a few frills and thrills, as you so eloquently put it."

She swallowed. "Thank you for saying so. When you're back in Phoenix, try to stay in touch. I'd love to hear how Emma is doing."

Try to stay in touch. She'd said it so casually he wanted to strangle her. And at the same time he wanted to slide that robe from her shoulders and take her on the kitchen floor. Well, he wouldn't play the fool. She wanted him gone. Out of her life. She wanted her space back. Why? So she could talk to that damn cat of hers? Probably.

Then why couldn't he leave? He leaned forward as if to kiss her good-bye and saw her stiffen.

"Libby," he whispered, only to be cut off by her.

"Ross, I'm tired and I have to get up early tomorrow."

He'd been dumped before, but never by someone he cared about as much as Libby. Her insensitive attitude irked him. "Well, Doc, I can certainly take a hint." He stepped onto the deck. "Have a nice life."

He heard the glass door slide shut behind him, the lock click into place. When he turned around, she'd already closed the blinds, shutting him out of her life.

SHE'D HANDLED THINGS badly, Libby thought, listening to Ross's footsteps trudge down the wooden steps from her deck. She'd planned to distance herself from him gradually. But he wouldn't take the hint. So she'd had to practically spell it out for him.

Smiley watched her as she sat down in the middle of the kitchen floor. After a few minutes, he stood up on the stool, arched his back and stretched, then jumped to the floor and made his way toward her. Gently, she ran her fingers through the cat's fur, listening to the purring sounds and feeling the vibration against her hand.

She hadn't been entirely truthful with Ross. She wanted to see him, but what would be the point? Why waste any more time with him when it would just make things harder when he had to return to Phoenix?

She thought he'd be relieved that she was the one to end things, rather than him. But he'd looked anything but relieved. If she didn't know better, she'd have sworn she'd broken his heart.

Fat chance! Remembering last week's picnic, and Emma's questions about babies and children, made her realize she'd done the right thing. Ross had made it perfectly clear to Libby that his daughter's fantasies were totally unrealistic. *Emma had this crazy idea that we were in love and should get married,* he'd said. *Crazy idea?* It had been like a slap in the face.

Oh, he'd been completely up front with her about their relationship, so she had no one to blame but herself. But she hadn't realized then that she could fall in love with him so easily. Or that she'd start developing maternal instincts for Emma and wishing for an extended family.

What a complete fool she'd been!

"LIBBY, WHAT ARE you doing here?" She was the last person Emma expected to see enter the bait shop. Libby didn't even fish.

"Since you've been avoiding me, I decided to stop by and see why."

Libby's bluntness surprised her. "I haven't been avoiding you," she lied, averting her eyes, pretending to straighten several items on the glass counter. "It's just that I know how busy you are with your practice."

Libby tilted her head to one side, wrinkled her

brow, and cast a wary look Emma's way. "I *am* busy, but I've always had time for you, Emma." She paused. "Just because your dad and I aren't seeing each other anymore—"

"What?" Emma flew around the corner and met Libby's eyes. "He dumped you, didn't he? Oh, Libby, I'm sorry. Sometimes my dad can be such an idiot." How could he have done such a thing? she wondered. They were perfect for each other. Why couldn't he see that?

"He didn't dump me," Libby said, smiling sadly. "It was a mutual decision."

"Yeah, right."

Libby brushed a curl from Emma's cheek. "Anyway, what matters is *our* friendship."

Looking down at her sneakers, Emma shrugged. "I guess I have been ignoring you a little." She chanced a look at Libby, hoping she wasn't mad at her. It would seem pretty unfair if two McLaughlins dumped her in the same week.

"Well, you probably won't understand it, but I thought that if I didn't see you as much that it would be easier when Dad and I go back to Phoenix. Silly, huh?"

Libby grinned. "No, it's not silly. But friends," she said, "close friends, like us, keep in touch. Letters, phone calls, e-mail. I thought that if you come back next summer that you might want to stay with me for a few weeks."

"Really? Cool!" She flung herself into Libby's arms and held on for dear life. She knew it probably wouldn't do any good to wish that Libby was her stepmother, but she wished it all the same. Just like she had so many times since meeting her.

20

"C'MON, DAD!" EMMA yelled down the hall. "We're going to be late for Grandma's birthday party." Lately, her father had been moving more slowly than normal. As if he were lethargic. And he'd been crankier than a bull, snapping at her for the least little thing.

She'd invited Zack to the party and was eager to see him. Last week she'd apologized to him for making excuses when he'd asked her out. She explained why she'd done it, and he'd said he could understand. They decided to take things slow. Just enjoy their friendship and see what happened. After all, he planned to start college in the fall, and he needed to concentrate on his studies.

Ross came around the corner dressed in khakis that looked a little loose and a white polo shirt. She'd noticed that he hadn't had much of an appetite the past two weeks, either. If she had to guess, she'd say he'd lost about ten or fifteen pounds. "Are you ready?" he asked.

She let out an exasperated sigh. "I've been ready for twenty minutes."

"Well, let's get going then. We're going to be late."

Rolling her eyes, she said, "You know, if you're that miserable without Libby, maybe you should apologize for dumping her and try to get her back."

"First of all, I didn't dump her, and secondly, this is none of your business."

"But Libby said—"

"I don't care what she said. Let's go."

"Jeez. What a grouch," she mumbled. Emma decided now was not a good time to tell him she'd invited Libby to the party.

IT WASN'T A big party. His mother hadn't wanted anything elaborate. Just family were coming as far as he knew. So when Zack Reese walked into the Marina restaurant, Ross had been slightly surprised. Not that it was any big deal. TJ had probably invited him.

But instead of the Reese boy heading for his nephew, he headed toward him and Emma. "Hi, Emma. Mr. McLaughlin," he said, offering his hand.

Ross took it and gave it a firm shake. Looking at Emma, Zack said, "Thanks for inviting me."

Ross watched as his daughter exchanged a smile with the kid. Neither of them spoke. Emma glanced his way several times and, after a few moments, Ross excused himself and left the two of them to talk. He could take a hint.

He studied his mother as he worked his way across the room. He hadn't seen her this happy in a long time. This was the first she'd had all her family under one roof since he'd returned to Falcon Ridge. He didn't want to think about it, but it could be the last time.

She'd wandered away from home twice last week and had given them all a good scare. Luckily they'd found her, once sitting on a neighbor's dock looking out at the lake, and the other time walking toward town. She'd claimed she was out of milk and had to get to the store before it closed. A full gallon was in her refrigerator at the time.

His father had spoken to him briefly about nursing homes. "If and when the time comes," Neil had said. "Do you think she'll ever forgive me?"

Ross hadn't wanted to discuss nursing homes. But he supposed that wasn't fair to his father. Neil just wanted support, and to know that he'd be doing the right thing, if and when the time came.

Leaning over, Ross placed a kiss on his mother's cheek. "Are you enjoying yourself?"

Bev looked up and smiled. "I can't remember having a better birthday." She lifted the lid to the box he and Emma had given her. They'd picked out the floral scarf together. "Look what Meggie got for me. Isn't it beautiful?" she said, running her fingers over the silk fabric.

Ross exchanged a look with his sister. "Yes, Mom, it's beautiful. Meggie has good taste."

"Mom, do you want to cut your cake now?" Meggie quickly asked.

"Oh, my!" Bev threw her hands to her face. "All this and cake, too? I don't deserve all this attention."

Ross was about to argue that point when Libby walked through the door, carrying a small gift-wrapped box. She met his eyes briefly, then glanced around the room until she'd spotted Emma.

Emma. He should have guessed. She just couldn't leave well enough alone. He stood there watching as his daughter and Libby exchanged a hug. Then Libby started his way. "Excuse me, Mom. I need to speak to Barry."

"It's so nice seeing you and your brother getting along," she said, and gave his hand a small pat.

Ross didn't respond. He nodded at Libby as he passed her. He'd let her greet his mother without crowding her. After all, she'd made it a point to tell him how important it was that she have her damn space.

He ignored Emma's sharp look and kept going. Pushing through the double glass doors, he sucked in a huge gulp of night air. Barry stood a few feet away, staring out at the lake. Puffing on a cigarette, he looked Ross's way.

"When did you start smoking again?"

"A few days ago." Barry took another drag and held out the pack. "Want one?"

Ross took the package, shook a cigarette free, and stuck it between his lips. Barry flicked a lighter and lit it for him. After taking several puffs, Ross made a face and dropped it to the ground, stomping it out with his foot. "I just remembered why I never got addicted."

"They are kind of nasty, aren't they? But after the third or fourth one, they start to grow on you."

"Something bothering you that you're out here trying to get lung cancer?"

Barry didn't answer for a long time. The sound of crickets hummed through the air. "Did you ever wonder what your life would be like if you could erase your mistakes? Start over?"

Ross had a pretty good idea where this conversation might be going, and he didn't want to go there. But instead of saying so, he answered, "A few times."

Barry nodded, took another puff, then flicked the cigarette into the air. Ross watched the flash of red sail through the darkness and land in the lake, the hot red embers disappearing. "I'm leaving April. I wanted you to know. I'm going to tell Dad later, but ask him not to upset Mom with the news." He turned around and faced Ross. "As far as she's concerned, we're still love-sick teenagers. We've been careful all these years to put on a good show in front of her. But I can't do it anymore."

Ross didn't know what to say. He knew their relationship was strained. But he couldn't imagine their getting divorced. They'd dated since high school. He wondered if they'd had children, if it would have made a difference?

Watching silently as Barry headed back inside, he cursed himself a hundred times for feeling helpless. He had so many questions without answers, and he'd kept silent all these years, a part of him not wanting to know the truth, and the other part desperately needing to know. There was no chance of closure when the truth had yet to be told.

Listening to the waves slap against the docked boats, he thought back to when Meri had died. Sheriff Reese, Dan's father, had asked him if he'd known Meri was pregnant. The truth was, he hadn't known. She was ten weeks along when she either fell, jumped, or was pushed off that cliff. And she and Ross hadn't slept together in nearly six months.

"What the hell did you say to your brother?" Neil demanded, interrupting Ross's thoughts.

He spun around to confront his father. "I don't know what you're talking about."

"The hell you don't!" he spat. "He just drove off and left April behind. He didn't even say good night to your mother." Ross started to say something but was cut off. "Why couldn't you just leave it alone? It's been fourteen years. He's paid enough for his sins, don't you think?"

Ross looked him squarely in the eyes. "That depends on what his sins are."

Neil fumed, sucking in huge gulps of air, and pointed his finger at Ross. "I don't want your mother upset. Your coming home with Emma was supposed to be a good thing. For all of us. Somehow I thought you might be able to forget the past and let it go. But you seem determined to spend the rest of your life with a chip on your shoulder, and wanting the rest of the family to pay. We were all sickened by Meri's accident, but we've gone forward. Why can't you?"

"Why are you so certain it was an accident?" Ross asked, seething inside.

"The sheriff ruled it an accident and closed the file."

"If it wasn't for all that money lying nearby, I'd probably agree with you—that Meri either fell or jumped to her death. But I don't believe that's what happened. And if I weren't scared shitless that Barry would tell me the truth, I'd probably ask him if he pushed her off that cliff." Ross's breath came in harsh gasps, and his palms felt clammy as he stared his father down.

"He didn't do it," Neil said softly.

"How do you know? That's what you said fourteen years ago, dammit. You stuck up for him then, too. But you don't really know, do you?"

Hanging his head, Neil turned his back to Ross and walked away. His silence was all the answer Ross needed. He was no closer to the truth now than he was the day Meri died.

An hour later, Emma's voice sung out to him in the darkness. "Dad? What are you doing out here? Everybody's getting ready to leave."

"I'm coming." Ross draped an arm around his daughter and walked her to the door.

"Are you okay? You've been out here forever."

Ross smiled thinly. "I'm fine, Em."

Emma stopped in front of the door and peered up into his face. "Are you sure you're okay?"

"I'm sure," he assured her with another smile. "Let's go home."

When he reached for the door, she said, "Would it be all right if Zack drives me home?"

"Well," he started, then backed off. He wondered when he would stop being so protective when it came to Emma. He'd sensed she had a crush on Zack Reese since the beginning of summer. He should feel happy for her. Besides, he kind of liked the kid. He seemed like a sensible young man.

"Dad, is it okay?"

"Sure. It's okay. But wear your seatbelt."

Rolling her eyes, she said, "Stop treating me like a baby. You know I always wear my seatbelt."

"I know," he admitted, leaning forward and kissing the top of her head. "I'll see you in a bit."

Emma raced inside the building. Ross followed behind at a slower pace. The place had mostly cleared out. He helped his father carry Bev's birthday gifts to the car, and said good night to the last of the guests. Libby was nowhere in sight. And his brother still hadn't returned.

In the parking lot, April headed toward him, a navy shoulder bag and a white cardigan sweater draped over her arm. "Would you mind giving me a ride home?" she asked.

"Not at all." Ross led her to his Cherokee and opened the passenger door, waiting for her to slide in. He walked around to the opposite side and got in, starting the engine.

The marina was on the opposite side of the lake from his brother and sister-in-law's place. They had to pass through the center of town before the turn-off that wrapped around the north side of the lake.

"You and Barry looked as if you were having

a serious talk earlier this evening," April said. "Anything I should know?"

Ross glanced her way. Barry hadn't told her he was leaving her, and *he* sure as hell wasn't going to tell her. For all he knew, maybe they'd patch things up by morning.

"We were just talking. It wasn't anything important," he lied. Passing the sheriff's office, he noticed the door hanging wide open, the lights on. A cruiser was parked out front. Someone was obviously working very late.

"Any idea why he just left me at the party like that?" she asked.

He looked at her apologetically. "I'm sorry, April. I don't really know why he did that."

"We were getting along so well the past two weeks. Then a few days ago, he started talking about the past. I know it's been a long time, but I just can't talk about . . . her."

Not only could she not talk about Meredith, but she couldn't say her name either, he noticed. Ross's gaze drifted her way, offering her a sympathetic look, before looking straight ahead at the road.

"I'm sorry. I'm sure you don't want to hear this." She fumbled with the knob on the radio, then flicked it off.

He started to say something, then changed his mind. As they continued in silence, he kept thinking about the sheriff's office. When he was a few houses away from April's, he stepped on the brakes, stopping his car in the middle of the road.

April looked at him sharply, as if he'd suddenly lost his mind.

"It's getting late," he said staring at the clock on the dashboard. "Almost midnight. What would Dan or his deputy be doing at the sheriff's office this late?"

"I don't know." The words had barely escaped her lips when Ross turned the car around and headed back toward town. "Ross?"

He shook his head back and forth. "Something's bothering me. I just want to check it out."

The car rolled to a stop in the middle of the parking lot at the sheriff's office. Ross flung the door open and raced toward the building. April hurried in behind him.

He saw Deputy Maloney lying face down on the tile floor. "Maloney?" he called out. At first, he thought the man must be dead, but then he noticed his hand moving slightly.

He had a nasty-looking gash on the back of his head. Ross dropped to his knees and peered into the deputy's face. "What happened, Maloney?"

"Lattimer," he groaned in response.

Ross's pulse raced. "Call an ambulance, April. But first call Dan Reese and tell him to meet me out at Meggie's place ASAP. Then find Barry and tell him to get his ass out there. Does he have a cell phone with him?"

Not hearing his sister-in-law's response, Ross ran out the front door and jumped into his car. He couldn't believe it; Lattimer had broken out of jail. He'd kill that bastard if he hurt Meggie again.

HER CAR WASN'T there. The place was dark and locked up tighter than a drum. Steve couldn't remember the last time Meggie had locked a door. She'd always been so damn trusting of everyone.

He went to the shed and found a shovel. He rammed it through their bedroom window, the sound of breaking glass echoing through the still night air. He was glad there were no nosy neighbors close by.

Dropping the shovel to the ground, he reached inside to unlock the window and lifted it open. Hefting himself up and over the ledge, he dropped to the bedroom floor with a thud. "Honey, I'm home," he called out in mock humor, then went in search of something to drink.

A few minutes later he went out the back door and to the shed again. Spotting the can of gasoline, he smiled with satisfaction as he picked it up.

"GRANDMA LIKED THE garden gloves I picked out, didn't she, Mom?" Jeremy boasted as Meggie unlocked the back door. Flipping on the kitchen lights, she tossed her purse and car keys on the counter.

"Yes, she did, very much. TJ, lock the deadbolt, would you?" Meggie asked.

TJ bolted the door, then jerked the refrigerator door open. "I'm starving."

"After all that food you ate at Grandma's birthday party?"

"Yeah. Besides, we ate hours ago." He pulled a green Styrofoam egg carton out of the refrigerator. "Who wants scrambled eggs?"

Meggie shook her head. "Not me. I'm going to bed. I'm pooped."

"I'll eat some," Jeremy offered.

"You boys clean up the mess when you're done. And don't forget to turn off the stove." She was about to aim her weary body toward the bedroom when the alarmed look on TJ's face stopped her.

"TJ, what is it?" she asked as she spun around to look in the direction her son was looking. "Steve," she gasped. "What are you doing here?"

Steve stood in the kitchen doorway, nursing a beer, his face flushed, hard and mean, his eyes glazed over. "Is that any way to greet your long-lost husband?"

Meggie didn't answer as she backed up a step, closer to her boys and away from Steve.

"Say hello to daddy, boys," Steve said with a sneer. Neither of her sons answered.

"How did you get out?" she asked, trying to think of a way to get her boys out of the house and out of harm's way. She wanted to appear calm so as not to frighten them either.

He laughed. "Why, I was such a model prisoner, they let me go on my good behavior."

He was lying. She was sure of it. "What do you want? Money?"

"That would be nice. We're going to need some until we get settled in California."

California? What on earth was he talking about?

"Are you planning on calling Mommy and Daddy to ask for a loan?" he asked, stumbling toward them. "They're sitting on a fucking fortune. What the hell do they need all that money for? They're gonna die soon, anyway." He tossed his empty can in the trash. "Your mom's already a loony bird."

He was drunk.

Jeremy grabbed her arm. "Mom," he said. "I'm scared."

Meggie hugged him close by her side. She didn't say anything. She was afraid she'd upset Steve, maybe set him off.

Steve stared at Jeremy, a disgusted look on his face. "Quit acting like a damn sissy. I'm not gonna hurt anybody. Unless one of you decides to be cute." His gaze shifted between her and her boys.

TJ came from behind. "Go away and leave us alone. We don't want you here."

"TJ," Meggie warned, but he didn't listen.

Instead, he moved closer to Steve. "I'll get you some money, and then you can leave."

"Not so fast," Steve hissed, grabbing at the boy's arm. But TJ managed to avoid his stepfather's grasp. "I suppose you were going to go looking for this, weren't you?" He pulled out the small silver pistol Meggie had purchased to keep them safe.

Oh, dear God, she thought, closing her eyes briefly. But then she remembered she'd taken the bullets out and had hidden them separately. There was a good chance he hadn't found them. "Put that thing down, Steve. It's not loaded."

"Wanna bet, sweetheart?" he asked, laughing at her. He pointed the gun directly at TJ, causing her heart to sink. "I found the bullets in one of your shoe boxes. Why, don't look so surprised, Meggie. That's the first place I looked. After all, you've been hiding your tip money there for months. Did you think I didn't know?"

Meggie hurled herself forward, pushing TJ slightly behind her. "Let them go. It's me you want to hurt, not them."

"Aren't you noble?" He waved the gun at her nose. "Isn't your mom brave, boys? But I told you," he said sharply, looking at Meggie, "I'm not going to hurt anyone. I'm sorry about that last time, Meggie. And things are going to be different from now on. I have a great plan. I should have thought of it before.

"You're going to call your parents and ask them to wire you some money in the morning. You'll tell them that you need to get away with the kids for a little while. I've already packed a suitcase for each of us. We're leaving tonight. Heading west. We should be in Kansas City by tomorrow. They can wire it there."

He took another step toward them. Meggie pulled TJ by the arm, and the two of them stepped to the side.

"California, here we come," Steve sang out, slightly off beat.

He grinned at each of them in turn. "Well, it's

going to be a long trip. You'll drive first, Meggie. And TJ, maybe we'll let you get some driving practice in. You're always complaining that I never take you driving. This is going to be fun. You'll see."

Moving toward the refrigerator, he said, "I need another beer before we go." When he reached inside to get the beer, TJ slammed the door on his wrist, knocking the gun to the floor.

"Owwww! You little bastard!" Steve shouted as he and TJ both scrambled to the floor to get the gun.

Meggie was knocked into a kitchen chair and nearly lost her balance in the struggle. Quickly, she pushed Jeremy toward the back door. "Run, Jeremy!" she whispered and was relieved when he flew out the back door. The screen door squealed, then banged harshly.

Seeing TJ holding the gun pointed at Steve caused the blood to drain from her face. Steve started to get to his feet.

"Don't move, asshole. Or you're dead," TJ threatened.

Steve stayed on the floor, sprawled against the refrigerator.

"TJ," Meggie said softly, her hand shaking as she held it out to her son. "Give me the gun."

He ignored her. "TJ," she repeated more firmly this time.

Shaking his head, he said, "No, Mom."

"Listen to your mother, you little bastard," Steve spat out, venom in his eyes.

If she had been holding the gun in her hand at that moment, she wondered if she could have shot him. Probably not. As much as she hated Steve, she doubted very much that she could kill him. Or anyone.

But what worried her was wondering if TJ could. "Honey, somebody could get hurt. Give me the gun."

Again, he shook his head, violently this time. "He deserves to die. For all the times that he hurt you."

"I should have taken you over my knee a few times," Steve hissed. "And your whiney-ass little brother, too."

"You say one more thing about my brother, and you're dead."

"TJ! That's enough." Meggie laid a hand on his arm. He felt steady, while she was unable to control her own shaking. Slowly, she pulled his arm toward her, inching the gun in her direction. She slid her hand toward his wrist, hoping her movements would convince him to release the gun to her. She almost had her hand on it when a car screeched to a stop outside.

Without thinking, she turned her head in the direction of the headlights shining brightly through her kitchen window. Then, suddenly, she was knocked off her feet by Steve.

During the commotion, Ross came charging through the back door. When she looked up, Steve was holding a struggling TJ by the throat, the gun pointed at his head.

21

ROSS DIDN'T MOVE. He didn't want to chance spooking Lattimer. He'd never forgive himself if anything happened to TJ.

"Oh, my God. Steve, please," Meggie pleaded, tears in her eyes, her voice no louder than a whisper. "Don't hurt him. Please don't hurt my baby."

"The sheriff's on his way. It's all over, Lattimer," Ross warned. "Why don't you put the gun down?"

"Why don't you shut the fuck up, hot shot?" Lattimer tightened his grip on TJ, and the boy's face reddened slightly.

Ross leveled his gaze on the man, wishing he could read his mind. He appeared to be thinking about something. Suddenly, his face and eyes lit up. "Okay, there's been a change of plans. Originally, I was going to burn this piece of crap house down. By the time anyone realized there weren't any bodies inside, we'd have been hundreds of miles from here. "But, hey," he laughed, "why not leave a body behind?"

Ross swallowed. He knew Steve meant Ross's body.

Meggie gasped. "Steve, you're drunk. You're talking like a crazy man."

"Hey, this would make a good scene for one of your books," Lattimer said, looking pointedly at Ross. "Too bad you won't be alive to write about it."

"Steve, stop it," Meggie said. "We can't go with you. Besides, we can't go anywhere without Jeremy."

"That's his problem. The little shit obviously didn't want to go to California. You know," he spouted, squeezing TJ's throat a little tighter, "I've tried to be a good father to these kids, but they're just too damn spoiled. All they ever did was complain and ask for more. They're the reason I started drinking and using drugs, Meggie."

"You don't have to father them anymore, Steve," Meggie said, tears slipping down her cheeks. "Please just go and leave us alone."

Steve shook his head in disgust. "You wouldn't be trying to get rid of me, would you, sweetheart? After all those words of love? Till death do us part and all that crap?"

Meggie was smart enough not to answer him. From the corner of his eye, Ross saw something move in the dark hallway. He hoped it was Barry or, better yet, Dan. Either way, he wasn't sure how they would get the gun away from Lattimer *and* keep TJ from being hurt.

But then an idea came to him, and he decided to go with it. "So, Lattimer, if it's me you want, then let the boy go and come and get me." Meggie's head whipped around sharply, but Ross didn't look at her. He kept his eyes trained on Lattimer and was careful not to look toward the hall again. Taking a step closer, he spoke. "Let him go."

Lattimer turned the gun in Ross's direction. Ross should have feared for his life, but instead he felt relieved that the gun was no longer aiming at his nephew's head.

"Don't come any closer, hot shot, or I'll shoot you dead."

TJ kicked his foot backwards, trying to connect with Lattimer's shin, but he missed. Lattimer tightened his grip on the boy. TJ's eyes started to water. He tried to work up a cough, but it came out as a soft hack instead.

"You're going to choke him to death, Steve!" Meggie shouted, reaching for her son. The man shifted his direction slightly. And at that moment, Ross took advantage and made his move. He ducked low and charged at Lattimer. He heard a shot, then a second one, louder than the first, before he noticed the sharp pain in his shoulder.

The next thing Ross knew, Lattimer fell on top of him, his weight crushing him to the floor. Ross pushed the man aside, but he still had trouble breathing.

He closed his eyes for just a moment and listened to the commotion around him. Someone gave orders to call an ambulance. It sounded like Barry.

Feeling a warm, sticky liquid covering him, Ross realized it was blood. He hoped it was Lattimer's and not his own. He looked up and saw Barry crouching over him, a horrified look on his face. "Hang on, little brother. You're going to be okay."

Meggie cried aloud and hugged TJ.

Dan Reese bent down, shook his head, and called Ross a fool before feeling for a pulse on Lattimer. "He's dead," Dan announced, not sounding the least bit sorrowful.

A woozy feeling came over Ross. Emma's face, and then Libby's, ran past him. Those were the last things he remembered before blacking out.

ROSS SLOWLY OPENED his eyes and took notice of the hospital room. There were floral arrangements and plants lining the window ledge. They seemed to have multiplied since the first day he was brought here. Several brightly colored Mylar balloons danced softly in the air. Those were new.

He could make out some of the cards, too. The balloons were from Emma and the large dish garden was from his agent, Sharon Richards. There was a huge vase of daisies. The get-well card said simply, "Libby."

Letting his eyes drift shut, he wondered briefly if she'd been by to see him. If she had, he couldn't remember. The last few days were a fog. They kept him loaded with pain killers most of the time. But he did remember seeing Emma and his brother at his bedside more than once.

Rolling to his side, he tried to get comfortable

but couldn't because of his shoulder. He realized that was the shoulder that had been shot. Anger stabbed at him, reminding him of that night, but he pushed it from his thoughts, knowing that he should feel lucky to be alive. He was thankful that his nephew wasn't hurt. That was worth a bullet in the shoulder any day.

Carefully, he shifted his weight and rolled onto his back. Within minutes, sleep overtook him once again.

LIBBY HAD HER back to Ross when he opened his eyes. He watched as she sniffed the floral arrangements. She took her time, lowering her head to each of the different blooms, sometimes lingering over a particular flower. He could smell their fragrant aromas from his hospital bed.

He ran his gaze up the backs of Libby's long bare legs. She wore a black and white striped shirt with the sleeves pushed up to her elbows, a black skirt that stopped a few inches above her knees, and black strappy sandals on her feet.

As if she suddenly realized she was being stared at, she pivoted in his direction. Her face was free of make-up, her eyes as clear a green as he'd ever seen. Smiling tentatively at him, she said, "You're awake."

Blinking his eyes, he nodded, then tried to reach for the water pitcher on the bedside table. He was so pumped full of medication it had left a sour taste in his mouth.

"Here, let me do that," she offered, pouring the water and melted ice chips into a clear plastic cup. She pulled back the paper from a straw, stuck it in the cup, and held it to his lips.

Lifting his head from the pillow, Ross drank a generous amount, then signaled that he was done. "Thanks," he rasped.

"You just missed Emma and Zack. They were here most of the afternoon waiting for you to wake up."

After clearing his throat, he asked, "Is someone keeping an eye on those two?"

"They're both good kids, Ross. And Emma's been staying with me. I hope that's all right."

It was more than all right. He smiled and nodded approvingly. "Thanks for looking after her. How's Meggie? The boys?"

"They're fine," she said clasping her hands in front of her. "None of them wanted to go back to that house after what happened. They've been staying with your brother and April. Next week, they're going to move into one of the cottages just down the road from them."

His eyes searched hers, but he didn't say anything. After a moment of awkward silence, she turned and reached for her purse, which sat on a blue vinyl chair at the end of his bed. "I should go," she said, coming along the opposite side of the bed. "Visits are limited. You need your rest."

Ross's arm shot out, stopping her. "I've been sleeping for three days. I'm plenty rested. Stay," he said.

Libby blinked several times, then set her purse on the bed beside him. "Let me raise your bed up a few inches; it'll make you more comfortable." She pressed a button on the metal arm of his bed, raising the head of the mattress. Gently placing her hands behind his head, she leaned forward, adjusted his pillows, tucked the sheet around him, and moved his IV tubing aside.

He loved the way she smelled. He didn't want her to leave. In fact, he wanted her to slide into bed next to him. But he knew that was out of the question.

A nurse chose that moment to interrupt their privacy. "Good evening, Doctor Larson." The woman's white shoes squeaked on the shiny tile floor as she moved about the room.

"Hello, Susan." Libby greeted her with a smile, then took a seat in the vinyl chair at the foot of the bed.

S. Fresch was etched on the nurse's name tag. "Hello, Mr. McLaughlin. How are you feeling today?"

"Like I'm going to live."

She laughed, and the loose skin from her neck and chin jiggled back and forth. She was round, plump, and had a head of curly black ringlets. Jabbing a thermometer in his mouth, she took his arm and wrapped a blood pressure cuff around it. She worked efficiently, pumping the rubber bulb. Ross noticed the pleased look on her face when she took the blood pressure reading. Apparently, she was happy with the results. She then pressed her forefinger to his wrist and studied her watch. After making some notations on the chart at the end of his bed, she said, "I'll let Doctor Shelby know that you're awake. He'll want to talk to you. In the meantime, can I get you anything? Are you hungry?"

"I could eat a whale."

She laughed again. "I'll have a tray sent up right away." With that, she sailed out of the room, her shoes squeaking all the way down the hall.

"She seems pleasant," he said.

"Susan's a wonderful nurse."

They stared at each other for a few moments. Ross noticed her hands fidgeting in her lap, which was totally unlike her. Libby was always cool, calm, and in control. He was the one who was usually a blundering idiot when he was around her.

"I," they both said in unison. Ross chuckled. Libby smiled.

"Go ahead," she said. "You first."

"I never told you much about my past. About my wife's death." In fact, he'd never told her anything about Meri. And Libby had never asked. She looked at him intently, her eyes wide with interest. So he went on. "She was young when I met her." He filled her in on their unusual meeting, the night she'd seduced him on the boat.

"I shouldn't have slept with her. But I was young, just out of college, raging hormones, et cetera. We saw each other a few times after that, but I quickly lost interest. She'd lied to me about her age. I found out she was only seventeen when we met, barely out of high school. I tried to avoid her, but she kept calling me, sending me notes, hanging around the marina. Then one day she showed up on my mother's doorstep and announced she was pregnant."

Libby sat up straight in the chair, offering him a sympathetic look.

"Our marriage was doomed from the beginning. I didn't love her. Hell, I didn't even like her much once I'd gotten to really know her." He told her about how he'd tried to make Meri happy, but that no matter what he did, it was never enough. "What she really wanted was to be loved."

He scratched his hand where the adhesive tape held the IV needle in his vein. "She loved Emma. She was the one thing that made Meri happy. But even the joy of Emma's birth seemed to be only temporary. Soon after we were married Meredith started inventing reasons to visit my brother. Every time I turned around they were together. And before long, Barry and April started having marital problems." He took a long breath, then a sip of water.

"I knew Barry and Meredith were having an affair. Part of me didn't care. I guess I thought they deserved each other. But then there was the part of me that just couldn't get past it. I wasn't surprised that Meredith was cheating on me, but Barry . . . my own brother.

"I wanted out of the marriage, but I didn't want to lose Emma. I couldn't stand the thought of only seeing my child every other weekend like most divorced fathers."

Libby smiled and nodded understandingly.

"I was afraid Meri would up and leave, and take our daughter clear across the country somewhere. I threatened to take Emma away from her. And she threatened to kill herself if I did. I told her to be my guest."

Libby's mouth dropped open. "Oh, Ross. Is that what happened? Did she...."

"I don't know. She was pregnant. The baby wasn't mine," he added quickly, seeing that wounded look in her eye. "They found her body at the bottom of Falcon Ridge. They also found stacks of money around her and a one-way plane ticket to L.A. I don't know where she got the money or the ticket. The sheriff at the time—who was Dan's father, by the way—suspected me."

"I know you didn't do it," she said softly.

He nodded in thanks. "If it weren't for the money and the plane ticket, I might have thought she jumped. But...."

"What do you think happened?"

"I wish I knew." He closed his eyes, then opened them slowly. "That's a lie. I guess I'm afraid of the truth. If she jumped, it was partly my fault. But if she was pushed...."

Libby sat forward. She seemed to be digesting his words.

"Do you understand now why I can't stay in Falcon Ridge? Some days, I can't even look at Barry, wondering if he's a murderer. And it wouldn't be fair to ask you to go back to Phoenix with—"

"Ross," she interjected, coming to her feet. "You said Meredith was pregnant."

"Yes. The baby must have been Barry's. That's another reason I—"

"But you don't know that for sure."

"Trust me. I'm sure."

"But, that's not possible. I thought you knew. . . ." her voice trailed off.

"Knew what?"

Libby shook her head. "Nothing. I shouldn't have said anything."

"What are you trying to say, Libby?"

"I think you should talk to your brother. Did you ever tell him your suspicions?"

Ross laughed bitterly. "What do you think I should say? *By the way, I was wondering. . . . I know you slept with my wife, but did you happen to get her pregnant and then push her off that cliff, too?*"

Libby stood up, chewed at her bottom lip. "He didn't do it, Ross."

"He was the only one who could have. Think about it."

She tossed her head back and forth and started for the door. "Talk to Barry."

"I've tried to talk him, dammit! Do you think it's easy?" He tried to reach for her, but she was too far from him. "Libby. . . ."

She stopped with her back to him but didn't turn around.

"What it is you're trying so hard not to tell me?"

"I shouldn't be the one to—"

"Please," he pleaded, then again, "Please, Libby."

Slowly, she turned to face him. "Barry couldn't have fathered Meredith's child."

"What makes you so damn sure?" he snapped.

She blinked her eyes twice. "Because he can't father anyone's child. He's sterile."

ROSS HAD BEEN home for two days. His left arm was in a sling to prevent unnecessary movement of his shoulder until it healed. He was thankful he still had the use of his right arm. He could at least feed and dress himself. And he could write—although it was somewhat awkward using only his right hand on the computer. Although he'd been managing. In fact, he'd been more productive in the past two days than he had been in weeks. He'd outlined his entire novel, something that usually took him weeks to do.

"Dad, do you want me to heat up some soup for you before I leave?" Emma yelled from the kitchen.

He cringed. He'd eaten nothing but chicken soup since he'd come home. Meggie, Libby and several different neighbors had each brought him a container. Why people thought chicken soup would cure a bullet wound was beyond him. Right now, he'd give anything for a thick, juicy burger, greasy French fries, and an ice-cold beer.

"No, thanks, Em. Any of those Pop-Tarts left?"

Emma came around the corner and gave him a

suspicious look. "You want Pop-Tarts for lunch?" She was dressed in a cute little blue sundress. She looked more feminine than he'd seen her look in months.

"No, not really," he said, settling himself on the sofa and reaching for the remote control. "I'm just tired of soup. You look very pretty, Emma. Just like your mother."

"Really?" she asked, her blue eyes sparkling. "Do you want me to stay home and make you something else?"

Emma had promised to keep her grandmother company while Neil took care of some boats at the marina. Zack had offered to drop Emma off, then help her grandfather with the boats. "No. Zack's coming to pick you up any minute. And besides, your grandmother would be disappointed if you didn't show up." Ross had no sooner stopped speaking than the doorbell rang.

Emma looked at the front door, then back at her father. "Last chance."

"Get going. Wear your seatbelt."

Shaking her head and rolling her eyes, she raced toward the door.

"WHAT ARE YOU doing?" April asked from the doorway of their bedroom.

Barry glanced at her over his shoulder, then resumed packing. "I'm moving out."

There was a moment of crystalline silence before April stepped into the room behind him. Barry pretended not to know she was there. Pulling open a drawer from his bureau, he grabbed several pairs of socks and underwear and tossed them onto the bed near the suitcase.

"Do you mind telling me why you're moving out and where you're going?" she asked quietly.

"I'm going to stay with Meggie and the boys for a few weeks until something opens up." Yesterday, he'd moved his sister and her boys into one of the lake cottages. "After what she's been through recently, she could use someone to lean on."

"So, this is just temporary? You're coming back, right?" she asked, her voice a little shaky.

Sucking in a large gulp of air, Barry turned around and faced her. "No, April. I'm not coming back." Her face grew tight with emotion, and her eyes filled with moisture. "Why not?" she asked, her voice barely above a whisper.

"Because I can't stand living this lie anymore." He could see her fighting to keep control, trying not to break down in tears. "Just tell me the truth," he demanded.

She looked at him, a questioning look in her eyes. "What are you talking about?"

Her act of innocence clawed at him. How could she keep pretending that he didn't know? This time he was the one who had to fight for control. "Dammit, April. Did you push Meredith off that cliff?"

22

HER GRANDMOTHER HAD been napping when Zack dropped Emma off at the house half an hour ago. It had been quiet ever since. Emma had already painted her nails and toenails and had flipped through all the magazines on the coffee table. She figured it was now time to check on her grandmother.

Peeking around the corner into their bedroom, she sighed with relief when she saw that her grandmother was still sleeping. The one thing her grandfather had warned her about was not to let her grandmother wander off, like she'd been doing lately. "Keep her indoors if at all possible," he'd said.

Emma prayed she wouldn't wander while *she* was watching her. She'd feel awful if something happened to her. What if she disappeared and got lost in the woods somewhere? Or fell down in a ravine? Or worse yet, got hit by a car?

Emma shuddered and tried to think about something else. Walking up the hall, she decided to make some Jell-O. She'd seen several boxes in the pantry just the other day. And she knew her grandmother liked it. Opening the cupboard door, her gaze roamed the shelf until she spotted the familiar boxes. Strawberry. Her favorite. Maybe she'd slice some bananas and stir them in, too, she thought, reaching for a bowl.

ROSS FLIPPED THROUGH the channels for the third time, then, feeling disgusted with the limited choices, turned the television off and tossed the remote aside. He was bored. He'd thought about calling Libby this afternoon, just to see how she was doing. But he knew that wouldn't be fair. She'd told him she wanted to end their relationship on a good note. And even though he didn't like the idea, he cared about Libby and wanted to respect her wishes. She'd dropped soup off for him a few days ago, but she hadn't come inside the house to even say hello. He hadn't talked to her since the day she'd visited him in the hospital.

The day he'd told her why he couldn't stay in Falcon Ridge.

The day she'd told him that Barry couldn't have children.

He'd tried not to let that information consume his thoughts, but it had. He'd thought all these years—without a doubt—that Barry had fathered Meri's unborn baby. He'd also thought his brother was somehow responsible for her death. That they'd met on top of Falcon Ridge and argued. That Barry had offered her money and a plane ticket so she'd leave town. Maybe he hadn't meant to kill her; maybe it was an accident.

April had known that Barry had cheated on her. Even before Ross had found out. And she'd decided to stay with him, anyway, and make a go of their marriage. So, if Barry wasn't the father of Meri's baby, why would he be so anxious to get rid of Meri? So anxious that he'd maybe kill her?

Ross scrubbed his hands over his unshaven face. What if he'd been wrong about Barry? What if it hadn't been his brother on top of Falcon Ridge that day? What if it had been someone else?

As his thoughts roamed, he started feeling sick to his stomach. Maybe he'd take a shower. But just as he stood to make his way to the bathroom, the phone rang. He thought about ignoring it, but then a small flicker of hope that it was Libby flashed in front of him. He answered on the third ring.

"Hello?"

His father's deep voice vibrated anxiously through the receiver. "Ross. Are Emma and your mother there with you?"

"No, they're not."

"Well, they're not here." Fear prickled at the back of his neck, but he told himself not to worry. They were fine. Probably just out for a walk. "And the car's gone," Neil added. "Your mother hasn't driven it in years."

Ross swore under his breath. Emma didn't have a license. So, why would she have taken the car? And where could they have gone? "I'll be right over." He slammed down the phone and started for the door, then went back and dialed Barry's number.

BARRY HUNG UP the phone and turned to April. "That was Ross. He said Dad just got home and can't find Emma or Mom. The car's missing, too."

"Oh, no. Emma should have known better than to take the car without asking Ross or Neil first."

"I've gotta go look for them."

"I'll go with you," she said, wiping her wet cheeks. She never had answered his question. He'd thought she was just about to when the phone rang. "Unless you don't want me to?"

He stared at her sad expression, then held out his hand. "C'mon. We'd better hurry."

On the drive to his parents' house, Barry glanced at his wife. "You know Mom's been acting pretty odd all summer. Especially when Emma's around her."

"She loves Emma."

"I know she does. But doesn't it seem strange that every time she seems to have some kind of . . . I don't know . . . breakdown, I guess you'd call it, that Emma's around?"

April didn't answer, but looked as if she were contemplating his words.

"And Mom's been running away lately."

"There's a difference between running away and wandering off," she said. "She probably just gets disoriented and then can't find her way back."

"The other day, when she wandered off—I

found her sitting at the top of Falcon Ridge," he said, eyeing April as the car rolled to a sudden stop in his parents' drive. "She was just sitting there with her feet dangling over the edge, staring out into space."

"Oh, Barry. She could have been hurt, or fallen over that cliff. What did your dad say?"

"I didn't tell him," he admitted.

April stared at him with a puzzled frown as they got out of the car. "Why not?"

"Because she begged me not to. She started talking weird. Saying things like he'd never forgive her. And he was never to know that she'd been up there. Ever." He shook his head. "It didn't make any sense."

Ross pulled up out front just as Barry and April entered the house. "Any word from them?" he asked his father, who was pacing the living room floor. Zack Reese sat on the edge of the sofa, a serious look on his face.

"No," Neil answered. "Before I called Ross, Zack and I drove around the lake. There was no sign of them."

When Ross came inside, Zack said, "I called my dad. He's going to take the cruiser out and look for them, see if he can spot Mr. McLaughlin's car in town."

"Well, let's go then," Neil said. "We should split up. Does everyone have a cell phone so we can keep in touch?"

They exchanged phone numbers and headed to their cars. Zack drove Neil and Ross. Barry and

April rode together. The two cars stayed together on the lake road. But at the edge of town, they went in separate directions.

"PULL OVER," BEV ordered Emma. "Right there." She pointed to a fork in the road. Emma turned off and brought the car to a stop when the road ended a few moments later. "Now where, Grandma?" she asked, her voice weak and tremulous.

"I told you to stop calling me that!"

Emma had no idea what she'd done to make her grandmother so angry. She'd been making Jell-O when her grandmother came into the kitchen and started carrying on about the dress Emma was wearing.

It was a blue floral sun dress. Libby had helped her pick it out while Ross was in the hospital. She'd said it looked good with her eyes. And her dad had told her she looked pretty earlier this afternoon. Like her mother, he'd said. But her grandmother didn't like the dress—not one bit. The first thing she'd said was, "Take that awful-looking thing off. How dare you come into my home dressed like that?"

Emma had almost cried. But then she'd told herself her grandmother was sick and she couldn't help herself. She didn't mean to be rude or nasty.

And when Emma had tried to pick up the phone to call her grandfather, her grandmother became hysterical, pushed her outside, and ordered her into the car.

She was stronger than her grandmother, and she supposed she could have refused. But Emma didn't want to fight with her, maybe hurt her. She'd wanted to go back inside and call her dad or her grandfather, but she was afraid her grandmother would wander off if she did. And, remembering her grandfather's warning, she'd stuck to her grandmother like glue. Maybe if she took her for a short ride, she'd calm down and then they could go back to the house.

She wasn't afraid to drive. Her grandparents' Chevy Impala was a lot bigger than the cars she'd driven, but she'd done okay. And her grandmother hadn't complained once about her driving. She hadn't asked her to slow down or anything. In fact, once she'd ordered her to speed up. They'd driven through town twice, and then her grandmother ordered her to drive up the road toward the cliff.

She'd never been to the cliff, although she'd heard TJ talking to Zack about it once. When Emma suggested they go up and take a look around, Zack said it wasn't anyplace she'd want to go, and that it was too dangerous. Instantly TJ had agreed, although only moments before he'd been bragging about going up to the top with some of his friends to drink a few beers. Emma hadn't been all that impressed. Drinking beer wasn't all that great; she'd tried it a few times already. In fact, she didn't like the taste all that much.

They'd been sitting in the car quietly for a few minutes when Emma stole a glance at her grandmother. She seemed to be looking up at the trail that apparently led to the top of the cliff, but she hadn't said anything, nor had she made the slightest twitch. Emma wondered what her grandmother would do if she backed up the car, turned it around, and headed home. She started to put it in reverse when her grandmother said, "Get out of the car, Meredith."

Meredith? Staring at her grandmother, Emma felt mortified. Why had her grandmother called her that?

A glazed look came over the woman's face as she said, "All these years, I thought you were dead. I've paid for my sin. I lost my son and granddaughter because of you. But they're back now. And I made my peace with God a long time ago. He's forgiven me for what I did."

Emma felt hot tears slip down her cheeks. She had no idea what her grandmother was talking about, or maybe she did, but just didn't want to know. "Grandma, it's me . . . Emma."

"Stop it!" She pointed a bony finger at her. "Stop trying to trick me. You think because I can't remember things sometimes that you can deceive me, but you can't." She opened the door, came around the car, and jerked Emma by the arm. Together, they started up the path.

"April warned me about you, and how you seduced Barry. I didn't believe her at first. She told me to be careful, not to turn my back on you, so I started watching Neil and how he reacted around you. The day you stopped by to show off that little blue sun dress. . . ." She stopped in her tracks and stared at Emma. "That one," she said, disgustedly. "Neil's eyes lit up when you arrived. I remember he told you how pretty you looked." The older woman's eyes bore into her granddaughter's with a disparaging look. "You were on top of the world, so thrilled with Neil's compliment. That's how I knew you were making a play for him. I tried to warn him, but he only laughed. He told me I was imagining things, and made me feel like a jealous fool." She started walking again, dragging Emma behind her.

"That was the summer he broke his leg in that car accident and was stuck at home all those months. He acted like a lovesick idiot every time you came to visit."

Emma's sandal tripped on a rock jutting out of the ground, but she managed to stay upright. Through her tears it was hard to see where she was going. She knew she could probably pull away from her grandmother. She could outrun her, too, if she had to.

But she couldn't just leave her out here by herself. What if she got hurt? She was in a very fragile state. And she was talking crazy-like. Saying things that just didn't make sense. It was almost as if she'd hated Emma's mother. But that couldn't be.

"Did you know you made Neil cry the last time you came to see him? I'd never seen him cry until that night. I'd told him I had a meeting to go to, but I lied."

She tugged harder on Emma's arm, and Emma winced in pain.

"I heard you tell him you were pregnant, and that you refused to have an abortion. I wanted to kill you that night, but instead I just sat in the bushes and watched you drive away. After you left, Neil cried like a baby. I watched him from the window. And I cried, too."

"No!" Emma shrieked, jerking her arm away. She'd heard enough. "Lies! All of them. My mother wouldn't have done those things you said. You're sick, Grandma. You don't know what you're saying." She rubbed at her sore arm. "Now, we're going back down the hill, and we're going to go find Grandpa. He'll tell you my mom didn't do those things."

"Emma!"

At the sound of her dad's voice, she turned to look over her shoulder. Her dad, her grandfather, and Zack started rushing up the hill toward them. Two more cars screeched to a stop simultaneously. One was the sheriff's car. Her Uncle Barry and Aunt April got out of the other car. By the time she turned to face her grandmother, the woman was several feet ahead of her—almost to the top of the crest.

"Grandma, come back!" she shouted, but was ignored. Emma hurried after her.

"Bev! Mother!" came the shouts behind them.

Because of her sandals, Emma had a hard time making her way over the tree roots and rocks. By the time she reached the top, Zack was beside her, breathing heavily, the rest of them just a few feet behind.

Her grandmother stood at the edge of the cliff,

her back to them. Zack took Emma's hand and held it tightly. When she started to move toward her grandmother, he stopped her with a gentle tug.

Ross touched Emma's shoulder. She spun around and clung to him, trembling as he pulled her close and hugged her. It was as if he needed to touch her to assure himself she was all right. Letting her go, he signaled to Zack and Emma to move back and stay out of the way.

Dan Reese kept his distance, allowing the McLaughlin men to handle things.

Ross nodded at his father to take the lead. "Bev," Neil said quietly. She didn't answer. "Move away from the edge before you fall." When she didn't move, Neil took a step closer. Ross stuck his arm out in front of his father, stopping him from going any farther. With a shake of his head, he told him that moving in behind her wasn't a good idea. She might panic and fall.

Ross had seen her dragging Emma up the hill. And he'd heard Emma shouting. He wasn't sure why and, right now, he didn't care. He just wanted his mother and daughter safe, and to get the hell out of here. As a teenager he'd been up here many times, but he'd never come back after Meri had died.

"Bev, please. You're scaring Emma. And me, too," Neil said.

Silence.

"Mom?" Ross tried getting her to speak to him. "Will you let us help you?"

"I didn't mean to do it, Ross. I swear," she

whimpered. Her eyes filled with tears as she spun around slowly. She seemed to sway once, then stood perfectly still, her eyes looking down at the ground.

Ross was afraid she'd fall backward. She looked so fragile, so helpless. "It's okay, Mom. I'm not mad. Neither is Emma. We know you didn't mean her any harm."

Lifting her head, she said, "Emma. Oh, dear God. What have I done?"

From the corner of his eye, he saw Emma bury her face in Zack's neck, her body quivering.

"Bev, please, take a step toward us," Neil said. "We want to help you."

She shook her head violently. "I didn't mean to do it. I just wanted Meredith to leave us alone. She destroyed our family. I wanted her to leave town and never come back."

She turned her head and looked pointedly at Neil. "I told her she had to leave Emma here with us—with Ross. I tried to give her money, but she wouldn't take it. She wanted to stay—to work things out with Ross. She claimed she still loved him, and she planned to have the baby. But it wasn't Ross's baby. It was *your* baby, Neil."

Her words sank in, burning a hole in Ross's chest. He closed his eyes for a moment, trying to block out what his mother had just said. He'd never dreamed in a million years that his father had slept with Meredith. Nor that his mother had been responsible for her death, and the death of Meri's unborn child.

"Bev, it was an accident. She fell while you were struggling," Neil said, as if he knew it for a fact.

Bev stared open-mouthed at her husband, as if to ask how he could possibly know that. He took a step toward her before Ross could stop him. April's gasp echoed across the still air as she clung to Barry.

"You talk in your sleep," Neil said, still moving toward his wife. "I know you didn't mean for Meri to fall, that you were only trying to make her go away. It's okay, honey, I forgive you."

"Stop, Neil. I don't want your pity."

"Bev, I've never pitied you. This terrible tragedy happened because of me. I have no excuse for what I did. I love you. I always have. And I love Ross. I had no right. . . ." He tossed his head back and forth, sighing. "No right to do what I did."

"Go away, Neil," Bev said, holding up her hands. Ross sucked in his breath as his mother took a small step back. But before she could take another, Neil grabbed her and pulled her to the ground with him.

Ross stood in a daze for several long moments while Emma cried on Zack's shoulder and April cried in Barry's arms. He'd never felt lonelier than at that moment.

Dan came up behind him, rested a hand on his shoulder. "Your family's all suffered enough, don't you think?"

Nodding his head, Ross turned to walk down the hill alone. Before he got to the bottom, Emma came rushing down behind him. Just as he turned, she crashed into his chest, and he squeezed her to him. It felt good to hold her like this—even if it was with one arm—and even though his injured shoulder hurt like hell. He held her longer than he'd planned, and she hadn't complained once. "I love you, Em."

"I love you, too, Dad."

So, now that he had all the answers, he wondered if knowing the truth was worth it.

23

BARRY HAD JUST finished shoving the last suit-case into the trunk of his car when Ross pulled into the drive.

"Emma just left. She said you'd be stopping by," Barry said as his brother got out. The poor kid, he thought. The look on her face when she'd come to say good-bye that day almost had him in tears. April *had* cried.

"I passed her on the way here. She's not speaking to me at the moment. She wants to stay in Falcon Ridge, and I think it would be best if we went back to Arizona," Ross explained.

Barry acknowledged him with a slight nod of his head. "So you're leaving tomorrow morning?"

"Yes. It looks as if you're going somewhere, too." His gaze drifted to Barry's open trunk.

April came out of the house carrying a small suitcase and walked toward them, her eyes red and swollen. She stopped a few feet away from Barry.

He pulled her close to his side and wrapped his arm around her shoulder. "April and I are going to Maui for a few weeks. Sort of a second honeymoon."

Ross smiled, his gaze wavering between the two of them. "That's great."

"We're going to miss you and Emma, Ross," April said, her eyes growing misty. "Promise you'll come back and visit us next summer."

"I promise," Ross said, leaning in to kiss her on the cheek. He looked at Barry, then dropped his gaze. "I don't know what to say."

Barry dropped his arm from April's shoulder. "We've got a lot of years to make up for, little brother. Hell, I haven't even kicked your ass yet on the basketball court."

"As if you could," Ross said jokingly, a grin on his face. Suddenly, he turned somber. "I'm really sorry—"

Barry cut him off with a slap on the shoulder. "Forget it. We've both apologized enough already."

Ross kissed April again, then shook Barry's hand before pulling him close for a hug. It felt good being embraced by his younger brother. It had been a long time. Afraid he'd turn to mush, he broke away and grabbed his wife's hand. "April and I have a plane to catch. And it looks like she's still got some packing to do."

Nodding, Ross got in his car and slowly drove off. Barry watched the car until it rounded the bend. He said to his wife, "I made such a mess of things. Between my brother and me, and you and me."

"It's over, Barry. Let's not beat ourselves up any longer."

"You're right," he agreed, pulling her into his

arms and holding her close. "How could I have thought that you—"

"Shhhh," she whispered. "I thought the same thing about you, remember?"

Yes, he remembered. They'd wasted fourteen years, going through the motions without really living. But things were going to change now. They'd been given a second chance, and he'd be damned if he was going to screw it up.

"So, how many more suitcases do you have in there?" he asked.

"Just a couple more."

Barry shook his head and laughed. "Well, let's go get them, so we can be on our way."

ROSS FINISHED LOADING the Jeep Cherokee, then went back to lock the front door of the cottage. Emma sat in the front seat, Max in the back. His daughter had been sitting there for over an hour, arms crossed over her chest. She hadn't spoken a word in all that time.

His shoulder was still slightly tender, but he'd managed to load the car by himself. There was no way Emma was going to help. Not in the mood she was in, anyway.

He hopped in behind the wheel, and turned the key in the ignition. "Ready?" he asked. Emma glanced his way, then turned her head to stare out the passenger window without speaking.

They'd said their farewells to the family. Ross

and Emma had gone together to see his mother in the nursing home. And Emma had gone alone to say good-bye to Zack and Libby. Ross had skipped seeing Libby. He'd asked Emma to say good-bye for him and wish her well. He felt like a heel for being so gutless, but he just didn't think he could say good-bye to her without making a complete fool of himself.

Emma hadn't talked about the day on the cliff. She'd said she wanted to forget about it. She wanted to think about her mother in her own way, she'd said. Although Ross knew that one day they'd have to talk about it.

After taking one last look at the cottage, he slowly pulled away. He'd gone only a few feet when he realized Emma was crying. He wondered if he should pull over or just keep going. As he passed Libby's place, he kept his eyes trained on the road. At the end of the street, he stopped the car. "Em—"

"Keep going. I'll be all right. Just go, quickly," she said without looking at him.

He sat there for a few moments, feeling like a louse, not knowing what to say to Emma to comfort her. Jerking the car into Drive, he stepped on the gas pedal, then swung it around in the opposite direction. He rolled the car to a stop in front of Libby's and placed it in Park.

Emma glanced at him sideways, tears streaming down her cheeks. "What are you doing?"

"I need to say good-bye to Libby." He patted her knee, then got out of the car. "I'll be back in a minute."

He'd never used Libby's front door before. When she didn't answer his knock, he tried the bell. After a moment the door opened and Libby appeared from behind it. Her eyes looked puffy and swollen. And her nose and cheeks were pink. Ross felt a stab of pain in his gut.

They looked at each other for a few moments without saying anything. It was he who finally broke the silence. "Can I come in?"

Rather than answer, she moved aside, allowing him to pass. She left the door open.

"You look like you've been crying," he said, asking himself if he'd really said something so ignorant. It was obvious she'd been crying.

She turned around and walked toward the kitchen. Ross followed her, his eyes staring at the backs of her long, bare legs poking out from beneath khaki shorts. "I'm going to miss Emma," she said over her shoulder.

"What about me, Doc? Are you going to miss me?"

She stopped in the middle of the kitchen, then turned around and leveled him with a look. "Yes."

Something happened to his insides just then. Something that wouldn't allow him to leave. The thought of moving two thousand miles away from her was no longer an option. Moving closer, he said, "I'm kind of dense. And I can be a real jerk at times."

"I know."

"Emma wants to stay." *Tell her you want to stay, too,* he said to himself.

She didn't answer, just looked at him with those sad green eyes.

"I was thinking...." *Just say it.* "Maybe we should stay. It's going to take time to heal, and it will only make it harder living clear across the country. Meggie needs someone to lean on, although Dan's been hanging around quite a bit lately. And my father ... I'd like to spend some time with him. He's not getting any younger."

Libby sniffed, nodded her head, and forced a thin smile.

"But," he said, taking a step closer, "the biggest reason of all to stay in Falcon Ridge is standing right in front of my face. What kind of fool would I be to leave you and what we had together?"

"A huge fool," she muttered.

He smirked. "What would you say if I asked you to marry me?"

He saw her swallow, the skin on her slender neck move up and then down, before she opened her mouth to speak. "I'd say ... yes."

His heart took a leap. Watching her with smug delight, he said, "You wouldn't want one of those big, fancy weddings, would you? The kind that take months, sometimes a year, to plan?"

Her eyes widened and began to tear as she shook her head.

"I didn't think so. I kind of had you figured for the small, intimate wedding type. You know, just family, maybe a few friends. One that could be planned quickly." He took her hands in his, brought them to his lips, and placed several open-mouthed kisses on her palms. "Libby, don't cry."

She lowered her head to his shoulder just as he pulled her to him. It felt so good holding her in his arms. He'd missed her terribly. He hadn't realized how much until he'd tried to drive away. "I couldn't leave. I tried to drive away, but I couldn't."

Gently, he lifted her chin and gazed into her watery green eyes. "I love you, Libby. I don't know how I ever thought I could live without you. Will you marry me?"

She was sobbing too hard to speak, but she managed a nod before placing her mouth against his. They enjoyed several drugging kisses before he pulled away. Breathing fast and hard, he asked, "Do *you* love *me*?"

Libby thumped him in the chest. "What do you think?" A huge smile formed on her soft, swollen lips. "Of course I love you, you big idiot."

An idiot he'd once been, but not anymore. He tugged her back to him. This time the kisses grew more urgent, but neither of them bothered to slow it down.

Someone cleared a throat behind him. Ross looked over his shoulder at Emma and Max.

"What are you doing?" Emma asked, her face a myriad of emotions.

"What's it look like I'm doing? I'm kissing my future bride."

Her hands flew to her face. "For real?" she shrieked.

"Yeah, for real. And if you expect to be a flower girl in the wedding, you'd better leave us alone for a few minutes," he threatened playfully.

Emma grinned and rolled her eyes at the same time. "I'm too old to be a flower girl," she said, hurrying toward them. "But I could be your maid of honor," she said, holding Libby's look.

Libby pushed away from Ross. "I can't think of anyone I'd be more honored to have stand beside me than you, Emma."

Ross stood aside while they hugged, laughed, cried, and, finally, jumped up and down together. He tried not to laugh, but he couldn't help himself. Even Max barked at all the excitement, although the dog couldn't have known what it meant. "All right. That's enough, you two," Ross said, pulling them apart and feeling a little slighted.

Emma swung herself around and kissed him hard on the mouth. "I love you." Ross squeezed her tight, winking at Libby over Emma's shoulder. "I love you too, Em."

"Okay, I'll disappear for a little bit," she said. "C'mon, Max."

"You said Libby had plenty of bedrooms upstairs," Ross said. "Why don't you go up and pick one out for yourself and one for my computer?"

"Okay. I'll even empty the car," she said cheerfully.

Libby grabbed his hand and held it in hers. "Are you sure you want to stay?"

"I've never been more sure of anything in my

life," he answered truthfully. Then to his daughter's retreating form he said, "Oh, and Emma, make sure there's an extra bedroom for a nursery."

Emma spun around and raced back to them. "We're having a baby?" she squealed with delight.

"Hopefully," he said. "Don't you remember? Libby likes babies."

He'd obviously said something to make them both cry again. The hugs started all over, followed by the jumping. This time Ross was the one to roll his eyes. Enough was enough. Slapping his daughter on the behind, he told her to scoot. Only when she'd disappeared did he grab Libby and kiss her thoroughly. "That's just a sample of what I have in store for you later. If we ever get a moment alone, that is."

"Hmmm, I have an idea," she said, smiling. "Why don't we call Zack? I'm sure he'd love to take Emma to a movie once he finds out she's staying."

"Good thinking, Doc. Good thinking." Ross grinned at her, then devoured her mouth again. With his lips against hers, he said, "Maybe we should call him now."

About the author

DEBBY CONRAD HAS been spinning tales since junior high school when she would force her younger sister and a few close friends to listen to her fantasies and dreams. Back then she had no idea her silly tales would end up in print, or that her later dream of becoming a novelist would come true.

Debby lives with her husband in Erie, Pennsylvania, has two grown daughters, three Chihuahuas, and a miniature Dachshund. *Lust's Betrayal* is her first published novel.